Money For Nothing

Money For Nothing

Donald E. Westlake

ROBERT HALE · LONDON

The events and characters in this book are fictitous. Certain real locations
and public figures are mentioned, but all other characters and events described
in the book are totally imaginary

Typeset in 10/13pt Plantin by
Derek Doyle & Associates, Liverpool.
Printed in Great Britain by
St Edmundsbury Press, Bury St Edmunds, Suffolk.
Bound by Woolnough Bookbinding Ltd.

The doggerel in chapter 50 is
by Arthur Hugh Clough, 1819–61

1

WHEN THE FIRST check came in, Josh Redmont, who was then twenty-seven, had no idea what it was for. The issuer name printed on the check was United States Agent, with an address of K Street NE, Washington, DC 04040, and the account was with Inter-Merchant Bank, also of Washington. The amount of the check was one thousand dollars.

Why? Josh had done two years in the army after college, but this didn't seem to have anything to do with the army. He was listed with a temp agency on Pine Street in downtown Manhattan that year, and so he asked Fred Stern, the guy he dealt with there, if the check had anything to do with them, and Fred assured him it did not. 'We don't give you money just for fun,' he said, which was certainly true.

But somebody did. Like most temps, Josh was financially shaky in those days, so he deposited the check into his checking account, partly just to see if it would clear, and it did. So he had an extra thousand dollars. Found money.

A month later, it happened again. Another check, another thousand dollars, same payer, same bank, same lack of covering letter or any other kind of explanation.

This time, Josh studied the check a little more intently, and saw there was a phone number under United States Agent's address, with the 202 area code for Washington, DC. So he called it. The phone rang and rang; no answer.

The next day, he called the number again, with the same results. The day after that, he deposited the check in his checking account, and it cleared. And a month later another one arrived.

Who was giving him all this money? A thousand dollars a month, regular as clockwork, the checks dated the first of each month, arriving in his mailbox between the third and the fifth. No explanation, never an answer at that telephone number. He thought about writing them a letter, but then he realized the address on the checks was incomplete. *Where* on K Street? Without a house number, he couldn't hope to send them a letter.

The checks had first appeared in August. In January, it occurred to him that the puzzle would soon have to be resolved because the United States Agent, whoever they were, would have to send him a 1099 tax form. So he waited for it. He got the 1099 from the temp agency, and from two other very short-term employers, but nothing from United States Agent.

Would he get in trouble if he didn't declare the five thousand dollars? But how could he declare it without the 1099? And what would he declare it as? And was he rich enough to volunteer to pay extra tax if he didn't absolutely have to? He was not.

A year and a half later he moved, to a better apartment on the West Side, having graduated from the temp life to an actual job as an advertising salesman for a group of neighborhood newspapers in Manhattan and the Bronx. He was sorry the monthly thousand dollars would end. But he had no way to send them a forwarding address, did he? So that was that.

Except that, the third of the following month, the check came in just the same, addressed to him at his new apartment. How had they done that? How had they known he'd moved? It was more than a little creepy.

If he hadn't been spending the money all along, he might have tried sending it back at that point, except he couldn't. He couldn't send the money back any more than he could write United States Agent a letter, not without more of an address than K Street NE. He considered writing RETURN TO SENDER on the envelope, but the envelope, too, bore that same incomplete address printed on its upper left corner. In the end, though he felt somewhat spooked, he deposited the check.

In the third year of the mysterious checks, he went to work as an account rep at Sewell-McConnell Advertising on the Cloudbank toilet paper account, and the following year he married Eve, whom he'd been dating off and on for three years and living with for four months. He didn't mention the checks to her – which followed him to their new apartment – neither before nor after the wedding, and he realized this must mean that, at some level, he felt guilty about taking the money. He hadn't done anything for it, he didn't deserve it, the checks merely kept coming in. And in not telling her, he doubled his guilt, because now he also felt guilty that he was keeping this secret. But he kept it anyway.

Which Eve made easier, it must be said, by having ceded to him exclusive control of their checking account, even though she'd lived and worked successfully on her own in New York City for five years before they'd gotten together.

Josh didn't need the thousand dollars a month by then, and had come to realize it wasn't very much money at all. Twelve thousand dollars a year; a nice supplement to his income, no more. And, of course, tax free.

The next year, when he and Eve had young Jeremy and she quit her clerical job with a cable network, planning to be a full-time mom until Jeremy entered nursery school at four, the annual twelve thousand became a bit more meaningful again, but by that time it was simply a part of his life, the check that came in every month, year after year, as natural as breathing. He had stopped telling himself he didn't deserve it, because if it came in so steadily, every single month, with no complaints, no demands made against him, maybe he did deserve it.

It was July fifteenth, a hot sunny Friday afternoon, and Josh was seated at the ferry terminal in Bay Shore, waiting for the ferry to take him over to Fire Island, where he and Eve had rented a small house for the month. She and Jeremy were out there full time, Josh spending long weekends. Jeremy was two, and on August first the checks would have been coming in for a full seven years, crossing with Josh into the new millennium.

Josh was secure enough in his job at the ad agency now to be able to take off Friday afternoons and Monday mornings, which meant he never had to ride the extremely crowded ferries packed with those whose weekends were shorter; the Daddy Boat on Friday evening, the Goodbye Daddy Boat on Sunday evening, or the so-called Death Boat at six-thirty Monday morning.

There were only thirty or forty people in the shade of the roofed dock, seated on the long benches waiting for the ferry, none of them anyone Josh knew. Then a man came over and sat down beside him and smiled and said, 'Hello.'

'Hi,' Josh said, and looked away. Most people didn't speak to strangers out here, and Josh agreed with them.

The man kept smiling at Josh. He was about forty, olive-skinned, fleshy-faced but muscular, with thick curly black hair. He was in chinos and a polo shirt and sneakers, like everybody else. 'I am from United States Agent,' he said.

Josh looked at him. Sudden dread clenched his stomach. His mouth was dry. He tried to speak, but couldn't.

The man leaned closer. 'You are now active,' he said.

2

ACTIVE? JOSH DIDN'T feel active, he felt paralyzed. He wanted to run screaming from the dock – but he didn't. He wanted to deny his identity, make up a name, give a friend's name – Matt Fairlough, not *that* good a friend – but he hadn't the strength for it. He wanted to promise to return the money – a thousand dollars a month for seven years, *eighty-four thousand dollars!* – but he couldn't do either of those, not say it and not repay it. He could only sit there, stunned, speechless, like the condemned man in the moments between the sedative and the axe.

Meanwhile, the man from United States Agent had hunched over a bit onto his right buttock so he could reach into his left hip pocket. Josh stared in horror, still frozen. What was going to come out of there? His imagination scattered, like raked leaves under a sudden gust, and the man brought out a small flat black book. It was almost square and very thin, and he couldn't think what it was going to be, and the man smiled and extended it toward him, saying, 'But first, per our agreement. You'll find it's all in order.'

No choice; Josh took the black book. Out there in the inlet, the white ferry slowly turned toward the dock. People stood, moved around, on this side of the barrier, and Josh lowered his bronze head on his oak neck to look at the book.

Silver letters curved above and below a swooshy sort of silver design, something familiar, simplified – wind-surfing. A wind-surfing board, the sail arcing against a strong breeze, silver on black. Above *Cayman*, below *Key Bank*.

What? Josh opened the bankbook, saw what it was, saw his own name and address – and Social Security number – on the first page, and below that a jumble of capital letters and lowercase letters and digits on a line marked *Account Number*.

11

Suddenly arthritic fingers fumbled page one away, and page two began the entry of deposits and withdrawals. 'All items in US dollars,' read a legend across the top of the page, but so far there was only the one item: A deposit, dated July 14th, the previous day, of $40,000.00.

His vision was darkening. The white ferry approached, out there over the sparkling water, but a black iris spiraled in, shadowing and obscuring everything in his vision except that small white page with its neat black gridwork of lines and that appalling number.

'What,' he whispered, not looking up from the little book, 'do you want me to do?'

'At the moment,' the man said, 'only a safe house. While your family is still at the beach.'

'A safe house?' Later he would remember the term *safe house* from a hundred spy movies, but at that moment, he couldn't think what a safe house might possibly be, except that he must be a million miles from one.

'The operation is beginning,' the man explained. 'We will be bringing people in, passing them into New York, traveling only on weekends because of course they are tourists.'

Something jocular in the man's voice made Josh force his eyes upward from the bankbook to see that he believed he had made a joke – 'tourists' – and was enjoying it. 'Oh,' Josh said.

'They will use your house only when you are out here on the island,' the man assured him. 'They will leave absolutely no sign, not even a fingerprint. We will merely move them through.' His hand made a graceful sweeping-away gesture, like a ballerina swatting a fly.

'I see,' Josh said, though he didn't, could barely see the man's smiling confident face.

The man gave him a sudden sharp look, as though realizing there was something a little off in Josh's reactions. But what should Josh's reactions be, to all this? He'd fake whatever the man wanted, he was willing to do that much, God knows, but what did the man *want*?

To move people through his apartment, on weekends, leaving no fingerprints. *Why?*

The man suddenly smiled and nodded and said, 'Of course. I beg your pardon.'

'Oh, sure,' Josh said. He could say that much.

'You were expecting Mr Nimrin,' the man said. 'It must have been very confusing to suddenly confront a stranger.'

'Yes,' Josh said, because that was something he could agree with, and then said, in a flat voice, because he didn't know how else to say it, 'Mr Nimrin.'

'Mr Nimrin is no longer with us,' the man said. 'Not for some time.'

'I'm sorry,' Josh said. It seemed the thing to say.

'Oh, he isn't dead,' the man assured him. 'Just . . . away. You could say, in retirement. But not to worry,' he went on, 'there was never a word out of him.'

'Ah.'

'Fortunately,' the man went on, 'the Americans don't go in much for torture, at least not when there's a public light on things, so Mr Nimrin never had to worry about *that*.'

'Good,' Josh said.

'So when I assure you,' the man said, 'that he never mentioned you, I can go further. Through it all, he never mentioned anyone or anything.'

'That's good,' Josh agreed.

'Well, you know Mr Nimrin,' the man said. 'He's like a rock.'

'A rock,' Josh said.

'But I should introduce my own self,' the man said. 'I am Levrin, and I am now your control. Well, I have been for some time, of course, but you wouldn't have known it.'

'No,' Josh agreed, and saw that people were getting on the ferry. 'My ferry's going to leave,' he said.

'Oh, you mustn't miss it,' the man told him, jumping to his feet. 'Now more than ever, you must not deviate in your patterns. Just give me your keys.'

Josh, in the process of rising, stumbled a bit. 'My keys?'

'I have to make copies, obviously,' Levrin told him. 'Now, don't miss your ferry. Give me the keys. I'll leave them with the cashier where you parked your car.'

For one mad second, Josh thought this whole thing was an elaborate scam to steal his car, the Toyota Land Cruiser parked a long block from here for the weekend, but of course it was not, he knew it was not. To begin with, the Toyota wasn't worth eighty-four thousand dollars.

One hundred twenty-four thousand now, according to this little book clutched in his left hand.

'Come on, come on,' Levrin said, hurrying him with quick little gestures. 'The last people are getting on the ferry.'

'Yes. Yes, of course.'

Panicked, frightened, completely without a will or a plan of his own, Josh fumbled his keyring from his pocket and gave it to Levrin. All his keys in the world, his car, his apartment, his apartment building mailbox, even his desk at Sewell-McConnell. Everything, his whole life, going into that man's fleshy palm; his olive fingers closed over it.

Josh ran – and just made the ferry.

3

EVE WAS AMONG the cluster of people on the Fair Harbor dock, waving as the ferry approached, she a vision of reward in her bright red bikini. He waved, and waved.

The first weekend, he had started to wave enthusiastically from well out in the channel when he'd seen her in her bikini – green, that week – and then, as the ferry slowed and turned toward the slip, had realized he was waving at the wrong woman, that Eve in *her* bikini – light blue – was a bit to the right, and he had immediately made the tiny shift in direction.

He didn't think Eve had noticed that error, and he had scrupulously avoided looking toward the green bikini throughout the docking process, and so had no idea which of his summer neighbors had a tall lithe body so like Eve's. And since then, he'd waited to be absolutely certain which of the half-dozen bikini-wearing women waving from the dock was Eve before he started to wave back.

Today, he had so much on his mind he almost forgot to wave at all. That hard squarish bankbook was a foreign intruder in the pocket where he usually carried his keys. Would the keys be there at the parking lot, as promised, on Monday morning, or would he have to take the train to the city, deal with the Toyota dealer, get another set of keys, train back out on Tuesday or Wednesday, having found the apartment stripped bare on Monday night?

How could he have given his keys away, just like that, to a perfect stranger, in return for this bankbook that could so easily be a fraud? Probably a fraud.

Well, not probably. He had seven years of checks to suggest that United States Agent was *something*, whether or not he could figure out exactly what, or even approximately what. Levrin had talked and acted with such assurance that Josh felt he had to believe him, even if he didn't know what it was he was supposed to believe. Safe house. People passing through. No fingerprints.

'At the moment,' Levrin had said, 'only a safe house.' At the moment? And then what?

Bump – the ferry met the dock – and the passengers off-loaded, and the smiling Eve folded him in her arms, his hands on the sleek curve of her waist. This summer vacation was good for her, freeing her from the ordinariness of ordinary life, making her more eager for enjoyment, for diversion.

And this was what he was putting at risk. But what else could he do?

'Jeremy's at Winchell's,' she whispered in his ear. 'Until we go get him.'

'Ah,' he said. 'Good.' Though it wasn't good, not really.

Mrs Winchell was an older woman, whose weekend-only husband was something in New York City government and whose children were grown and gone away. She provided baby-sitting and day care in her home up by the beach, and Eve had taken to leaving Jeremy there before Josh's Friday arrivals, so they could, as she said, 'get acquainted again.'

Usually, his heart and so on leaped up at the idea of an hour or two alone with Eve, re-creating their pre- Jeremy relationship, but not today. Today he had too much on his mind.

And one thing more to plague him: He couldn't tell Eve about this, either. Having hidden the checks from her all this time, how could he tell her about this? 'I've loaned our apartment to some foreign spies or something, I don't know who they are or what they're doing.' He couldn't open that can of worms, not at this point, it was far too late. He was going to have to be a spy himself, for the weekend, protecting his secrets.

Eve put an arm around his waist, her eyes sparkling, and they started the walk to the rental, a little two-bedroom bungalow half a block from the beach. As they walked, Eve told him the gossip of the week, and for the first time in his life Josh thought: Will I be able to perform?

The weekend was not a disaster. He kept up his part, as it were, or so he thought. Everything seemed normal and fine. On Saturday, at the beach, he and Jeremy spent a few hours playing the game they seemed to have invented, in which first they made a village, by upending pails of wet sand and shaping their tops to be the houses and poking fingerholes into their sides to be windows and doors, and then watching as a giant – Jeremy – with many a, 'Ho ho ho,' and, 'Har har har,' tromped through the peaceful village, destroying it and, presumably, all of its peaceful villagers.

Josh had never minded this game before, had known that other little boys up and down the beach were also taking the opportunity of summer in the sun to improve their skills as homicidal maniacs, but today, after United States Agent had made him 'active,' he found himself regretting that it was too late to train Jeremy in the ways of pacifism.

Not that Jeremy was at the outer extreme of homicidal mania among two-year-old boys. He was basically a sunny kid, agreeable and friendly except when tired, and from the beginning Josh had been amazed at the depth of the bond he felt with this new life. He looked for signs of himself in Jeremy's movements and reactions, and at times he thought he caught glimpses, but more often the boy reminded him most of Eve. Not in an effeminate way, of course, but in a kind of hurtling grace, an almost off-balance surge into life, that reminded him of certain things about Eve.

So, what with playing one way with Eve, and another way with Jeremy, and seeing their friends out here in the evenings, and lazing Sunday away with the *New York Times*, it seemed to Josh he was behaving with his family exactly like someone who had not been made active. But then, Monday morning, as they walked toward the 11:10 ferry, Eve pushing Jeremy in the stroller their son was aching to grow out of, she said, 'Phone me tonight.'

'Sure,' he said. They always talked on the phone once or twice a week, but she hadn't ever made it a request before.

'Call me every night,' she said. 'Will you?' And then he realized he must not have been perfect this weekend after all. His distraction had been noticed. She's beginning to wonder, he thought with astonishment, if I'm having an affair, separated in New York with her stuck way out here.

How to deal with that? The worst thing, he knew, would be to deny an accusation that had not been directly made. That would confirm her in her belief. He said, 'Sure, I will. But, you know, you ought to do it.'

She raised an eyebrow at him. 'Do what?'

'Make the call,' he said. 'I wouldn't want to call, and Jeremy's just about to go to sleep, or something like that. You could call, any time after I get home. I'll always be there.' He grinned at her, stroking her shoulder. 'I'd like you to call,' he said. 'I miss you.'

Her smile was sunnier. 'You'd better miss me,' she said.

The keys were waiting for him at the parking lot cashier's shack. When the woman handed them out to him through the window, he felt immediate almost astonished relief – Levrin *had* been telling the truth – followed by almost as immediate depression: Levrin had been telling the truth. 'Tourists' had been in the apartment all weekend, not leaving fingerprints.

In New York he kept a monthly outdoor parking space in a vast lot in the West Sixties where some day another huge building would rise, but not in the foreseeable future. It was an eight-block walk home, during which he tried to think of courses of action. Tell the police; phone his mother and father in Muncie, Indiana; grab the forty thousand dollars and Eve and Jeremy and run for Canada; plot to be here next weekend to *catch* the tourists, see who and what they were. But finally he realized that inaction was his only possible move. Wait and see. Hope things wouldn't turn very bad.

His Monday routine this month was to have a sandwich and a cup of coffee at home, then get to the office by two-thirty, around the time everybody else would be getting back from lunch. But today, before going into the kitchen, he searched the apartment for signs. *Had* anybody been in here while he was gone? It wasn't really possible to stay in a residence and leave absolutely no trace at all, was it? But he searched the foyer, the living room, his and Eve's bedroom, Jeremy's tiny room, the bathroom, and there was nothing, just nothing, not an area rug scuffed, not a washcloth out of place.

Had there *been* nobody in here? After all that mystery, all that tension – all that money – had this apartment *not* become a safe house?

He went into the kitchen last, to make his lunch, and it was in the kitchen that he found it. He and Eve kept their cups and glasses upside down on the shelves, so their insides wouldn't get dusty. Two water glasses, on the shelf just above eye level, were precisely in their places, right side up.

He didn't eat lunch that day.

4

'**F**ORTUNATELY THE AMERICANS don't go in much for torture, at least not when there's a public light on things.'

Levrin's words never did say very much, as Josh remembered them, or tried to remember them, but they hinted at a great deal. A public light on things?

After a sleepless night, he spent Tuesday morning not engaged in Sewell-McConnell's affairs, though he was using their computer, in the terminal at his desk. Nimrin. Was that the way it was spelled? No other combination looked right, so that was the name he inserted into data banks at the *New York Times*, the *Washington Post*, the *Boston Globe*, and the *Los Angeles Times*. Whatever it was that had shed a public light on things, presumably it had happened sometime in the last seven years, because, at least at the beginning, according to Levrin, Mr Nimrin had been his 'control,' another word from spy movies, all those glum Le Carré characters dragging themselves out of their Tartarean beds every morning. Or afternoon.

He found it in the *Washington Post*, because it was in a federal court in the District of Columbia that the public appearance had taken place, almost a full seven years ago, on August eighteenth. This Ellois Nimrin – surely Levrin's man – seemed to be nothing but a minor walk-on in an industrial espionage case. The question was, had or had not advanced computer technology been illegally exported by this agglomeration of beetle-browed moustachioed men with strange-sounding names lined up at the defendants' table here?

Ellois Nimrin didn't appear in the body of the news story, nor in any of the other items on the case Josh scanned, but was only a name in a photo caption: 'Defendants' – and then three difficult names, and then – 'Ellois Nimrin' – and four equally difficult names, under a photo of the eight seated at the defense table, bunched together shoulder to shoulder, almost moustache to moustache, and looking as glum as any character in Le Carré.

Mr Nimrin, as Josh still thought of him, following on Levrin's respectful references, should be fourth from the left. The photo wasn't that clear, and its reproduction on the computer screen didn't help much. Josh had an impression of a burly man, hawknosed above the moustache, with a high gleaming forehead and eyes that, even in this poor reproduction of a side-view medium-distance shot, seemed to glare in unrepentant rage and contempt in the general direction of the bench.

All the other defendants, to one extent or another, seemed cowed by their circumstances. Mr Nimrin seemed energized. It was hard to believe he wasn't a principal in the case, was just another spear-carrier, but judging from the news pieces that did seem to be the situation.

As for the case, Josh couldn't make heads nor tails of it. Laboratory technicians had been bribed or coerced, allegedly. Secrets had been stolen, allegedly. Diagrams and other documents had been smuggled out of the country, allegedly. These eight defendants were somehow part of the plot, allegedly.

But this was where it got tricky. The government lawyers, in presenting their case, asserted that national security was an issue here, and that much of the evidence against the defendants was too sensitive to be revealed in public; some was too sensitive to be revealed to a jury or to the defense attorneys; and some was so sensitive it couldn't even be revealed to the judge.

What had brought these defendants from the 'federal facility' where they were being held into this courtroom was not the trial, but a hearing as to whether a trial was even possible. The defense argued, and Josh could see the justice in the argument, that it was impossible for a person to defend himself against evidence he wasn't permitted to see or even hear described. The prosecution, speaking for the government, essentially argued that the defendants would get a fair trial because the government could be trusted – would they lie?

Mr Nimrin appeared by name only the one time, under that photo, but the story itself took up space in the Post for ten days, that space becoming briefer and briefer toward the end, then petering out before the judge had given his decision as to whether or not they could all, in a phrase Josh had grown used to in the coverage, 'proceed to trial,' which made it sound like, after the cocktails, they would go in to dinner.

Nothing else about the trial, or the case, or the defendants ever appeared again, so far as Josh could tell from the Post's records. So it

seemed unlikely there had actually been a trial. Still, this was clearly what
had ended Mr Nimrin's career, whatever that career had been.

What else had Levrin said about Mr Nimrin? That he had not been
tortured, and that he was not dead. 'Just . . . away. You could say, in retirement.'

By the time Josh had gone this far, it was time for lunch; today, an
important one. Not in the world of Levrin and Mr Nimrin, but in the
somewhat more real world of Sewell-McConnell. A representative of
Amalgamated Pulp, manufacturers of Cloudbank toilet paper, in objecting
last week to a mock-up of a print ad, had described the clouds pictured
there as looking 'like white turds,' which, given the nature of the account,
had led to some unfortunate wordplay, ruffling the rep's dignity before
maturity was reimposed.

As Josh had not himself been guilty of ribaldry on that occasion, and
had spearheaded the forces of seriousness, so it had fallen to him to take
the rep to lunch and smooth his feathers. It was a thing he was good at,
which was one of the reasons he'd been hired by Sewell-McConnell in the
first place, and he handled it as well as usual, though in fact he was
distracted throughout the lunch by the questions to which he had no
answers.

What was the United States Agent? If Mr Nimrin and Levrin were
spies, whom did they work for? If people were being brought into New
York because the 'operation' had started, what was the operation? What
did they want from Josh beyond the use of his apartment?

But the most serious question, and the one that kept him most from
concentrating on the job at lunch, was: Why him? Why had they chosen
to send him all those checks? Why was he the one they were now activat-
ing? If Mr Nimrin had been his control, back at the beginning, why is it
he'd never met the man nor heard his name before in his entire life?

If he'd ever been recruited as an undercover spy, he'd have remembered
it. He was sure of that much.

The lunch at last came to an end, with the rep's feathers once more in
an unruffled state. They shook hands outside the restaurant, assured each
other of their continuing unity in the pursuit of more consumers of
Cloudbank, and Josh returned to the office where, apart from a memo
about the lunch to Sid Graff, his immediate boss, he again did nothing for
Sewell-McConnell but use their computer.

This time, he wanted to know about Cayman Key Bank. He typed the
name into a search engine and was somewhat surprised to find that the
bank not only existed but had a website. He went there and found an airy

world of white and pastels, mostly pale blue and pale green, and suggestions he buy himself a piece of the sun.

Account Holders was one of the destinations he could click on. He did – and found a place that offered him an opportunity to type in his account number. He'd brought the bankbook along to the office, so he copied the number, which was mostly letters, into the space provided, and noticed that no matter what he typed, another x appeared in the box on the screen.

He was then asked his mother's maiden name, which surprised him a lot. How would they know his mother's maiden name? All right; he typed in *Hansforth,* which became *xxxxxxxx,* and then the screen segued to a place that said, 'Welcome to Cayman Key Bank, Mr Redmont. Please select from the menu below.'

He had not given his name. The fourth item on the menu below was *Account Balance.* He clicked on it. The site considered the question, then numbers began to appear in the box to the right of where he'd clicked: *$40,000.00.*

It was real.

5

THERE WERE DAYS when Josh took the subway home from Sewell-McConnell at the end of the day. Some days, when the weather was good and his spirits were up, he walked. But on days when he felt harried or low or faintly sick or – like this Tuesday, after the *Washington Post* and Cayman Key Bank – all three, there was nothing for it, coming out of the office building on 3rd Avenue in the 40s, but to hail a cab.

It was almost six by the time he came out, having finally done some work for his employer toward the end of the day. The late afternoon sun glared like a dormitory proctor down all the side streets, and the city was full. Since it was July, the city was full mostly of people who didn't speak English or, if they did, spoke it with one of those mashed-potatoes-in-the-mouth twangs. The sidewalks were full of people and the streets were full of vehicles of all sorts. It would surely take longer to get home by taxi than by subway, and would be more expensive as well (not that a man with a bank account in the Cayman Islands would care about *that*), but it would be soothing. And he felt a need for soothing right now.

The only problem with getting a cab at 6 P.M. on a weekday, of course, was finding a cab. Josh marched to the curb, where other people stood and waved their arms at cabs, and he waved his own arm, and eventually his turn came and the yellow car angled to a stop in front of him. He opened the door, slid in, and somebody slid in right behind him. One of the other people who'd been waving at taxis; got right in after him, shoved him over.

'Hey!' Josh cried. 'This is *my* cab.'

'I am Mr Nimrin,' the man said, low and fast, still pushing Josh left-

23

ward on the seat so he could bring his body in far enough to shut the door.

Josh stared. Mr Nimrin, now successfully aboard, flashed the profile Josh had been studying in the *Washington Post*, except without the moustache, as he leaned toward the driver to say, '137 Riverside Drive, near 86th Street.'

'Wait a minute,' Josh said. 'That isn't where I live.'

'Your place is no doubt under surveillance,' Mr Nimrin told him, and sat back as the cab started forward. 'We will talk when we are alone. You will pay for the taxi.'

Josh said, 'I was told you were retired.'

Mr Nimrin gave a scornful snort. 'We shall see,' he said. He raised a warning finger. 'No talking now.'

'My wife will be calling me,' Josh said.

'You will call her back,' Mr Nimrin said. 'No talking.'

So they didn't talk. Uptown and crosstown, through the park at 64th Street and then up Broadway, they were in the middle of heavy honking traffic all the way. This was one of those days when it might have been faster even to *walk* home.

Though home wasn't where he was going – was it?

He took the opportunity of the long ride to study Mr Nimrin, at first covertly and then openly, as it became clear the man didn't care if he was stared at. That same glower he'd seen in the photo, aimed at the off-camera judge, was still visible in his large-headed sharp-featured profile, though damped down, as though Mr Nimrin's disapproval of all he saw was so natural to him that he himself hardly remarked on it anymore. He had that eagle's nose, that high gleaming forehead, that powerful shock of black hair. He was older than fifty, perhaps younger than a hundred. He wore a lightweight black suit, white shirt, maroon tie with geometric figures. He didn't look diplomatic enough to be a diplomat, but he certainly had some kind of foreign-office air about him. His accent was quite noticeable, though it didn't interfere with Josh's understanding, and he couldn't tell what Mr Nimrin's original language might be.

Riverside Drive, high over the Hudson, is peaceful but windy, even in July. The cab stopped at one of the tall broad apartment buildings placed here to take advantage of the view, and Mr Nimrin impatiently clambered out while Josh paid the fare. Then he levered himself out, the cab fled, and Mr Nimrin said, 'Well, come along.'

There was a doorman, who saw them coming and opened the door. Mr

Nimrin ignored him, so Josh did, too, and followed Mr Nimrin at a left oblique across the gold lobby, not toward the elevators. Mr Nimrin walked like a man pleased to deliver bad news; a flatfooted heavy tread, arms moving a bit more than necessary at his sides, eyes and face following that eagle beak in a straight line, implacable, ignoring everything to left and right.

On the left wall of the lobby was a door, darker gold, with two white marble steps and a delicate wrought iron railing that led up to it. Mr Nimrin mounted the steps, pushed open the door, and stepped through, not looking around to see if Josh were still in his wake. He was, and heard a bell ring faintly, somewhere farther ahead, when the door was opened. It sounded again when he let the door snick shut behind himself.

This was a waiting room, windowless, in calming grays and pale greens. Two gray vinyl sofas at right angles faced a square wooden coffee table on which magazines were lined in orderly display. Floor lamps flanked the sofa, beaming gentle illumination upward. Reproductions of Hudson River school paintings were grandly framed on the walls. The carpet was a curly light green that looked like Velcro's gentler cousin.

'Sit there,' Mr Nimrin said, with a shooing gesture at the righthand sofa, while he himself headed for the one on the left.

As they sat, Josh said, 'What is this place?'

'A psychiatrist's office,' Mr Nimrin told him. 'No one knows I know her. We will not be spied upon here.'

Josh said, 'So you can tell me—'

'One moment,' Mr Nimrin said, again raising that warning finger. 'She will be coming out.'

He looked past Josh at the interior door, which obediently opened, and a woman leaned out. She was about sixty, stocky but striking looking, with thick waves of gray hair around a strong-featured face. She wore a high-necked bulky gray sweater and black slacks. She peered past Josh and said, without surprise, 'It's you. Are you all right?'

'Fine,' he told her. He was curt, but not as though he meant to be insulting.

'I'm with a patient,' she said.

'We will be brief,' he assured her, which sounded to Josh like a dismissal.

To her, too. 'Take your time,' she said, smiled meaninglessly at Josh, and left, closing the door.

'Now,' Josh said, 'you can tell me what's going on.'

'That I cannot,' Mr Nimrin corrected him. 'What I can tell you is that it all depends on you.' He looked more stern than ever. 'What you do,' he said, 'over the next days and perhaps weeks, will determine whether or not we are both terminated.'

6

'YOU DON'T MEAN fired,' Josh said.

'Fired *at*, perhaps,' Mr Nimrin told him. 'In any case, dead.'

'But ... why?' Josh made vague hand movements. 'Why am I even *in* this?'

'I must accept some of the blame for that,' Mr Nimrin said.

'Really?'

'You shouldn't be in it at all,' Mr Nimrin said. 'It was very stupid of those people to activate you. What's the point? You're an amateur. You have no training. You're a lamb led to slaughter.'

'Oh, God.' Josh pressed his palms onto the vinyl sofa seat on both sides of himself, praying for balance. A lamb led to slaughter? Mr Nimrin didn't look like a man who made jokes.

'If it were only you,' Mr Nimrin went on, 'I would never concern myself. Let them embarrass themselves, having put some babe in the woods through the meat grinder.'

Meat grinder – it was getting worse. Josh said, 'Mr Levrin didn't seem—'

'*Mister* Levrin?' Mr Nimrin snorted. 'Levrin is an idiot,' he said, 'as even you probably noticed, but he is also savage and ruthless and merciless. I have seen him at his bloody work.'

'Oh, have you?' Josh said. This is a nightmare, he told himself. I've fallen asleep at my desk. If I don't wake up, I'll be in trouble.

Big trouble.

'Levrin,' Mr Nimrin was going on, 'is capable of the kind of cruelty only possible to those with absolutely no imagination.'

Trying to remember back to that encounter at the ferry terminal, trying to remember Levrin's face and words and manner, Josh said, 'He didn't *seem* like that kind of person.'

'Of course not,' Mr Nimrin said. 'If he *seemed* like that kind of person, he'd be no use to anyone at all. It's because he can seem like no more than the idiot he is that he is effective.'

'But—' Floundering, Josh tried to find firm footing somewhere in all this. 'You said, you're partly to blame, for me being in whatever this is.'

'Well, of course.' Mr Nimrin shook an irritated head. 'I'm the one who recruited you. But no one was ever supposed to make actual *use* of you.'

'What do you mean, you recruited me?' Here at last, surprisingly enough, there *was* firm footing. 'I've never seen you before in my life.'

'Well, yes, you did,' Mr Nimrin said. 'You wouldn't remember. I was in disguise.'

Disguise? Josh almost laughed. How could a powerful presence like Mr Nimrin disguise himself? Fake beards and beauty marks, humpbacks. He already had an accent.

But then the urge to laugh faded, to be replaced by a fresh fear. Why were they in this psychiatrist's office, who 'they' didn't know Mr Nimrin knew? Was he just crazy, after all? Was this some paranoid fantasy? But if so, whose?

Mr Nimrin caught the unexpressed thoughts and said, 'You know nothing about disguise, that's obvious. Nothing is easier than disguise.'

Josh had to ask: 'What were you disguised *as*?'

'A bartender.'

'A what?'

'This was nine years ago,' Mr Nimrin told him. 'There was, at that time, on Sixth Street in the East Village, a bar known as Uncle Ray's.'

'Oh, sure,' Josh said.

'It is no longer there,' Mr Nimrin said, 'but at that time it was popular with NYU students. You were there as well sometimes, though I don't believe you were an NYU student.'

'I was there to pick up NYU students,' Josh said, remembering, with some nostalgic pleasure.

'I was there for a similar reason,' Mr Nimrin told him. 'To collect young people. You were one of the ones I collected.'

'What do you mean, collect?'

Mr Nimrin sat back on the sofa, frowning at the coffee table. He seemed all at once not quite so certain of himself. He said, 'At first, I wasn't going to tell you your part in my scheme, but then I realized, if they're interrogating you it won't matter what you give them because I'm doomed either way. Whereas, if you have a clear idea of the situation, it will certainly encourage you to do your best not to become an innocent victim.' He looked at Josh. 'Believe me,' he said, 'you do not want to be an innocent victim.'

'I believe you,' Josh said.

'Very well. We must go back,' Mr Nimrin said, 'to the collapse of the Soviet Union. The confusion, I would even say devastation, created in the intelligence communities in the east by that disaster was beyond belief. Before, there had been easy alliances, cooperation, a world of known friends and known enemies. Suddenly, it was as though we'd entered a world of warlords, none of us secure in our territory. Who did we work for? Who did we report to? Who would provide our funding? Who was with us, and who against?'

Mr Nimrin sighed and shook his head. He adjusted himself on the sofa. Clearly, these memories were painful ones. He said, 'It took years, I must say, before the situation was sorted out, even a little. We turned out to be Ukraine, surprising many of us, and linked to Naval Intelligence. The so-called Russian navy, you see, is mostly in the Ukraine, the Black Sea having been the Soviet Union's primary access to open water.'

Josh said, 'What do *I* have to do with any of this?'

'Nothing!' thundered Mr Nimrin, suddenly enraged. 'That's the aggravating thing of it!' Calming himself, he said, 'I could see that our future, in our new Ukrainian guise, was extremely unstable. It seemed to me that I should first feather my nest and then retire, before things got worse. This is where you come in.'

'I do?'

'One of the things that carried over to the new order,' Mr Nimrin said, 'was the sleeper fund, moneys to be spent on deepcover operatives, maintained on standby wherever in the world we might have an interest. These sleepers were mostly a joke, as we in the field knew. Our dread was always that we might have to wake one of them and depend on his help in an emergency. So the sleepers were *not* wakened.'

'Is that me?' Josh asked. 'A sleeper?'

'Yes, of course.'

'But I've been wakened.'

'That's the infuriating part of it!' Mr Nimrin said, pounding his knee. 'I have no idea what this operation can be. How could they be so stupid as to activate you? What can they have in mind?'

Josh said, 'What did *you* have in mind?'

'What, me?' Rage gone, Mr Nimrin smiled at his former self. 'I was quite clever,' he said. 'I arranged to become a recruiter of sleepers, each of whom would be paid one thousand dollars a month while on standby, then more, of course, if ever activated. I needed people who would look plausible to my superiors, who would vet them once and then never think about them again. Rootless young men, single, with a reputation for radical politics.'

'*I* wasn't in radical politics,' Josh protested.

'You forget,' Mr Nimrin said, 'I was your bartender. I heard the loose talk around that bar, and you were very much a part of it. One of my first candidates, in fact.'

Josh sank back on the sofa, trying to remember how much of an idiot he'd been in those days – then, trying not to remember.

Mr Nimrin went on, 'My goal was to accumulate twenty sleepers, and of course I would divert their payment checks to myself, because none of them would ever know he'd been recruited. Twenty thousand dollars a month, two hundred forty thousand dollars a year, for ten years. I felt I could maintain the fraud for that long, and then, with two and a half million dollars US., I could very easily disappear. Buy an island, for instance, in the Caribbean. There were many choices.'

Josh said, 'I was one—' and the inner door opened again. This time, what came out was male, short, skinny, about forty, with a face speckled in acne and a nose like a can opener. He wore a New York Mets cap, a New York Knicks T-shirt, baggy dragging green running shorts, white tube socks, and large white sneakers. He scuttled across the waiting room, not looking in their direction, pretending he was alone, his pocked cheeks twitching. He fumbled in panic with both hands on the knob of the lobby door, finally managed to pull it open, and scuttled away, the door snicking shut in his wake.

After this apparition had gone, Josh got back to the topic at hand: 'I was one of the people you pretended to recruit. But I *got* the money.'

'This was absolutely unforeseeable,' Mr Nimrin said. He sounded very irked. 'Less than two years into the project, I became caught up in a ridiculous case of industrial espionage.'

'I read about the trial,' Josh told him.

'There was no trial,' Mr Nimrin said. 'It was all ludicrous.' Then he gave Josh a keen look. 'You read about it? Very enterprising. In the *Washington Post*? You saw that photo.'

'You had a moustache then.'

'The only public picture of me extant.' Mr Nimrin sounded bitter about that. 'Forced to make a change, I did away with the moustache. In any event, that farrago cost me my position with the agency. My desk was taken over by others, who of course had no idea what I'd been up to. I'd

30

only managed to insert six of my false sleepers into the system, including yourself, and now all six of you began to receive my money.'

'Every month.'

'Infuriating,' Mr Nimrin said. 'Three of the six never cashed their checks, so it was assumed they'd had a change of heart and were dropped from the program. But the other three, including you, have done very well off me the last seven years.'

Josh said, 'You couldn't take charge again?'

'They no longer trusted me,' Mr Nimrin said. 'A secondary effect of that ridiculous federal case was that certain things came out that made my employers suspicious of me. That's why I'm still in this country. They've taken my passport so they won't lose me. I have fine quarters at a safe house in nearby Long Island, and they're waiting to find out what I've done. I have developed ways to elude them temporarily, as I have done today. Until now, I've been safe, if bored. But *now!* Now they've activated *you!*'

'Yes, they have,' Josh said.

'You! A guileless naif! An artless witling! An unskilled, untrained, unqualified marplot! A—'

'Hey,' Josh said. 'Enough.'

Mr Nimrin lowered a brow at him. 'Do you disagree?'

'No, not really. But you don't have to rub my nose in it.'

'But I do,' Mr Nimrin told him. 'I have to make certain you understand the part you are now to play.'

'I've been activated,' Josh said.

'Yes, that's all well and good,' Mr Nimrin said, 'but the *part* you have to play is someone who has been an undercover mole all these years. A willing traitor.'

Josh sat up. 'Traitor?'

'You took our money,' Mr Nimrin pointed out.

'I didn't know it was yours, I didn't know *what* it was.'

'You do now,' Mr Nimrin told him, 'and let me tell you what you must do about it.'

Go straight to the authorities, Josh thought, but kept the thought to himself.

Or did he? 'If you try to go to the authorities,' Mr Nimrin said, 'who wouldn't believe you anyway, or would believe you were an actual turncoat trying to turn back—'

Josh moaned.

'And you have nothing real to tell them anyway,' Mr Nimrin added.

'But if you did make the move, you would almost certainly be stopped. They are watching you. If they think you're betraying them—'

'They think I'm betraying America!'

'Yes, exactly,' Mr Nimrin said. 'And your only salvation, and mine as well, is to keep them thinking that. You sold out your country nine years ago, you've never had doubts, you've taken the agency's money, and you are now prepared to be activated and to serve your foreign masters in any way they see fit.'

'Oh, Jeez,' Josh said.

'Yes, indeed,' Mr Nimrin agreed. 'If for any reason they begin to doubt you, of course they will kill you, to protect their own security. But before they kill you, your mild friend Levrin will torture you to find out what you know, and you'll get to see what *he's* really about. If we had not had this conversation, and you continued to know nothing, that would soon come out under torture, and then they would come for *me*. Now we have had this conversation, and it, too, would soon come out under torture, and once again they would come to me.'

Mr Nimrin leaned back, the better to survey Josh. 'You are my only hope for survival,' he said. 'I can't say I'm encouraged.'

7

NEITHER WAS JOSH. All the way home in the new cab, Mr Nimrin's story kept circling in his brain, and he could find nowhere in it a way out for himself.

Was the story true ? Well, the checks had been true, and the Cayman Islands bank account was true, and Levrin's appearance on the ferry dock had been true, and Mr Nimrin looked exactly like the only extant public photo of himself, absent moustache. So it was undeniably true that he was caught up in *something*, but who knew what? It was like one of those dreams that begin in the middle: you're running, something's chasing you, and there's a cliff dead ahead.

I'll have to tell Eve this weekend, he promised himself. I can't carry this by myself, and who else is there to tell? I've been betraying my country for seven years without knowing it, and now they want me to *do* something, I don't know what, and if I don't do it, or if I let them even suspect the truth about me, they'll kill me. After torturing me, let's not forget that part, because *they* won't.

Will it be possible to pretend to go along with them, and yet not actually *do* anything? Anything, uh, treasonous.

Too late, he realized. I've already done something. I've provided a safe house for foreign agents coming into America to do something America won't like.

He overtipped the cabby, to start the belated process of becoming a good guy, and went up to his apartment, where of course there was a phone message from Eve: 'Josh? It's six thirty. Can you still be at the office? I'll try you there.'

Well, no, she wouldn't find him there, and the time was now seven-forty, so where had he been all this time? He fully intended to tell her the truth this weekend, somehow or other, but he couldn't possibly tell her any truth at all now, not on the phone.

He wasn't used to lying to Eve, had never lied to her except about birthday presents; that he wasn't going out to buy her one, that he liked the one she'd bought for him, things like that. It's true he hadn't told her about the checks, but that hadn't been a *lie*. He hadn't made anything up in that instance, he'd merely left something out.

Now, he would have to make something up. When Jules Verne was asked what he thought of the science fiction writings of H. G. Wells, he'd indignantly said, '*Il invent!*' Why did he now remember that one little item from college, when he'd forgotten almost everything else? Whatever; he would now have to reach down and find that inner H.G. Wells. Time to invent.

When he phoned, after first drinking a long glass of water to calm himself, she said, '*There* you are! Where are you?'

'Home,' he said, still searching for an invention, and suddenly thought of Jack Crisp. 'I was having a beer with Jack Crisp,' he said. 'You remember him.'

'He's somebody at the agency,' she said, sounding confused. 'But you don't like him.'

'I don't *dis*like him,' Josh said, which was sort of true. 'And, turns out, we're in the same boat.' Which was absolutely true, and the reason, he suddenly realized, that Jack Crisp had come into his mind in his moment of need. All at once, he liked Jack more than before.

'In the same boat?' He could almost see Eve turn to look out the window, seaward, for a boat.

'His family's away this month, too,' Josh explained. 'At the beach. He's commuting weekends, same as me.'

'Oh. Out here?'

'No, the Jersey shore. Down around Barnegat Bay. I think it's an easier commute.'

'I wouldn't like the Jersey shore.'

'No, neither would I,' Josh agreed, thinking, good, we're changing the subject.

But she stayed with it a bit longer: 'So you were two abandoned husbands, having a beer together.'

'That's it.'

'Are you going to do that all the time?'

'No, I don't think so.' Josh forced a laugh that he certainly hoped didn't sound forced. 'He is kind of boring, to tell the truth.'

'So you'll probably be home at the regular time tomorrow.'

'Oh, sure,' he said. 'You know, if nothing unforeseen comes up.'

8

NOTHING UNFORESEEN KEPT him from going straight home on Wednesday. The something unforeseen was already in his living room, and it was Levrin. He had made himself a drink, with ice cubes and what looked like watered scotch, and he was seated in comfort on the sofa, leafing through the *New Yorker* that had been on the coffee table. He smiled pleasantly at Josh, lifted his glass in a toast, and said, 'Hello.'

The pleasant smile and the easy pose did nothing to soften the sudden dread that gripped Josh's chest, squeezing it like a rubber ball. 'What is it?' he asked, and imagined himself doing a U-turn, sprinting for the elevator. No, the stairs; no waiting for the elevator.

'Oh, one or two things,' Levrin said, and lifted his glass again. 'Do you want to get yourself a drink first?'

'Yes,' Josh said, and went to the kitchen to fall apart, shaking and trembling all over, gripping the sink, staring out the window at the apartment building across West End Avenue. When at last his breathing calmed, and he felt he could let go of the sink without falling over, he got a bottle of beer from the refrigerator, opened it, and carried it to the living room, where Levrin had the *New Yorker* open on his lap and was smiling at a cartoon. He looked up when Josh entered, and said, 'I understand about half the cartoons in this magazine, and they are usually very good.'

'Yes, they are.' Josh sat in *his* armchair and rattled the beer bottle onto the side table.

'If I lived in America all the time, I would understand more of them.'

'Sure.'

Levrin tossed the magazine onto the coffee table, put his glass on the end table to his left, and reached for something on the floor. Josh tensed, and Levrin came up with a thick briefcase, black, scuffed. The snaps opened like pistol shots, and Josh kept thinking of Mr Nimrin's description of this man. Levrin reached into the briefcase, and Josh stared at that forearm, forgetting to breathe. Levrin brought out a large self-closing plastic bag, about the right size for a head of lettuce, and Josh saw that in a way it did contain lettuce; money, cash, American bills. Levrin held it up for Josh to see, and then, as he put it on the sofa beside himself, said, 'I'll ask you to hide this somewhere until you leave on Friday, and then put it under your pillow. It will be gone next week, when you return.'

'It looks like a lot of money,' Josh said.

'Ten thousand dollars,' Levrin told him, smiling fondly at the package. 'And the other thing,' he said, as he focused on Josh again. 'I don't want you to be startled, so I thought I should tell you.'

Startled, Josh said, 'Yes?'

'There will be some matériel, when you return next week. Temporarily stored here, but not for long.'

'Matériel?'

'Yes, not a lot.'

'Bombs?' Josh was instantly sorry he'd asked.

In any event, Levrin looked at him in surprise. 'Of course not,' he said. 'We don't want you blown up or this apartment.'

'Good,' Josh said.

'The things will be here for just a little while,' Levrin assured him. 'Gone before your family comes back from the ocean.'

'Good,' Josh said.

9

THIS WAS THE first year they'd tried this kind of summer vacation, and the first year on Fire Island. Before Jeremy, they'd automatically done everything together, and the first year after Jeremy's arrival they did nothing. Now, it had become necessary to plan some sort of summer vacation that would get the increasingly active Jeremy out of the apartment for at least part of the season. Josh would take his own vacation time in midwinter, as usual, and the family would do something in the Caribbean, but that meant this summer had to be their first extended separation.

They'd chosen Fair Harbor because it was a summer beach community, supposed to be good for kids, and because they already had some links to the place, two couples who regularly summered there, the Frasers, who were childless, and the Welshes, with daughters, four and six. It was enough of a nucleus so Eve wouldn't be lonely out at the beach during the week. Not as lonely as Josh in town.

Usually, the trip out from the city on Friday afternoons was a simple pleasure, no matter what the traffic or the weather, because he was on his way to a reunion with Eve. But today everything was different – anxious and unnerving. Today was the day he'd tell her everything, and try to decide, with her, what to do about it all. Driving out, he tested various fantasy conversations in his mind, but everything he imagined himself saying sounded awkward and false.

'I'm being asked to be a traitor, and if I don't do it they'll kill me.' No, he'd have to ease into the story from some other direction, if he didn't merely want to sound like a lunatic. But he had no idea what, neither in the car nor on the ferry.

There she was on the dock, as usual, waving. He could recognize which bikini was hers by now, and so he could start his own waving from farther out in the channel, and as he did so he realized that telling her his problem could not be the first thing he did out here this weekend. It would have to be the second.

Yes. She kissed him, and smiled with her eyes that certain way, and said, 'Jeremy's with Mrs Winchell until we pick him up.'

'Good,' he said.

'The Welshes invited us for dinner,' she said. She'd just come out of the shower and, naked, stood in the middle of the bedroom to pummel her wet hair with a large green towel.

He was half-seated, half-sprawled on the bed. 'Tonight?'

'Yes, of course.' She let her hair alone long enough to peer out at him from inside the towel. 'What's wrong?'

'Wrong. Well...' He couldn't tell her like this, in this situation, but if they were going out to dinner with other people he had to tell her soon.

She shook her head, lowered the towel, and said, 'We'll talk later. I can see something's bothering you. Take your shower and I'll go get Jeremy.'

'No,' he said. 'Don't get Jeremy, not yet.'

She looked at him. 'Why not?'

'We do have to talk,' he said, getting up from the bed. 'Just wait. I'll take a quick shower, and then we'll talk.'

Dressed in khaki shorts and a blue T-shirt, he went out and found her on the back deck, in white shorts and a green halter. She was drinking iced tea. She pointed at it, and said, 'Want some?'

'Maybe later.'

He sat at the rusted white table with her, and looked out at the scrub pines that incompletely hid the neighbors. The houses were too close together here and the vegetation too scrubby, but people made up for it by leaving one another alone. There were people in the houses all around them, but no one could be seen, and nothing could be heard except somebody's electric saw half a block away. The owners did their own carpentry all summer. The rising and falling shush of the ocean sounded in a different way, hardly a noise at all, but always present.

Eve watched him, a little worried. 'You have something to tell me,' she said.

'I've been trying to think where to start.' It was easier if he looked at the bits of white clapboard siding he could see past the scrub pines. He said, 'I think maybe I should start with the checks.'

'Checks?' She was utterly baffled. 'Josh? What is this about?'

'Seven years ago, before I met you—'

'Josh!'

'Please,' he said, 'let me figure out how to tell this.'

'I won't say a word,' she said, and folded her arms, which meant, he knew, that as soon as she had it straight in her mind what she should be mad at, she intended to be *very* mad.

Much safer to look at the white clapboard. 'Seven years ago I got a check in the mail for a thousand dollars. No explanation, nothing. From something called United States Agent.'

'You get envelopes from them,' she said. 'I've seen them sometimes.'

'Every month. A check for a thousand dollars.'

'But—'

'Let me tell it, Eve. It's hard enough anyway.'

'I won't say a word,' she said, and unfolded her arms.

'Seven years ago,' he told the white clapboard, 'I was broke, I needed the money, I thought maybe it was government somehow, something to do with the army. I deposited it, and it cleared, and the next month I got another one. And ever since.'

'And you never knew who sent them or why?'

'Not until now.'

'Something happened,' she said.

'Oh, boy.' He shook his head. 'I tried to find out who they were, years ago, but their phone never answers, and the address just says K Street, no house number.'

'In Washington,' she said. 'I thought they were something to do with the government.'

'So did I, at first.'

'But they're not. What are they?'

He said, 'Here's where it gets weird. It turns out, there's this guy, I don't know, he's Russian or Ukrainian or something, I'm not sure what, but he's a spy.'

'A spy,' she said, in a flat voice, and he knew, if he were to look away from the clapboard he would see skepticism on her face.

'It's true,' he said. 'It's just as true as the checks. Nine years ago, this man started a scam to steal from his government or his spy funds or whatever – for when he'd retire. So he pretended he'd recruited these people to be what they call sleepers, deep cover spies they could activate if they ever needed them, and he pretended to pay them each a thousand dollars a month, but he was actually keeping it all for himself.'

'But you *are* getting it.'

'Because he got involved in a spy trial, I read it online in the *Washington*

Post, you could read it, too. And it meant, he lost that job he had, and somebody else got that desk, who thought the sleepers were really sleepers and started sending them the money.'

'Including you.'

'Including me.'

'You mean,' she said, 'for seven years you were being paid to be a spy.'

'And never knew it.'

'But now you do.'

He sighed. 'They activated me,' he said.

There was such silence from his left that he had no choice; he had to look at her. Her face now was a study in complexity, or abstraction, or something. Like a person eating a Fig Newton for the first time? Or a person not sure if that dog is friendly.

He said, 'It's serious, Eve. Take a look at this,' and drew the bankbook from his pocket, to slide it across the rusty table to her.

She looked at it for ten or fifteen seconds before picking it up, as though not sure she wanted to be a party to this thing. But then she did pick it up, studied the cover, studied the first page, studied the second page, and then, holding it open, frowned at Josh. 'It says you have forty thousand dollars there.'

'And I do,' he told her. 'I went to their website, and it's real. The money's there.'

She studied the bankbook some more. 'Opened on July fourteenth,' she said.

'The man who activated me,' Josh said, 'gave it to me last Friday over in Bay Shore. While I was waiting for the ferry.'

Her frown deepened. 'You knew about this for a *week*?'

'I didn't know what to do,' he said. 'I knew I was in some kind of trouble, but I didn't know what kind, and then the man who started the scam came to see me this week, and told me about it, and it's *big* trouble. So I have to tell you about it.'

She turned the bankbook this way and that. 'What do they want you to do?'

'I'm not sure yet. Last weekend, they had people staying in our apartment, I don't know who, I never saw them. And right now there's a bag with ten thousand dollars in cash under my pillow, that's supposed to be gone by the time I get back. And—'

'Under your *pillow*?'

'That's where he told me to put it.'

'The man that started the scam.'

41

'No, there's two of them.'

'I'm not getting this,' she said.

'The man that gave me the bankbook is my control,' Josh explained. 'His name is Levrin. The other one, that started the scam, is Mr Nimrin. And *he* says, if Levrin finds out I was never really a sleeper at all, his people will kill us both, Mr Nimrin and me, him for punishment and me for security.'

He watched her, expecting a reaction, astonishment, fear, *something*, but all she did was watch him back, as she took another bite out of that Fig Newton. Slowly, she lowered her frown to the bankbook in her hand. She turned it over. She riffled its pages. She read every word and every number on every page. She raised her frown to focus on him. 'Did you have the graphics people put this together, at the agency?'

'What?' He couldn't believe it. 'No! For what?'

'As a joke.'

The finger he pointed at the bankbook trembled. 'That's no joke,' he said. 'Go on their website. Read the *Washington Post*.'

'I could, you know.'

'Do! Do!'

She considered him, considered the bankbook, then said, 'These people are real.'

'Yes. Yes.'

'And there were people in our apartment last weekend.'

'Yes.'

'And you put a bag of money under your pillow.'

'I suppose it's still there,' Josh said.

She thought about it. For quite some time, she communed with the clapboard. Then she sighed and faced him and said, 'You can't have anything to do with those people.'

'But if I don't,' he told her, 'they'll kill me. I mean, Mr Nimrin was very clear on that.'

Stubbornly, she shook her head. 'I believe you, you somehow got into this mess—'

'Just stupid, I was just stupid.'

'You wouldn't do anything *this* elaborate, just for a joke.'

'Of course not!'

'But you can't do it,' she said. 'They can make threats all they want. You just can't help them.'

'That's what I've been trying to think about,' he said. 'What are my choices? What can I do? I thought, maybe take the forty thousand dollars out of that account, and the three of us go to Canada and change our names. I bet I could get an ad agency job in Toronto.'

'No, Josh,' she said. 'You're not somebody who lives on the run. You're not a fugitive, you're not the type.'

'Then what else do I do?'

'Go to the police. The FBI.'

'Mr Nimrin says I'm being watched, so they'd probably grab me before I could get to the police, or the FBI. And if I *do* go to them, what do I say? There are spies in New York. Everybody knows there's spies in New York. What are they doing? I don't know. Mr Nimrin says the FBI would probably think I'm just a turncoat trying to turn back, lost my nerve after I was activated.'

'But you can tell them the truth!'

'What's the truth?' he asked her. 'I cashed the checks for seven years. Are they going to believe I never found out who was paying me, never worried about it, just cashed the checks?'

'It really wasn't very smart,' she said.

'It was the easiest thing to do,' he said. 'For seven years, it was easy. Money for nothing.'

She shook her head. 'But why *you*? Why did they pick you?'

'I have no idea,' he said, because the one thing he couldn't tell her was his early history as a loudmouth barroom radical. 'Just the luck of the draw,' he said.

She thought about it. Now she, too, studied the white clapboard across the way, while Josh studied her face, realizing how important that face was to him, how important their life together was, how little he'd really needed that thousand dollars a month over the years, and how abruptly and unexpectedly he'd put everything from their life at risk. Including life itself.

'All right,' she said at last, and looked at him. 'Here's what I think you should do.'

'Just tell me.'

'Well, you're part of the decision-making, too,' she said. 'Don't put it *all* on me.'

'Tell.'

'All right. What I think you should do is open a file in the laptop here, and put in it everything you told me, and put the date. The people's names, and what you did, and what they told you. And say in there, you're afraid for your life—'

'I am.'

43

'And I think you're right,' she said. 'So you say in there, you're afraid, and that's why you'll go along with those people unless they ask you to do something really illegal or wicked, and you'll keep that file as a diary, and tell it everything that happens. *Then*, if the time comes that you have to go to the police, or they come to you—'

'Oh, God.'

'You can show them the file. So they can see for themselves the fix you were in. That should count for *something*.'

'So I should write it all down,' he said, 'and I should go along with those people unless they want me to do something really bad.'

'And,' she said, 'we should have a glass of wine before we go to the Welshes. To calm us down.' Gesturing at the glass in front of herself, she said, 'This is no time for tea.'

'I'll bring it out,' he said, rising.

'Take your bankbook,' she said, extending it toward him.

He took it, reluctantly. 'For the first time in my life,' he said, 'I don't really want money.'

In the kitchen, he got the wine bottle from the refrigerator and glasses from the shelf, and was pouring the wine when it occurred to him he hadn't told her about the 'matériel' he was allegedly going to be storing next week.

Well, enough for today. He could tell her about the matériel later, when he knew what it was.

10

GUNS. UNDER THE bed were four long wooden boxes, about the right size to carry a pair of ski poles each. Numbers and letters were stenciled in black on the boxes, and when he pulled one out from under the bed it had a square of paper glued to the top, containing several lines of words or numbers, the most important of which were AUTOMAT-KALASHNIKOVA and AK-47.

Josh sat heavily on the floor in front of the box he'd pulled out. Assault rifles. He was storing in his bedroom, under his bed, the favorite weapon of terrorists and guerillas and revolutionaries all around the world. Four of them.

And what else? No bombs, Levrin had assured him; but AK-47s? What else?

Under Jeremy's crib, four cardboard boxes, heavily taped, which had markings and words on them Josh couldn't understand, but also one drawing he understood completely: The curved metal magazine that would contain the AK-47's bullets. Many of the consumers of these products around the world would be illiterate, of course, or would only speak some obscure local language, so the picture was meant to be helpful to the customer, and Josh was sure it was appreciated.

And what else? In the closet in his bedroom, hanging in black plastic garment bags, four uniforms, a very dark green-brown, with black-and-red boards on the shoulders and silver lightning-bolt pins on the lapels and red chevrons on the sleeves. On the floor in the closet, a box of tall black lace-up boots. On the shelf in the closet, four white cardboard boxes, each containing an officer-type military hat, with a longer hard brim and higher front peak than usual, so that the hats all by themselves, without uniforms or people or anything underneath them, already looked evil.

He couldn't have this. He still hadn't actually *done* anything, hadn't participated in anything bad, but these things were not here for the staff

45

picnic. He couldn't let this go on.

But what to do? Make a run for the FBI, downtown? Or maybe even phone them from here.

No. Even if *they* weren't watching him every second, they were surely tapping his phone and no doubt had people around Foley Square, looking to see who approached the FBI offices.

He couldn't go back to Fair Harbor to discuss this with Eve. She'd be horrified, and she'd have to blame him for this mess, and besides, he'd just come to town. He was supposed to have lunch now and after that go into the office. He was supposed to be thinking about Cloudbank toilet paper, not AK-47s.

Well, he couldn't go to the office today, he was sure of that much. He'd have a hysterical fit in the elevator, he'd faint at his desk, he'd blurt out his problems to everybody in the place.

He did have to go out now, but it wouldn't have anything to do with lunch. Food would lie like cannonballs in his stomach, he couldn't even think about it.

But before he left here, he had to deal with the office. He phoned, and Martha the receptionist answered, and he said, 'Martha, hi, it's Josh. Listen, I can't come in today, I think I got food poisoning or something.'

'You're still out on the island?' If there was an accusation in that, she hid it well, with a flat delivery.

'No, I came back to town this morning,' he told her, 'but I just keep feeling worse. Maybe it's the clams I had.'

'Seafood,' she said. 'That can be the worst.'

'I'm gonna nap, and maybe see a doctor. I'm sure I'll be all right tomorrow.'

'You don't sound good,' she admitted.

'I'm not good.'

'I'll tell Mr Grimsby,' she said.

'Thanks,' he said, and left the arsenal his apartment had become.

Riverside Drive was still windy, as he crossed the sidewalk from the departing cab to the doorman opening the entrance. 'Hi,' he said, being unable to ignore people as totally as Mr Nimrin could.

'Sir,' the doorman said.

Josh crossed to that inner door, with the marble steps and the wrought iron railing. If the door's locked, he thought, if she isn't there, I won't know what to do. I don't know her name, I don't know anything.

The door wasn't locked. He opened it, and heard that distant bell sound, and again when he shut the door. He walked over to stand beside the coffee table and look at the interior door, through which, as Mr Nimrin had pointed out last time, she would come.

She did. She looked at Josh in mild surprise, without recognition. 'Yes?'

'I was here with Mr Nimrin. I need to see him again.'

'I am with a patient,' she said. 'Do sit down, it won't be long.'

She nodded, maybe to encourage him, and withdrew, shutting her door. He sat, fidgeting, on the same sofa as last time, and looked over at the magazines on the coffee table. But he couldn't read, he couldn't do anything but sit and feel his nerves unstring.

It was nearly half an hour before a stunning redhead of about thirty came out, gave him a cool look she might have offered to a caged parakeet, and left, her little pink summer skirt twitching around her thighs.

'You wanted to see *me*?'

Oh – he'd been staring at the redhead. He turned and the older woman was in the interior doorway, giving him a somewhat skeptical smile. 'Sorry,' he said, and stood.

'That's all right,' she assured him. 'Even matters of life and death must take a back seat to sex. Come in.'

The next room was like an antique shop, crowded with armoires, desks, hutches, sofas, armchairs. Two windows would look out on Riverside Drive through vertical iron bars, except that they were so heavily swathed in drapes.

The woman gestured to a maroon empire settee, saying, 'Sit there,' while she sat in a bulky black leather armchair at right angles to it. Handy to her right hand, he noticed, was a round table with notepad and pen. And handy to his own settee was a small table with a box of tissues on it.

He said, 'I have to get in touch with Mr Nimrin. Right away.'

'Yes, I understand,' she said. 'I don't know your name.'

'Josh Redmont. I don't know yours, either.'

She smiled at that. 'I am Harriet Linde,' she said. 'Elwah didn't tell you much about me, I see.'

Elwah? Then he remembered, from the *Washington Post*, that Mr Nimrin's first name was Ellois; so that's how it was pronounced. He said, 'I think there's a lot Mr Nimrin doesn't tell people.'

'I have never asked him his business,' she said, 'and he has never volunteered. But he is something sub rosa, that much is obvious.'

'Can you help me talk to him?'

'Perhaps.' She studied him, and he struggled to contain his impatience.

47

'You are not,' she decided, 'the sort of person I usually see with Ellois.'

Probably not. Josh said, 'If he doesn't tell you his business, maybe I shouldn't tell you his business, either.'

She laughed at that, and said, 'No, I wouldn't ask. But let me tell you how we met.'

Any other time, Josh would have been happy to hear how Harriet Linde and Ellois Nimrin met, but not now. 'It's kind of urgent,' he said.

'No, I don't believe it is,' she told him. 'I can see that you are in deep distress, but if your problem were *urgent* you wouldn't be here, going all 'round Robin Hood's barn. You are here because you want to maintain secrecy, not because your problem is urgent.'

'All right,' he said, and tried to calm himself.

'Take deep breaths,' she suggested, 'and I will tell you the story. This was, oh, almost thirty-five years ago. I was in Vienna for the first time, at a conference. It was very cold, but beautifully sunny, and I was walking by myself in the park, because I was very young and knew no one at the conference: Then suddenly a man was beside me, grasping my arm, and very urgently – *this* was urgency – he said, "Pretend you know me." '

'No,' Josh said.

Again she laughed. 'Exactly,' she said. 'My reaction exactly. I thought, immediately, has any man ever in the whole long history of the world actually used that as a pickup line? Impossible.'

'It wasn't a pickup line,' Josh said.

'Well, it was,' she said, and he could see that all at once she was very nearly blushing. 'Not primarily, no, but yes, it was that, too.'

'And I guess it worked.'

'He said he would buy me a torte. We went to a café, and he wanted to sit inside, of course. He asked me where I was from, and when I said New York he said he was often in New York and asked for my phone number, which of course I gave him. I asked where *he* was from, and he said, "I am a man of the world." '

Now Josh laughed. 'He gets all the good lines,' he said.

'But spoken with such conviction,' she said, 'that they lose their absurdity. I believe Ellois *is* a man of the world, if that is another way to say no fixed abode.'

'Okay,' Josh said.

'We spent a little while in the café,' she went on, 'and slowly he relaxed. Then he paid our bill, and said he'd no doubt call me in New York, and asked me to stay at the table a little longer, and he went away to the back of the café. I took it for granted I'd never see him again.'

'But you did.'

'The next day,' she said, 'at my hotel. And from time to time, over the years. Sometimes here in New York, sometimes places where I'd be at a conference, San Francisco, for instance, or once Sao Paulo. Once, years ago, he asked if he might use my waiting room on occasion, if he had a private conversation he needed to keep private, and I said of course. Over the years, I would guess he's done that fewer than half a dozen times, and I must say, you were the first reputable-looking person I've seen him with.'

Josh said, 'Aren't you curious?'

'Of course,' she said. 'But curiosity would kill more than the cat in this case. Whatever Ellois is involved in must have some sordid elements I wouldn't want to know about. And if he found me expressing curiosity about him, I *know* I would never see him again. For instance, something changed with him seven or eight years ago—'

'Seven,' Josh said.

She paused to give him a bright-eyed look. 'Thank you,' she said. 'But do not tell me things I don't want to know.'

'Sorry.'

'Seven years ago, as you say,' she said, 'something changed in Ellois's life. He doesn't travel the way he used to. His spirit is not broken, but is more . . . defensive. May I ask what your trade is?'

'I'm an advertising copywriter.'

'Ah.' She nodded. 'There's a great deal of self-hatred in that occupation, I understand.'

'I don't hate myself,' Josh told her.

'Good. To be associated with Ellois suggests self-destructive behavior.'

'I'm trying to save myself,' he promised her. 'That's why I need to talk to Mr Nimrin.'

'Good,' she said. 'I can reach him, but indirectly, and not at once. I will let him know that you feel the need to meet with him, and then it's up to him.'

'Oh,' Josh said.

'I'm sorry, that's all I can do.'

'Okay.' He looked around, at the overstuffed but somehow comforting room. 'So I guess I should . . . go home.'

'Or to your work. Work can be a great solace.'

'If it doesn't make us self-destructive,' Josh suggested.

Laughing, she said, 'I'm glad Ellois's grade of associates has risen. Nice to meet you, Mr Redmont.'

'And you, Ms Linde,' Josh said, all at once realizing she'd told him that story because he'd come in here hysterical, and it was the way to calm him down. He hadn't known he was hysterical, but he could feel the difference in himself. Maybe he *would* go to work this afternoon. Food poisoning all gone.

As he got to his feet he said, 'Thank you. I hope I haven't taken time from a patient.'

'This is my lunchtime,' she said. 'And for you, too.'

'Lunch and work,' he said. 'Thank you for the prescription.'

11

THEY'D NEVER GOTTEN more than the standard TV channels for the apartment in New York – out in Fair Harbor these days, Eve wallowed in the luxury of a dish – because they'd never thought of themselves as people who stayed indoors to watch television. Once Jeremy came along, it looked as though they might have to rethink that, but inertia had so far won the battle, so these evenings, alone with his AK-47s, he didn't have much choice in his TV-watching.

But he really did want to watch TV. In the first place, if he didn't fill his evenings with moving pictures, no matter of what, he'd get bored out of his mind, alone here in this little apartment. And in the second place, waiting for Mr Nimrin to make contact – and knowing he might never make contact – would be completely unbearable if he didn't have something to distract himself.

Which is why, at ten that evening, still having no word from Mr Nimrin, he roamed restlessly among the channels available to him and at last settled on a news-magazine program, mostly because it seemed to be the only thing on offer without a laughtrack. The first segment was about advances in geriatric health care, which, along with the attendant commercials for denture glue and worse, made it pretty clear what demographic he had now fallen among. All right, go ahead; those earnest white-coated people speaking to somebody just off Josh's right shoulder were at least soothing.

Harriet Linde had been soothing today, hadn't she? He guessed she must be a very good psychoanalyst, the way she almost casually diagnosed his immediate problem and went about treating it. And she was exactly the kind of very strong person that Mr Nimrin needed, who would never invade his privacy and who would never ask more of him than he was capable of giving. And he would treat her with the same distant respect.

Sooner or later, I guess, he told himself, we all find the right person out of the five billion. Or most of us do. Like Eve and me.

I am being, he next told himself, bored into philosophy. Cut it out.

So he focused on the television set, where they had gone into the second segment of their program, this one concerning the upcoming visit to New York City of someone called Fyeddr Mihommed-Sinn, the premier of Kamastan, one of the smaller shards created when the Soviet Union got smashed, yet another Stan in among the Stans. It seemed that Premier Mihommed-Sinn would be leaving Kamastan for the first time in his life, as a result of the Olympic gold medal won by its ace sprinter, Drogdrd Ozak, the first Kamastanian athlete ever to compete in the Olympics, much less win. Footage was shown, with the sprinter's name superimposed on the screen as Ozak sprinted by.

It had now turned out that Premier Mihommed-Sinn was a mad sports fan, who had almost died with elation when young Ozak had won the sprint. In the footage of the premier going about his official duties at home, he looked in fact very little like a man who would die with elation and very much like a man who would kill with impunity. Short, muscular, glowering, he looked mostly like the kind of super who disapproves of the way you handle your garbage.

A man who had never before seen a reason to leave Kamastan, the premier would fly to New York City now because his first-ever Olympic gold winner would be receiving a special United Nations medal at a ceremony in Yankee Stadium. Athletes and politicians from around the globe would be present at the event.

It was hoped, the announcer explained, that this trip would be the beginning of a thawing process between Premier Mihommed-Sinn and the rest of the world. He was considered the most despotic of the despots who ran the Stans, and was roundly hated both inside his country and without. That sports had been the way to melt his icy heart was considered a wonderfully hopeful sign all over the place.

Premier Mihommed-Sinn had received other invitations for his stay in America, to visit the White House and the United Nations and Universal Studios, but had turned them all down. He would fly in Kamastan Air Force One into JFK, with a planeload of bodyguards right behind him. He would spend a night at the Kamastan Mission to the United Nations on York Avenue, he would autocade to Yankee Stadium, he would take part in the ceremonies there, he would spend a second night at the Mission, and then he would sky homeward. Taking with him, it was hoped, a clearer gentler understanding of the outside world.

All of this would occur over this coming weekend. The premier would fly in on Friday the twenty-ninth of this month, spend that night at the Mission on York Avenue, attend the ceremony promptly at two on Saturday afternoon, and would then sky back to his lesser Heaven on Sunday. The Saturday afternoon events would be shown live on this channel beginning at one-thirty. Various sporting exhibitions would be a part of the festivities.

File footage was also shown of Premier Mihommed-Sinn reviewing some of the troops of his giant army. Apart from sports, his giant army was the only thing in the world the premier was known to love. These troops wore uniforms of a very dark green-brown, with black-and-red boards on the shoulders and red chevrons on the sleeves. Their military hats, with a longer hard brim and higher front peak than usual, made the tough faces under them look even tougher.

Josh gaped. The footage changed to Yankee Stadium, where a security expert talked about the extraordinary measures that would be taken to protect the world-hated premier during his visit, but Josh just went on gaping.

He knew.

12

TUESDAY HE DID go into the office again, where he wasn't much use to anybody, including himself. But he felt that he ought to keep up his regular schedule as much as possible, both to keep Levrin and his people lulled into believing everything was still all right with Redmont, and also as the best way to make it possible for Mr Nimrin to get in touch. If Mr Nimrin ever wanted to get in touch.

Mr Nimrin *had* to want to get in touch! Josh was on the verge of blowing this whole thing up, out of nothing but blind fear and maddened panic. If there was a way to survive this mess without a whole panoply of bloodshed and madness, Mr Nimrin would know it. Mr Nimrin, it seemed to Josh, was a survivor. The thing to do was stand next to Mr Nimrin.

But where *was* he? Hadn't Harriet Linde told him the state Josh was in? And yet, nothing all day Tuesday. He didn't particularly want a taxi home tonight, would have been happy to walk, clear his head, but since Mr Nimrin had used a cab to make contact that first time, Josh – with difficulty – hailed one again today, and rode all the way home alone.

But he wasn't alone once he got there. He walked in his front door into the living room and this time, sitting on the sofa there, drink in hand, completely relaxed and at home, was not Levrin with his scotch and water but a very lanky long-haired brunette in a silver sheath, holding in one hand a tall champagne glass he recognized as one of his own, containing no doubt champagne. Yes; there on the coffee table, atop a Tweety potholder, was their white ceramic icebucket, with an opened champagne bottle angled up out of it, very like, he suddenly noticed, a howitzer out of a fort.

This woman, who might be thirty in a minute or two, rose when he came into the room, and was very tall indeed, probably six foot three, at least an inch taller than Josh, and about a hundred pounds lighter. Her nearly black hair fell in long folds to frame a long but delicately beautiful face and to brush her bare shoulders as she moved. Her smile was frank, but not quite suggestive. 'You are Josh Redmont,' she said, with a charming hint of accent.

He almost said, *I'm married*, but a more appropriate moment for that statement would arrive eventually, he was sure. So all he said was, 'Yes, I am. I live here.'

'It is a charming little apartment,' she told him. 'I am Tina Pausto. I am to be billeted with you for a while.'

'Billeted? You're moving in?'

'Andrei Levrin thought,' she told him, 'you would be too lonely here, without your family. As the day approaches, you see, we must all concentrate. You will forgive me if I say nothing about the operation itself.'

'Sure,' he said, because she didn't *have* to tell him anything about the operation itself. He already knew far too much about the operation itself.

With a graceful gesture, and a slight dip of the knee, she said, 'Would you join me? Champagne at vespers.'

An empty glass stood on the coffee table beside the icebucket. Josh looked at it, looked at the half-full glass in Tina Pausto's hand, and said no, thank you. Or that's what he thought he was saying, but what he heard was, 'Yes, thank you.'

She did a perfect bunny dip, emphasizing her breasts by not displaying them, and poured him half a glass, then topped up her own, then, as the bubbles receded, topped up his. As she put the bottle back into the icebucket and he reached for the glass, their arms did an intertwining thing, all in motion, never quite touching, that Josh found stunning, as though he'd just entered some sort of electric field. Like those science fiction movies where people shimmer through doorways because they're entering a different dimension.

Well, he didn't *want* to enter a different dimension. Levrin and Mr Nimrin had him in trouble enough, with the FBI and no doubt the CIA and all the police departments of the world, and the giant army of Kamastan, and who knew who all; he wasn't going to let them get him in trouble with Eve.

So, as Tina Pausto resumed her place on the sofa, gesturing for him to join her there, he stayed on his feet. He said, 'How many people are going to live here now?'

'Just we two, at present,' she said. 'When you go away for the weekend, others may drop by.'

To suit up, no doubt. Desperate to quantify the dangers that surrounded him, and even eliminate one or two of them if possible, he said, 'Are you supposed to sleep with me?'

She raised an eyebrow at him, with the faintest of smiles, as though he were guilty of some breach of politesse, as though he'd raised a topic that would not have been voiced in gracious company. 'That was not discussed,' she said.

'Well, where *are* you going to sleep?'

'Wherever we decide,' she told him. 'The apartment is small, but not *that* small. I'm sure the living arrangements will sort themselves out.'

She *was* supposed to get him into bed! To keep his loyalty, to interrogate him when he was befuddled, for whatever reasons spies had when they employed femme fatales.

Damn damn damn. If he were tired of Eve, or if he were by nature an unfaithful kind of guy, what a hell of a week he could have before the shit hit the fan.

But, no. 'Maybe that sofa'd be okay,' he said, nodding at it.

She patted the cushion beside her hip. 'Very comfortable, I should think,' she said, not as though she believed it, and the phone rang.

Josh leaped like an adulterer. 'That's my wife! She calls every—' In motion, he said, 'I'll take it in the bedroom.'

'I shall not listen in,' she assured him, and he ran to the bedroom, shutting the door, thinking that it hadn't even occurred to him that she *might* listen in.

'Eve—'

'Barnes and Noble,' Mr Nimrin's voice said. 'Broadway and Sixty-fifth Street. An author reading on the third floor at seven P.M.'

'But—' Josh said to the dial tone, then broke the connection and, before he could think about it, speed-dialed the Fire Island number.

'Yes?'

'Eve, it's me, I couldn't wait to talk to you.'

'Just a minute, I'm feeding him. Hold on.'

'Should I call back?'

'No no, we're almost done. Damn! Oh, that's all right, sweetie, Daddy never liked that plate anyway.'

'Our damage deposit,' Josh said, 'is going to look like the far end of a Ponzi scheme.'

'There!' she said. 'Just a little clean-up . . .'

Josh heard water running, a baby crying, more water, more baby, then just baby, then receding baby, then door closing. Not slamming, closing. But forcefully.

'*There!* How are you?'

'Things are getting worse around here, to tell the truth,' he said. 'I'll give you the ugly details on Friday.'

'Should I come back for a day? I could leave Jer—'

'No no, that's fine,' Josh said, preferring to describe his new roommate to Eve from afar on the weekend than have her see Tina Pausto in situ and in the flesh. 'What's going on out there, anyway?' he asked, because it was always possible to change the topic to the latest beach gossip.

They chatted a few minutes, about nothing at all. During it, Josh fervently wished that nothing at all was all they could possibly chat about, and when they were finished, winding down, he said, 'Tomorrow, I'll wait for you to make the call.'

'That is better,' she said.

'Love you.'

'Love you.'

In the living room, Tina Pausto, like her predecessor on that sofa, sat leafing through the *New Yorker*. Josh said, 'I have to go out for a while. You'll take care of your own dinner?'

She gave him a comfortable smile. 'I am very self-sufficient,' she assured him. 'Like a cat.'

13

THIS POSTER-STYLE sign rested on an easel beside the ground-floor escalator. Josh rode up, the bookstore becoming more open to him as he rose, with a few dozen customers visible, none of them apparently here for Volume VII of the Farbender Netherbender Series.

It was a little trickier to find the next escalator, and then there he was on 3, where a more generic poster read AUTHOR READING with an arrow. Josh followed the arrow to a corner of the building, where the late summer twilight showed Broadway beyond the windows. Within, a carpeted lecture area had been constructed. Within an L of bookshelves about thirty wooden chairs faced a lectern beside a small desk, on which hardcover books were stacked, their spines all reading *ENCHANTRESS* in large letters, and on a second line *of Nyin* in smaller letters, and then some even smaller letters that were presumably the author's name.

It was not quite seven P.M., and half the chairs were occupied, none of them by Mr Nimrin, unless he was even more a master of disguise than he claimed. Anyway, nobody here looked either like Mr Nimrin or a bartender, so Josh took the last chair on the right in the last row and looked around to see who *was* here.

Strange people. There appeared to be some sixties flower children who'd been cryogenically stored for thirty years and then imperfectly thawed. Scruffy round-shouldered baggily-dressed people of both sexes – or indeterminate sex – carried an unmistakable aura of homelessness about them. Others looked like people who'd lost their luggage, but decided to come anyway. And down front were half a dozen burly guys in dark-toned T-shirts and light-toned windbreakers and ponytails and scraggly beards and bent eyeglasses in either tortoise-shell or black. Josh originally assumed those guys must be a group, but then he saw nobody here knew anybody else, though most people, including the ponytails up front, were amiable about it.

'Ladies and gentlemen,' the store's loudspeaker informed them, 'best-selling author David L. Fogware is about to read from *Enchantress of Nyin* from his best-selling Farbender series in our author area on 3. The reading will begin in just a minute at seven o'clock in our author's area on 3.'

This announcement produced another half-dozen people, smiling, glad not to be late, scuttling in to take up more of the chairs, giving more of a sense of a full house. Then a slim bespectacled man with a black moustache, white shirt, penguard and pens in shirt pocket, and black slacks, stood at the lectern and spoke into the microphone there:

'We are very proud to present,' he began, and read David L. Fogware's press release with a certain enthusiasm, while Josh suddenly came to the conclusion that David L. Fogware would turn out to *be* Mr Nimrin.

But no. Introduction finished, the spectacled store employee smilingly made his exit, and a fellow carrying a book came out to take his place at the lectern. *He* was David L. Fogware, and he looked exactly like the half-dozen fellows in the front row, who gave him the most enthusiastic applause of all, the rattle of hand-clapping that greeted his presence. He, too, was a burly guy with specs and beard and ponytail and windbreaker over T-shirt over baggy jeans over L.L. Bean boots, and he accepted the acclaim with becoming modesty.

Josh hadn't had occasion to notice this before, but there are in this world two kinds of burliness. There's the burliness of muscle and brawn and large bone, and there's the burliness of beer. These fellows, applauders and applaudee alike, represented the burliness of beer.

When the group quieted down, David L. Fogware opened his book, which was hardcover and very tall and thick, and briefly studied its first page. Then he looked up and said, 'You know, when I first started the Farbender Netherbender series, I had no idea it would take me this far. In those early days, I used to say I was at work on a trilogy.'

He chuckled at himself, shook his head at his earlier innocence and the vagaries of fate, and then said, 'But what happened was, the deeper I got into the history of the Netherbenders, the richness of those worlds, the tapestry of it all, the implications just kept coming on. Folks would say to me, "David, what about this implication? What about that implication?" And I could see just what they were talking about. Every road I took, in this journey through the Netherbender epos, every road I took left who knew how many roads *un*taken? Unexplored. Unrealized. It became clear' – here he chuckled again, nodding at his audience – 'that three wasn't going to be my lucky number after all. We left trilogy behind us in the Lind of Lirt!'

His audience, who must all be his readers, did their own chuckle at this in-joke, and they had a moment of everybody smiling around at everybody else in comfortable in-group companionship, while Josh looked around in increasing desperation. Where was Mr Nimrin?

'Well, now, we've reached volume seven of the trilogy,' Fogware announced, stretching his joke a bit beyond capacity, 'and we're all about to meet the Enchantress of Nyin.' He lowered his head toward his book. 'It was Finwards Day, and the princess Li-Whon would birthe, all the scholars said so. But where was Gahorn? "He has never failed me before," Li-Whon told the faithful Muglurk, "and I know he will not fail me now, no matter what unimaginable perils he must go through to return to Elgadaare." And even as she spoke, in the forests of Mahrsohn on faroff Hilvet V, Gahorn himself urged his fleet Silverdart onward. "Hi!" he cried. "The portal, Silverdart! We must not fail!" And the powerful six-legged steed galloped up the quegs.'

By this point, Josh was regretting the lack of a laughtrack almost as much as the lack of Mr Nimrin. Looking around for the thirtieth time, the only one in this little isolated group, this separate world, not mesmerized by Volume VII, he saw, shambling down an aisle in his direction, then slowly and painfully turning off, a fat elderly woman with a walker. As she turned leftward into a side aisle, the right forefinger on the walker twitched.

Poor woman. Josh looked back at David L. Fogware, for whom the implications of wedding Arthurian romance with Buck Rogers in the twenty-fifth century would never exhaust themselves.

He thought, That was Mr Nimrin.

14

SINCE HE WAS already at the outer edge of the enchanted forest, Josh didn't disturb anybody when he rose and sidled away, in cautious pursuit of the old lady with the walker. He reached the aisle where she'd turned off, and there she was, straight ahead, bumping along, just reaching the far end of the aisle, where an empty armchair stood beside a small round table. Making the turn, she/he glanced back at him, then dropped a sheet of paper on the table and continued on out of sight.

Josh hurried down the aisle, slid into the seat, and looked at the sheet of paper. It was a copy of a newspaper item, datelined July 25, yesterday, apparently from a smalltown paper:

HANGING DEATH
LABELED SUSPICIOUS
by Edward Tassel

Moore, Jul 25 – The discovery of the hanged body of Robert Van Bark, 34, of Moore and New York City, suspended from the rafters of a barn adjacent to his property on Wiggins Road, has been labeled suspicious by state police investigators.

The body of Van Bark, a weekend resident of the area the last four years and a computer technician in New York City, was discovered by his wife, Wendy, 31, at six-thirty P.M., when she could not find him in or near their home when it was time to return to their apartment in New York City.

The piece went on for another three paragraphs of incidental detail and fuzzy speculation. Josh read it all, wondering *why* he was reading it all, then sat there for a few minutes, watching the other customers and wondering when the old lady would come back. Surely that was why he'd been directed to stay here.

But it wasn't the old lady who came back. It was an overweight workman in paint-spattered bib overalls, a full black beard, thick black hair, a black canvas backpack, and a Benjamin Moore cap worn backward, carrying a short metal ladder on his right shoulder, who paused for one significant second in front of Josh and then moved on.

Startled, Josh almost forgot to grab the copy of the clipping before he stood to follow the workman down the maze of aisles. Along the way, he realized the ladder was made from the same pieces that had once been the walker. And the old lady's dress and wig would be in that backpack.

The workman took the down escalator, Josh trailing, and went out to Broadway. He turned right, Josh well behind him, and they made their way into the pocket park where Broadway crosses Columbus Avenue. There the workman found an empty bench and settled wearily onto the far end of it, leaning his ladder against the armrest.

As Josh approached, the workman made a quick moving-away gesture while looking elsewhere. When Josh paused, not sure what he meant by that, he impatiently pointed down at the seat, then did the move-away again.

Oh; sit on the bench, but at the other end. Josh did so, and Mr Nimrin looked out at all the noisy traffic and the big blocky buildings of Lincoln Center and said, 'You wished to see me. But I wished to see you. And so we are together.'

'What they're—' Josh said.

'One moment. You read the news item.'

'I never heard of him,' Josh said.

'I did,' Mr Nimrin told him. 'There were three of you taking my money these last seven years. He was the second.'

'Oh,' Josh said.

'Clearly,' Mr Nimrin said, 'he did not behave as wisely as you. They felt their security was threatened. They act swiftly, these people.'

'Hanged him,' Josh said. He felt nauseous.

'That was handiest, where he was. You they might drown. After torture, of course.'

'Good God,' Josh said.

'If you are to be helped,' Mr Nimrin told him, 'you must look elsewhere than the Almighty. And *I* must look for Mitchell Robbie. You don't know him by any chance, do you?'

'Mitchell Robbie? No. Is he number three?'

'Yes, of course.' Mr Nimrin was very irritated. 'I need to get to him before he makes the same sort of mistake Van Bark made. If two of my sleepers turn out to be rotten, they'll come for me in a trice. Frankly, your cooperation with them is the only thing at this moment that allays their suspicions.'

'I can't go on with this,' Josh said.

Mr Nimrin snorted. 'You want to finish like Van Bark?'

'There's guns in my apartment,' Josh said. 'AK-47s. There's uniforms, ammunition. There's a slinky woman called Tina Pausto.'

'Tina? She's here?' Mr Nimrin gazed skyward over Lincoln Center. 'She had barely begun when I was taken out of the action,' he said. 'I imagine she's fairly something by now.'

'Yes, she is,' Josh said.

'Then,' Mr Nimrin told Lincoln Center, 'whatever their operation, it must be of top importance.'

'I know what their operation is,' Josh said. 'That's why I can't go on with it.'

Mr Nimrin actually looked directly at Josh, one withering instant of scorn, before addressing Lincoln Center again: 'You? How could you possibly know?'

'There was a thing on television last night,' Josh told him, 'about the premier of Kamastan.'

'Freddy?' Surprised, Mr Nimrin said, 'What about him?'

'Mihommed-Sinn, they said his name was.'

'Yes, yes,' Mr Nimrin snapped, more impatient than ever. 'Fyeddr Mihommed-Sinn, Freddy to those who know him. An animal. A beast. Exactly what those tribesmen deserve.'

'They're going to kill him,' Josh said.

Mr Nimrin frowned mightily in the direction of the Metropolitan Opera. 'Who? *My* people?'

'That's what it's all about.'

'Nonsense.' Mr Nimrin was always certain about everything, but he'd never been as certain as *this* before. 'They'll never get a team across the border.'

'They're going to kill him *here*,' Josh said. 'In New York.'

'Impossible.' Mr Nimrin's certainty had not been dented. 'He won't leave that rubbish tip of a country, it's well known. Never.'

'He's leaving,' Josh said. 'He's coming here Friday. It seems, he's a sports fan.'

'Oh, please.' Mr Nimrin shook his head, now very nearly laughing openly at him. 'Freddy Mihommed-Sinn is coming to the United States

63

to attend a *sports* event?'

'At Yankee Stadium.'

'A baseball game? I know Freddy, young man, I haven't seen him for years, but I know him, and Freddy Mihommed-Sinn knows *nothing* about baseball.'

They won a gold medal in the—'

'The runner!' Now it was Mr Nimrin's turn to be astonished. 'Freddy's coming to New York because of the *runner*?'

'There's a big ceremony,' Josh told him. 'Thousands of politicians and sports stars. He's a big sports fan. Maybe not baseball, but—'

'For baseball,' Mr Nimrin said, 'you need a larger flat expanse than exists in Kamastan. But why would he go against the curse?'

Feeling all at once that he'd somehow slipped into some other segment of the Farbender Netherbender Series, Josh said, 'The curse?'

'When Freddy was born,' Mr Nimrin said, 'an old gypsy woman told his mother that Freddy would never die so long as he stayed within the borders of his own country. It's very well-known.'

'So that's why he never left before.'

'That and his own provincial bloodymindedness,' Mr Nimrin commented. 'But he must be going soft. He *knows* if he leaves Kamastan he risks death. Has he stopped believing in gypsy curses?'

'In my apartment,' Josh said, 'are four uniforms of the Kamastan army. And four AK-47s.'

'Tell me his itinerary,' Mr Nimrin said, 'and routes.'

'I don't know the routes,' Josh said. 'He's flying in on Friday, with a second plane full of bodyguards—'

'Sensible. And probably no one will know which of the two planes he's on.'

'I don't know about that. Anyway, he's staying Friday night at the country's United Nations Mission—'

'On York Avenue. Yes, yes. And?'

'Saturday, the autocade takes him up to Yankee Stadium, then back to York Avenue, then Sunday he flies back to Kamastan.'

'If still alive.'

'Yes.'

'Well,' Mr Nimrin corrected himself, 'in either case. If we succeed in dispatching him, they'll ship the body home for the state funeral.'

'*We!*'

Mr Nimrin gave him another lightning disgusted glance, then told Lincoln Center, 'Where do you think the staging area is? Who do you think is hosting the assassination team?'

'Oh, goddam it!' Josh cried. 'I can't tell you how much I'd like to just give the money *back*.'

'We're beyond that.' Mr Nimrin pondered. 'There are two possible venues. Not the autocades, to and fro, they'll have doubles in dummy cars, New York Police Department protection, far too much. So either in the building on York Avenue before or after the ceremony, or at Yankee Stadium during the event. If it were my operation, of course, I would choose the stadium.'

'The stadium!' Josh was horrified, his imagination filling with sprawled and bloodied sports enthusiasts. '*Why?*'

'Easier to get close to your target in a crowd, easier to make your escape in mass confusion. Four uniforms, you say.' Mr Nimrin nodded, considering the options. 'How *I* would do it,' he said, 'is insert those four substitutes into the honor guard that will fire off the salute. Everyone else in single-shot mode, armed with blanks, aimed at the sky. My four, in full automatic mode, armed with live ammunition, aimed at the last second at the target. Spray him and the entire reviewing stand, or wherever Freddy might be. Then spray the nearby honor guard members, release the blood packets within your own uniforms, and fall to the ground as though a victim rather than a perpetrator. Later, kill the ambulance attendants and make your getaway.' He nodded, satisfied with himself. 'Yes, that's how I'd do it.'

15

'THEY'D NEVER GET away with it,' Josh said.

'Oh, come now.' Mr Nimrin was insulted. Glowering at Lincoln Center, he said, 'Of course they'll get away with it. These are not some religious fanatics, determined to kill themselves and sail off to some matinee heaven. These are professionals. Do you think this is the *first* assassination I've been connected with, in thirty years of service?'

'It's my first,' Josh said, 'and I don't want it.'

'Though it *isn't* mine, is it?' Mr Nimrin said. 'They're keeping me out of the loop on this, aren't they?' Then he offered a bitter laugh and said, 'Oh, yes, we say "out of the loop", too. Everyone does now, though many have no idea what it means. Part of the Americanization we all so bravely struggle against is the Americanization of slang. It started many years ago with OK, which seemed to be all right, since OK didn't mean anything in English, either. But it was the thin end of the wedge. See? There's another.'

'Mr Nimrin,' Josh said, 'I don't want to talk about *slang* with you. I want to talk about how I get *out* of this mess.'

'Well, you don't,' Mr Nimrin told him, 'and we'll both be much safer if you simply accept the fact. You are in this now, through my bad luck and your own cupidity, and it would be—'

'My what?'

'Cupidity,' Mr Nimrin repeated. 'It's a word in your language. It means greed.'

'I didn't know it,' Josh said, apologetic, but then bridled a bit: 'A thousand dollars a month doesn't seem like an awful lot of greed.'

'Enough greed to land you where you are now,' Mr Nimrin reminded him. 'And enough to leave Robert Van Bark hanging from a barn rafter.'

'Ohhh.'

'You should look on the bright side,' Mr Nimrin suggested.

'Bright side?' Josh stared wildly at the traffic thundering by. Maybe a bus would hit the bench and make *all* of this go away. 'What's the bright side?'

'Freddy Mihommed-Sinn,' Mr Nimrin said, 'is one of the most despicable persons on the planet. I doubt there are even three others who deserve to die more richly than he does. It's not as though the target were a Princess Diana or a rock-and-roll singer, although some of those might make it onto a slightly longer list. Believe me, your own government will not be sorry to see Freddy go.'

'They'll be sorry to see him go at Yankee Stadium,' Josh said. 'With a whole lot of innocent bystanders along for the ride.'

'Collateral damage is always a possibility,' Mr Nimrin said comfortably.

'No,' Josh said, 'I'm beginning to get the idea. Collateral damage isn't a possibility, it's dessert. You may all be professionals, but you still have to have your fun.'

'Poppycock,' Mr Nimrin said. 'We've risked security quite long enough, sitting here, pretending not to converse. They may not recognize me, but they'll certainly recognize *you*.'

'I wanted to say,' Josh told him, 'you are a master of disguise, I'll give you that—'

'It's simple,' Mr Nimrin told him. 'Become someone people don't want to look at. Crippled, deformed, ill. Or a workman.'

'Thank you, I'll remember that,' Josh said.

'Come to Harriet Linde's office tomorrow at six,' Mr Nimrin ordered. 'I may have further news, or I may not.'

'You'll be there?'

'I will or I will not.' Mr Nimrin shook his head at Lincoln Center. 'Go home,' he said. 'But, one word of advice.'

Bitter, Josh said, 'Only one?'

'Do not drink with Tina Pausto.'

Remembering that one glass of champagne, Josh said, 'Okay.'

16

BUT IT WASN'T Tina Pausto waiting for him in the living room at home, it was Eve, and she was coldly furious. 'What an elaborate liar you are,' she greeted him.

Josh finished shutting the apartment door. 'Eve? I told you don't come back.'

'Yes, and now I know why,' Eve said. 'I've seen her overnight bag.'

'Over—'

'On Jeremy's dresser. *Jeremy's!*' As though some really arcane blasphemy had just occurred.

'Oh, for God's sake,' Josh said, realizing what it had to be and what conclusion Eve had jumped to, 'that must be some bag of Tina's.'

'Her name is Tina?' Frost lay thick on every syllable.

'Tina Pausto, she just showed up today, she said she was being billeted here.'

'That's a new word.'

'Oh, come on, Eve. Is this the bankbook out of the graphics department again? Do you think I made everything up, so I could sleep with Tina Pausto? And am I sleeping with AK-47s, too?'

She blinked at him. 'With what?'

'Oh, *those* you didn't notice,' he said. 'Just come here and look.'

And he marched off toward the bedroom, because he wanted to nip this idiotic misunderstanding in the bud, so they could go back to the serious job of keeping him out of a grave and out of jail. And off barn rafters. And out of the ocean.

Halfway to the bedroom, Eve frowningly following, he had the horrible thought, What if they took everything out of here while I was gone? But no, there they were, those four wooden crates peeking modestly out from under the bed. 'Look at this,' he said, and knelt to pull one of the heavy boxes partway out.

She stared at it. 'What *is* that?'

'Assault rifles. Didn't you notice those boxes under Jeremy's crib?'

'All I saw was that Prada bag with all those Victoria's Secret things in it.'

'Well, those boxes are the ammunition for these babies,' Josh told her. 'And the closet is full of uniforms. Kamastan army uniforms.'

She shook her head, gave a very good impression of someone recovering slowly from a concussion, and went over to open the closet door. 'Uniforms,' she said.

'Believe me, honey,' Josh said, 'I did not import all this stuff in here myself just so I could con you into thinking I'm *not* having an affair with Tina Pausto. In fact, I *am* not having an – wait a minute! We've got to get out of here! *You've* got to get out of here!'

She looked ready to be offended. 'Why?'

'She's going to come back, Tina Pausto's gonna come back.' Saying her complete name seemed safer somehow, created more distance. 'If she sees *you* here, she'll know security's been breached, you've seen all this, you know everything, and she'll make one phone call and we'll *both* be killed!'

'But—'

'Also,' he said, reaching for her arm, pulling her toward the doorway, 'it's dinnertime. You're hungry, I'm hungry.'

'But—'

'We'll have the conversation,' he told her, as he shoved her at a half-trot through the apartment, 'in the restaurant.'

They did. He told her what he'd learned from television last night, and about his conversation with Mr Nimrin, and about the appearance of Tina Pausto, who seemed prepared to either sleep with him or not, depending how things went. A flexible girl, you might say.

Eve said, 'You *asked* her if she was supposed to have sex with you?'

'Well, I wanted to know.'

'What did she say?'

'Apparently, the question was, in poor taste. She looked down her nose at me and said, "That was not discussed." '

'Ha,' she said. 'That's funny, really,' and the waiter came, to take their order.

After he left, Josh took the newspaper story from his pocket and handed it to her. 'Mr Nimrin gave me this.'

She read it, saying, 'Oh, that's awful. Oh, the poor wife.'

'Well, the both of them, okay?'

69

Holding the story, she frowned at him across the table. 'But who is he?'

'There were three of us that kept the money these last seven years, that they thought were their sleepers. He was one of them. It looks like, he gave a wrong answer when they woke him up.'

Awed and horrified, voice hushed, she said, 'This could have been you.'

'Well, the barn is because it's upstate,' he said. 'Mr Nimrin said me they'd probably drown. After torture.'

She gave him back the story, and as he put it in his pocket she said, 'These are horrible people.'

'Dangerous horrible people. Eve, I don't know what to do. They're going to assassinate this guy, he's supposed to be a very bad guy, but still.'

'*I* could go to the FBI,' she said. 'Maybe they're watching you, but they aren't watching me. They aren't watching everybody in the world.'

'Okay,' Josh said. 'Let's say you go to Foley Square, you get out of the taxi, in a car across the street is a guy with a rifle and a bunch of pictures of people they don't want talking to the FBI. *Your* picture is there. If they're that worried about betrayals, and they're using me to – what did Mr Nimrin say? – host the assassination team, then, sure, they're keeping that much of an eye on you.'

'You can't—' Eve said, and the food arrived. When they were alone again, Josh said, 'I know I can't. I have to find some way to get clear of these people without setting off their paranoia. And you know, I'm already in this so deep. I *am* hosting the assassination team. I *am* storing their guns and their uniforms. I *have* had people staying in the apartment, though Tina Pausto's the first one I've seen.'

'She's there to watch you,' Eve said.

'Sure. In case the sleeper loses his nerve, or makes a mistake like Van Bark did.'

She said, 'I don't think I can stand this.'

'Neither can I. One way or another, it's over Sunday, maybe Saturday. If they come in and do it and get away, then I'm probably okay, and I can say look, I did it, but it was too nerve-wracking so please don't use me anymore, don't send me any checks, take back the forty thousand from the Cayman Islands bank, and maybe they won't think I'm a security risk.'

'Oh, Josh.'

'But what if they get caught?' Josh stared down at the food he wasn't eating. 'They get caught, that means *I* get caught. Up to now, when I didn't know anything, I could maybe get out from under with that diary in the laptop out on the island, but can I put this assassination plot in there? Mass murder at Yankee Stadium, and I never mentioned it to anybody? Guns and uniforms in my apartment, and I never had any idea what they were for? Eve, if I try to get away from this thing, they're gonna kill me, but if I *don't* get away from it, I'm likely to spend an awful long time in a federal prison.'

'Oh, Josh, there has to be a way, some way, something we can do. You have to get *out* of this.'

'I took the money,' he said. 'I keep thinking that. Money for nothing, and now look. There is no free lunch.' He shook his head at the food he wasn't eating. 'I wonder . . .'

Hopeful, wanting a straw to clutch at, she said, 'What? You wonder what?'

'Mr Nimrin hasn't found the third guy yet, who took the money,' Josh told her. 'Robert Van Bark, and me, and somebody named Mitchell Robbie. I wonder if it would do any good if *I* found him, talked to him, found out if they're using him, too. Maybe the two of us . . .' He shook his head. 'No.'

'No?' She acted as though this *was* a straw to cling to. 'Why not?'

'If Mr Nimrin can't find him, how can I?'

'Dick Welsh could find him, I bet,' she said, meaning their friends out on the island, who had Jeremy with them now. 'Dick's something in insurance downtown,' she pointed out, 'they have databases on everybody, I bet he could find him. Mitchell Robbie? How do you spell it?'

'I dunno,' he said. 'I guess like Robbie the Robot.'

'Fine,' she said. 'When we get home, I'll—'

'You can't come home with me,' he said.

'Oh.' She looked at him. 'Because that woman's there.'

'And if she knows you know,' Josh said, 'we're in major trouble.'

'*Damn* it!' she said. 'We can't *move*.'

'You'll have to take the late ferry back to Fair Harbor.'

'I can't even stay in my own *home*,' she complained. 'I know it isn't your fault, Josh, but—'

'Well, it is my fault,' he said. 'I took the money.'

17

TINA PAUSTO WAS in the living room, watching television. A laugh track could be heard. She had changed into voluminous maroon pants and a black scoop-neck blouse that revealed tan lines that were somehow very sexy. 'You do not have HBO,' she said, by way of greeting.

'No, I know,' he agreed. 'We don't have anything.'

'Only these awful networks. Why are you so behind the times? I expected more from a New Yorker like you.'

'We never watch television much,' he said. 'We didn't think it was worth it.' I'm apologizing to a foreign spy femme fatale for not having HBO, he told himself. I don't believe this. I don't believe any of this.

And this is a decided change from the glass of champagne and the silver sheath from a few hours ago, isn't it? Once she isn't going to seduce me, she doesn't have to pretend to be a nice person anymore.

With a disgusted look at the television set, which again laughed at her, she offed it with the remote and said, 'You had a nice evening?'

'I went to a reading at a bookstore,' he said, understanding that he was now reporting to her, 'and then to a restaurant.'

'By yourself?'

'Sure.'

She nodded, then got to her feet, a tall lithe woman, graceful without emphasizing it. 'I have spent some time on this piece of furniture now,' she said, with a little dismissive wave at the sofa, 'and I have decided it would not be comfortable for me for the night.'

'Oh.'

'It would be too short, for one thing.'

'Yeah, I guess so.'

'I shall sleep in the bed,' she told him, 'in the bedroom. You shall sleep wherever you wish.'

'I guess I get the sofa,' he said, thinking that it would also be too short for him.

She smiled, in a wintry way. 'Faithful husbands are so relaxing,' she said. 'You may wish to get some things from the bedroom.'

So he did.

18

THE LIVING ROOM was not perfectly dark. Amber streetlight-glow angled upward through the windows, around the edges of the shades, to make long diagonal convict stripes along the ceiling, reflecting down to give a hazy dark honey-tone to everything in the room. Lying on his side on the sofa, knees bent in a not completely comfortable way because the sofa truly was too short, Josh looked out at his muffled sidewise living room, listened to the far clatter below of late-night traffic on West End Avenue, and thought, I'm losing my life. Not death, not being killed, the loss of my *life*. The life I've constructed for myself.

Everything he looked at now, turned ninety degrees, swelled with his life. The furniture choices he'd made with Eve, the pictures they'd chosen to put on the walls, even the inadequate television set, whose very inadequacy helped to define his life, his and Eve's lives together, all of these things were at risk, now at risk.

No, *he* was at risk. The objects of his life were safe, but he was not. Driven from his normalcy, now even driven from his bedroom, pushed into this horrible parallel universe where all the decisions were monstrous and none of the roads led anywhere, what was he to do? How could he somehow clamber back onto the raft of his real existence?

I am privy to something I shouldn't know, he thought, inner workings that a little guy like me isn't supposed to have even an inkling of, until after it's all over and we proles can safely be told about it on the evening news. When you're one of those who is out of the action, when every bad thing that happens in the world has been muted by the safety of distance and time and your own unimportance, when the horrors are all done and over with before you know anything about them, then you can stand the particulars of the news, absorb them like a form of entertainment, forget them, get on with your life. The newscaster will describe this plot, after the events, these villains with their evil designs, and it will all make

74

perfect sense, because after all there *are* villains in the world, and they *do* plot, and our only job, we crowd-extras, spectators, is to know about it afterward.

I'm a rabbit, Josh told himself, and I'm running with the wolves.

The first hour of tonight's insomnia was spent in variants on this self-pity, mourning the loss of himself as though the loss were already complete, as though the living room he gazed at edgewise already belonged to some new tenant, that the furnishings were fading in the faint light, to be replaced by someone else's objects, someone else's taste.

After an hour, the increasing ache in his knees made Josh try another approach to the sofa, rolling over onto his back, stretching his legs out – aaahhh – and resting his ankles on the sofa arm. This position tried to bend his knees the opposite way, downwards, which they couldn't do, but it was better at least for a while, so he lay there, now looking not askant at his possessions but upward at his light-striped ceiling; a different view.

Which somehow gave him a different view, as well, of his situation. He'd been bemoaning his fate, on the basis that outrageous things did not happen to ordinary people, but now, focusing on those long narrow strips of yellowy light from the outside world below, bars of butter across the dark ceiling, he reminded himself that anything could happen to anybody, and that only science contains impossibilities: Time does not reverse, for instance, the apple does not fall up, the sun does not circle the earth.

He had been careless. He had lived his life as though there were no consequences. If he could forgive his seven-year-younger self for cashing the checks, back when he was footloose and single and broke, what excuse could he find for going on with it as his life had changed, as he had taken on responsibility and maturity? It had just been passivity, from the very beginning. As the years went on, he could tell himself he'd *tried* to find United States Agent in the beginning, he'd done what he could, and the checks had always cleared, there had never been a consequence. So why change?

Because now he had a life worth protecting.

The ankles on the sofa arm didn't work. The sofa arm was too firm, it cut off blood to his feet. Also, the downward pressure on his knees never relented. Finally, he shifted again, staying on his back but bending both knees, the left knee upright and leaning against the sofa back, the right knee down to the side, hanging off the edge of the sofa cushion. That position was acceptable, at least for a while, and once he'd settled into it he started another line of thought.

Responsibility. If, in the past, he'd been careless about his responsibility to his own life, he now had to acknowledge that a brand-new responsibility had arrived, thrust horribly upon him. A responsibility to all the intended and collateral victims of Levrin and Tina Pausto and their assassin friends.

What could he do about it? Going to the FBI, or the New York City police, or any other authority figure, it seemed to him, would be both pointless and dangerous. Even if he got through, if he eluded Levrin and who knew how many others, even if he managed to tell his story as completely and honestly as he could, what then? Where was his proof? Come to that, where was his knowledge?

'We turned out to be Ukraine,' Mr Nimrin had said, 'surprising many of us.' Which meant, it seemed to him, that Mr Nimrin was *not* Ukraine. Russian? Some other onetime Soviet Socialist Republic? What were they all? Moldava. Belarus. There must be more.

Come to think of it, he didn't suppose he could really exclude Finland. Or the three Baltic States, What'sitsname, What'sitsname and What'sitsname.

And what sort of name was Nimrin? Or Levrin? Or Pausto?

The point was, what could he give the authorities that had any heft or weight? The AK-47s? Maybe, if he could actually get through to an official somewhere, tell his story, be believed, and be checked on before Levrin and company had whisked the evidence back out of the apartment; unlikely.

Lying there, knees splayed, toes increasingly uncomfortable against that damnably firm sofa arm, Josh tried to create the dialogue of his confession – no, no, information – to some receptive police ear: 'The people who've paid me all this money over the years, that I never questioned and never tried to track down, are from somewhere in what used to be the Soviet Union, or maybe one of its satellites.' (Hungary, Bulgaria . . .) 'They intend to kill Fyeddr Mihommed-Sinn of Kamastan, though I have no idea why, nor for whom. The one who was in trouble seven years ago on an illegal technology-exporting case that never came to trial, Mr Ellois Nimrin, says he lives in a safe house somewhere on Long Island. The others . . . I have no idea how many of them there are, I've only seen two of them face to face, but others have been moving through my apartment the past two weeks, and I'm holding uniforms for four of them, and I have no idea where they're staying in the United States. I don't know the details of the murder plot, but I could tell you what Mr Nimrin says is the way *he'd* do it if he were in charge, but he isn't in charge.'

Should he mention Harriet Linde? That seemed unfair, somehow; she had even less to do with the situation than he did. Well, yes, a lot less; nothing, in fact. But on the other hand, if he were going to make a clean breast of it all, how could he hold *anything* back? What if they later found out there were things he hadn't mentioned?

The muscles on the insides of his thighs were feeling the strain of his spread-legged position, and his toes against the sofa arm were beginning to cramp. Maybe it would be better if he slept on the floor. It had a carpet, anyway.

Reluctantly, aching in many joints, Josh sat up and pushed the coffee table out of the way, then transferred his pillow and the sheet he was sleeping on and under to that part of the floor. He lay down on his back, legs stretched straight down, arms over the sheet, hands folded on chest, and it was amazing how much farther away those stripes on the ceiling looked. He contemplated them for a while, trying at last *not* to think about his problems, to think about the comforts of sleep instead, and gradually came to the realization that the hard floor hurt his back. It grated against his shoulderblades, and left a gap at his waist that made his skeleton warp slightly.

I can't start all over again on the sofa, he told himself, and turned painfully over onto his right side, back to the sofa. There, three inches from his eyes, stood a narrow wooden leg of the coffee table. He gazed at it, and something about the rigidity of that leg, its narrowness and its verticality, changed his mood yet again.

It's up to *me* to make things right, he told himself. I took their money, incurious as to whose money it was or what it meant, and now I'm suffering the consequences. And one of the consequences is that it's up to me to stop this mad assassination from taking place.

Could it even *happen* without him? If Levrin and the others and their superiors had not believed they had three sleeper spies fixed in place in New York City, ready to provide a base and support for their operation, could they have assembled the operation anyway?

He couldn't know, not really. So it was possible they couldn't do it without him, and that possibility meant he had to assume that, without him, and without Robert Van Bark, and without Mitchell Robbie, these people would not have been able to plan and put together this monstrous assault. Van Bark had paid for his carelessness, and Mitchell Robbie might yet do so (or might have already), so it was down to himself, to Josh Redmont. He was going to have to do something.

All right, what? Wide awake, he stared at that coffee table leg, waiting for inspiration. If he couldn't go to the police, what *could* he do?

What about reporting the situation to the Kamastaners? Kamastanis;

whatever they were. What if he were to go to that place of theirs on York Avenue and tell them, listen, some people intend to kill your premier when he comes to the States, so maybe you should warn him and tell him *not* to come to the States, what if he were to do that? After all, if Premier Mihommed-Sinn didn't leave Kamastan, the assassination wouldn't take place.

They're watching the Kamastan embassy, mission, whatever it is. That's for sure. If there's one place in New York City that Levrin's group is keeping a close eye on this week, it's the Kamastanish outpost on York Avenue. I'd never get to the door.

All right. What else?

Sabotage. Louse them up some way. Steal their bullets or pack sand in their AK-47 barrels. Something along those lines.

And run his own investigation, so he could learn the things the police *would* find useful. Who these people really are, where they're really from, who they work for, where they're hiding in New York. Other than my apartment, of course.

But how to do that? Befriend Tina Pausto, for one thing. Not sleep with her, no, no, still not that, but *talk* to her. Be friendly with her, drink with her – regardless of Mr Nimrin's warnings – get her to tell him more about the plot and her co-conspirators. The same with Levrin, next time they met. And *find* Mitchell Robbie.

He couldn't go out to Fair Harbor this weekend, he realized, though he was supposed to be there to help pack for the end of the rental. But he couldn't leave New York, not with this unresolved. Eve would understand.

So he was to become a spy himself. A *counterspy*.

Sure. An over-the-counter spy, he amended his thoughts, and offered that coffee table leg a rueful smile. But at least – at the very least – he had an idea now of something to do. Clutching tight to that thought, more or less comfortable at last lying on his side on the floor, he dropped, with a silent thud, into troubled sleep.

19

WHEN HE WOKE, his head was under the coffee table. The reason he awoke is, he'd set his travel alarm, and where he'd set it was on the coffee table. The vibrations from the alarm found some sort of harmonic in the wood of the coffee table, and the result was to give him some idea what it would be like to live inside an amplified guitar. He only hit his head slightly while getting out from under, but then eased his feelings by hitting the alarm clock's head very hard.

He struggled to his feet, stiff in many joints, and hobbled into the bathroom. Back in the living room, he found his clothes on the chair where he'd put them last night, and dressed, ignoring as best he could the sand behind his eyelids.

He'd hoped Tina would be up, so he could start his campaign of worming his way into her confidence (and nothing else), but she was still asleep, or at least still in bed, those long legs, that long lithe torso, that long and beautiful face framed on the pillow by waves of thick almost-black hair. So he left home early instead, planning to have a diner breakfast somewhere along the way.

He walked quite a while, wanting the exercise, needing to work his mistreated body as well as his overloaded mind. As for his body, he found that everything eventually loosened up except the tense muscles across the top of his shoulders and the back of his neck, as though a wooden hanger had been surgically implanted there while he slept. While he dozed. And as for his mind, last night's conclusions – take responsibility, spy on the spies, see it out here in the city instead of spending the weekend at the beach, stop the assassination – still seemed to him right, though perhaps not quite as easy as, lying on the floor, he might have thought.

He found a not very good breakfast and ate not very much of it, then went on to the office, arriving early, and tried to concentrate on what he was supposed to be doing there, the statistical breakdowns on the results of the new campaign in selected parts of the country. Generally it was doing well in the southwest, poorly in the southeast, so-so in the northwest. Why? Why these regional differences? Why didn't people just stop making trouble? Everybody go out and buy the same thing and stop making us *think* about you.

At ten-thirty his phone rang and it was Eve: 'Got him,' she said.

'What?'

'You know what we talked about.'

And then he did. 'Oh, right! You got it? Really?'

'And truly. I told you Dick Welsh could find out. His address is 856A East Second Street.'

'Not a great address,' Josh said. Already he didn't like the idea of going there.

'It's a theater,' she said.

Again he was lost. 'And he *lives* in it?'

'This is where Dick is so wonderful,' she said. 'The company couldn't get insurance, for all their lights and sets and costumes and things, because they're such a marginal operation, not unless somebody was living there. So they got all kinds of variants from the city, and put in a little apartment, and Mitchell lives there, behind the stage, and that way they can get insurance. No wonder your friend couldn't find him.'

'Let's hope nobody else can,' Josh said.

The Good Rep Classic Theatrical Company was in half of the bottom of an old tenement on the Lower East Side, the part of town that has been the first home in America for immigrants from all over the world for nearly two hundred years. This southern end of the island of Manhattan is one of the two parts of town that extend east farther than the numbered avenues can accommodate. Uptown, east of First Avenue, there's York Avenue, a pretty good neighborhood, with the Mayor's residence, Gracie Mansion, toward one end and the Kamastan Mission to the United Nations at the other, but downtown the eastern bloat is more pronounced, creating, east of First Avenue, a new Avenue A, then B, then C, and even D before the East River puts a stop to it.

Alphabet City, it's called, and as a neighborhood it could not be more mixed. The remnants of the waves of immigration can still be seen, fused with newer arrivals. Parts of the area have become more valuable, but it still contains plenty of pockets of poverty.

Poverty and art have always been more than nodding acquaintances, so another part of life in Alphabet City has a certain LaBoheme atmosphere, with coffee shops and performance artists and poetry bars and the most minor of publications and the most marginal of theaters. Good Rep fit right in. It was in a corner building, six stories high, the tallest you can erect a building without an elevator in New York City, with a crumbling stone outdoor staircase leading up to a wide entranceway that looked as though it had been gnawed for many years by giant rats, which was probably true. To the left of the stairs, toward the corner, was a bodega crowded with inexpensive food in very bright packaging, and to the right of the stairs, with a marquee the size of a Honda hood, was Good Rep.

It was one slate step down to the tiny forecourt of the theater, which featured an enormous handmade poster for *Arms and the Man*, in which the gaudy uniforms, meant no doubt to be Ruritanian or Graustarkian, struck Josh as uncomfortably Kamastanish. There was no doorbell to be seen, so he tried turning the knob, and the door opened, just like that.

What he entered now was small, dark, and hot; you wouldn't expect much by way of air-conditioning from Good Rep. Posters of previous productions, along with professional shots of the actors involved, filled both side walls. Ahead, over a lumpy black linoleum floor, a box office window was at the right, a closed black door on the left.

Josh went over to look through the box office window at an empty shelf, a kitchen chair, and a black wall. Moving to his left, he tried the door, but this one was locked.

Knock, or shout? He tried both, knocking first and then, getting no answer, moving over to lean down and call through the arched hole in the window, 'Hello! Hello?'

Nothing. He looked around, and on a small table just inside the entrance was an open cardboard box full of throwaway sheets describing the current production, with copy on only one side. He took a sheet, folded it with the print inside, and used the little ledge in front of the ticket window to write his note:

Dear Mitchell Robbie,
　My name is Josh Redmont. I too have been getting United States Agent's checks the last seven years. If you haven't

'Box office opens at five.'

Josh looked up, and in that narrow space back there had materialized a short very thin narrow-faced man with black hair slicked straight back. He wore a black turtleneck and black jeans and a red-and-white bandanna knotted gracefully around his throat. He nodded briskly, having delivered his information, and started to sidle away.

Josh said, 'Mitchell Robbie?'

Deep suspicion creased the man's face into a walnut shell. Peering intently at Josh, he said, 'Does he know you?'

'No, but I need to—'

'About what?'

Josh met him, suspicious gaze for suspicious gaze: 'Are *you* Mitchell Robbie?'

'I could take a message.'

'I, too, have been receiving those checks every month from Uni—'

'*What?*' The man actually jumped up on tiptoe as he frantically patted the air downward with both hands. 'Are you *crazy?*'

'Did they activate you?'

'I have absolutely—' More bewildered face-crinkling: 'What?'

Josh said, 'Did Mr Levrin come here? Did he activate you?'

'I have no idea what you're talking about,' the man – who Josh was now certain was Robbie – said, 'I think you want professional help, but you won't find it here. I suggest you leave.'

'Take a look at this,' Josh said, and slid the Van Bark clipping through the slot in the window.

Robbie didn't want to look at it. He didn't want to have to do anything about anything, but clearly he understood he had no real choice. Leaning far back, as though to lessen the possible contamination, gazing down along the line of his nose and his fully extended right arm with the fingertips on the shelf, he read the clipping, and partway through it his face crinkled with distaste. 'What an ugly thing,' he said. 'But what is it to me? I mean, no man is an island, but he's an island, you certainly don't think I *know* that person.'

'Three of us get the checks, every month,' Josh told him. 'For seven years. A thousand dollars a month. You, and Robert Van Bark, and me. I never knew why. You never knew why either, did you?'

'I still don't know what you're talking about,' Robbie said. 'What checks?'

'We don't have time for this,' Josh told him. 'Ten days ago, they activated me, and I was just lucky, I didn't say the wrong thing. Then they went to Van Bark, and I guess he *did* say the wrong thing. And pretty soon Andrei Levrin is gonna come here, and from the way you're acting, you're gonna say so many wrong things you'll be dead in ten minutes. Which would be very bad for me.'

A false nervous smile played over Robbie's mobile features. 'I see what it is,' he said, 'it's an audition. You have a play, and of course you want to star in it, and this is how to attract—'

'Van Bark is dead,' Josh said.

Robbie shook his head, drawing his shoulders up like a matron in a comedy. 'I have never heard of the man.'

'He cashed the checks. Every month.'

Robbie cast around, this way, that way, for some other reaction to offer, something to make this scene go away. At last, he merely sighed, and looked Josh head-on, and said, 'What do you *want?*'

'Let me in there,' Josh said. 'I'll explain the whole thing. Maybe we can help each other.'

Robbie thought it over. Then sudden suspicion hardened his face again, and he said, 'Are you *wired?*'

'What? Oh, you mean carrying a recorder? Of course not.'

'Or a transmitter,' Robbie told him. 'Any little *gadget.*'

'I'm not carrying anything,' Josh told him.

Robbie nodded. 'Strip,' he said.

'Strip?' Josh couldn't believe it. 'Here? In the lobby?'

'No one will come in. If you're clean, I'll let you in and you can tell me your story, whatever it is. Up to you.'

He was this far into this situation, Josh told himself, he might as well go through with it. 'Oh, all right,' he said, and peeled off his shirt. 'Okay?'

'Everything,' Robbie said.

Josh frowned at him. 'What do you mean, everything?'

'I mean everything,' Robbie insisted.

'Oh, the hell with you!'

'Goodbye,' Robbie said, and turned away.

'All right! All right!'

The next part of the experience was grim enough. Pirouetting starkers in front of Robbie's intense gaze, Josh said, 'I suppose you've played a doctor on TV.'

'Not yet,' Robbie said. 'I'll unlock. Come in when you're decent.'

20

INSIDE, THE THEATER was narrow but deep, like a shoebox, with the stage at the far end. Facing it were two stepped wooden platforms with an aisle between them from the entrance, and on the platforms were rows of black metal folding chairs.

No curtain covered the stage, where the set was as minimal as possible. To the left were a bed covered with scratchy-looking throws and a battered dresser with a candle on it, unlit. To the right, a green settee and a mirrored dressing table, fronted by a round piano stool. On the dressing table stood a large framed photograph of Robbie, in a doorman's uniform. Centered, upstage, was a doorframe connected to nothing, with a door open back toward a tall narrow painting of a snowy mountain. Beyond that, the rear wall seemed to be sheets of plywood painted flat black.

Robbie, also in flat black unlike his photo, led the way to the stage, saying, 'Take the settee, it's more comfortable than it looks.'

It would have to be; and it was. Josh sat on it, facing all the empty chairs, and Robbie sat on the piano stool, leaning his back against the dressing table. 'Those checks have meant a lot to me,' he said, 'over the years.'

Josh said, 'Did you ever try to find out where they were coming from?'

'Called the phone number on the checks a few times, never got an answer.' Robbie shrugged. 'I don't know about you, but for me, an extra thou a month is a godsend.'

'Not from God, though.'

'All right,' Robbie said. 'So now I'm gonna find out about the money. Does this mean it stops?'

'Let me tell you the story.' Casting around for a starting point, Josh said, 'Did you used to hang out in a place down here called Uncle Ray's?'

'On Sixth Street?' Robbie nodded. 'Sure. What about it?'

'The bartender there,' Josh told him, 'was a man whose real name is Nimrin. He's actually a spy.'

Robbie frowned, crinching his face up. It was really a very mobile face, throwing expressions that could have hit the back wall of a space much bigger than this theater. 'What do you mean, a spy?'

'A spy. For the Soviet Union or somebody back when. I don't know who after that.'

'He was spying in Uncle *Ray's?*'

'He was collecting *us*,' Josh said, and sketched in Mr Nimrin's scheme and their oblivious position in it, followed by his own removal from the plot, so that the beards actually got the money. And now the piper was here, ready to be paid.

Robbie was a good listener, watching Josh's face intently, almost never blinking. When Josh finished, Robbie let a little silence go by and then said, 'That's crazy, you know. That's completely crazy, all that story.'

'Getting a thousand dollars a month for seven years with no explanation isn't crazy?'

'I wouldn't plot it this way,' Robbie told him. 'You have to at least make a *stab* at believability.'

'What don't you believe?' Josh asked him. 'The money?'

'I mean, *spies*,' Robbie said. 'Come on. I could believe somebody stashed stolen diamonds down in here a hundred years ago and now his grandson is coming looking for them, and you and me, we're in his way. *That* I could believe.'

'United States Agent,' Josh told him, 'is not looking for missing diamonds. You are a deep cover sleeper spy, in the pay of a foreign country for the last seven years, and now they're on their way to activate you.'

'No,' Robbie said. 'I don't want to be activated.'

'I guess Van Bark didn't, either,' Josh said.

Robbie's eloquent face twisted into an expression of almost physical agony, as though he had fleas. He said, 'You're raining on my *parade*, buddy. A grand a month, no questions asked, and I can *live* in this shithole, my pals and I can put *on* our low-rent little productions. Do you know we have not *once*, in eight years, got a review in the *New York Times?*'

'Well, this is pretty far off the beaten track,' Josh suggested.

'BAM is farther.'

Josh shook his head. 'Bam?'

'Brooklyn Academy of Music,' Robbie said. 'Brooklyn is farther from Times Square than *here*.'

Josh said, 'Wait a minute, you're switching things around. I'm not here to talk about your theater troubles, I'm here to talk about your *Levrin* troubles.'

Robbie cracked his knuckles, thinking hard. The reports bounced off the walls. He said, 'He's the activator, huh?'

'In my case,' Josh said. 'In Van Bark's case, more the terminator.'

Robbie said, 'Ugh. So what are you saying? Time to lower my standards and go to the Coast?'

'I've thought about running away,' Josh said, 'and maybe I could. My wife doesn't think so. And you know, to tell the truth, it isn't that easy these days to completely disappear. Not and still be alive.'

'But what you're telling me,' Robbie said, 'is now I gotta go *along* with these people, and really do a Benedict Arnold number. I mean, for real.'

'Maybe they won't ask you to do much,' Josh said. 'I've just had some people staying in my place, when I wasn't there, and I'm kinda storing stuff for them.'

Robbie's keen eyes bored in. 'What stuff?'

'Well . . . guns.'

'*Oh*, no!' Jumping to his feet, pacing the stage like Hamlet, Robbie said, 'I don't *like* guns, man, I even have trouble with the props on the stage, I try to stay away from Mamet, I don't like any of that stuff, maybe you should just go away and—'

'Wait, wait,' Josh said. 'You can't just pretend this isn't happening, because it's *happening*. Levrin is gonna show up, because he obviously still needs somebody, because Van Bark didn't work out—'

'Ugh.'

'If you can't make him believe you've been part of the sleeper thing all along,' Josh said, 'honest to God he's gonna kill you. Same as Van Bark. And then he'll come get *me*, because he knows the truth. And then Mr Nimrin.'

'This Nimrin sounds like—'

'*Hello!*' yelled a voice from offstage; from the lobby, in fact. '*Anybody here?*' yelled the voice, and Josh recognized it, the accent, the intonations.

Suddenly on his feet, he hissed, 'It's him! It's him!'

Robbie gaped at him. 'The terminator?'

'*Hello!*' Rattling of the locked door.

'He'll break it down!' Josh said, in a shrill whisper. 'You've gotta go out there, talk to him!'

Robbie stared up the aisle. '*Talk* to him?'

'*Hello!* What's the matter with this door?'

'You're an *actor!*' Josh whispered, frantic with haste. '*Act!*'

'Act? But—' Robbie waved his arms, acting frazzlement. 'What's my – what's my throughline?'

'You're a *spy!*'

'*Anybody there?*' More door rattling.

'Answer him, before he breaks in.'

'Be right out!' Robbie yelled.

'*Mitchell Robbie?*'

'Be right there!'

Robbie started to move, but Josh grabbed his arm. 'Where do I hide?'

'Behind the stage,' Robbie said, distracted, and called again, 'Here I come!' Instead of which, he did three quick deep kneebends, then straightened, having become somehow taller, thicker. 'Be right there,' he called, in a considerably deeper voice, and marched up the aisle.

21

'I COME FROM Mr Nimrin. Of course, you *remember* Mr Nimrin.'
'Yes, of course. How *is* old Nimrin these days?'

Hide behind the stage. Behind the stage?

'Retired. Enjoying his retirement. I am Andrei Levrin.'

'Among his roses, eh? Good for old Nimrin,' Robbie said, his voice becoming more upper-crust English with every sentence. 'Come in, old chap, come in.'

But the back wall was blank black plywood. How could he—?

'Not much comfort in these digs, I'm afraid.'

The voices were so *close*. And there, at the right rear corner of the stage, on the plywood wall, a round black wooden knob, the same color and texture as the wall, almost impossible to see. Push, or pull?

Push; which was why no hinges showed. Josh stepped through into a different kind of darkness, and the voices just kept getting nearer.

'I suppose you thought the call might never come.'

'One stands ready. As the poet says, one also serves. Take the settee, why don't you, you'll find it more comfortable than it looks.'

'Thank you. But first let me—'

'Ack!'

'Mitchell? What's the matter?'

'Nothing, not a thing, I wasn't certain what you were reaching for, I didn't want you to miss your footing on the— What's this?'

'Per our arrangement.'

He's looking at the bankbook now, Josh thought, as he himself looked around at where he was hiding. Robbie's quarters, it must be, the living space that made it possible for Good Rep to get insurance.

It was a fairly large room, very messy, overcrowded with furniture, boxes, lamps, paintings, posters. It appeared to be a living room plus bedroom plus theatrical storage room, with two filthy windows in the far wall through which the remnants of daylight diffidently oozed, not helped much by the walls, which were painted in the pale grayish color variously known as landlord white or cockroach white, because it goes on the walls dirty and therefore it's very hard to know when it should be repainted. An open doorway in the left wall suggested an even grungier kitchen beyond.

But Josh's attentions were all behind him, on the conversation taking place just beyond this thin sheet of plywood, its hairy surface on this side also landlord white. Josh touched it with a palm, leaned close, and listened.

'Quite a lot of money.' Robbie now sounded like a strangled Englishman.

'That was the agreement with Mr Nimrin, as you recall. You do recall.'

'Yes, of course. Memory like a steel trap.'

'You are now, what this means is, activated.'

'Yes.' Thoughtful now, in control, no longer strangling. 'One understood the situation at once, of course. What are my orders? Oh, and by what rank shall I refer to you?'

'Rank?' Josh could imagine Levrin frowning through lowered brows at Robbie. Don't overdo it, he begged. Don't get into the part too much.

'Well, Major, Colonel, whatever. One likes to do these things properly.'

'Oh, I see.' Wonderful; there was no suspicion in that voice at all. 'Very considerate of you, but no, we don't do military ranks, we aren't that sort of group. In the old days, we might have said "comrade," but that doesn't seem to have the . . . *ring* it once had.'

'So shall I call you Andrei? No cover name? Or possibly that *is* your cover name.'

'Andrei will do very nicely,' Levrin said, sounding just a bit nettled. 'And you? Mitchell, or Mitch?'

'Oh, Mitch, Mitch is fine. But now to the assignment.'

'You seem eager, Mitch.'

'Well, it has been a long time between drinks, as the Governor of North Carolina said to the Governor of South Carolina. Or was that the Gov—'

'It's very simple, really.' Levrin seemed in more of a hurry than before. 'All you're going to do is rent a car.'

'Rent a car? Is it a, is it a *long* journey?'

'No, no, not even out of the state. Can you take a note?'

'A what?'

'Write a note. Write the information.'

'Oh, yes, of course, I'm sorry' – the voice getting even *closer* – 'I'll just get a pen and—' another sudden strangled noise, an inch from the plywood. 'No no, what am I thinking, silly me, pen and paper in the box office. I mean, ha ha' moving away – 'where else would it be? Half a sec.'

The voice faded and jounced, as though Robbie were leaving at a dead run. Josh waited, ear to the plywood. Was that the sound of Levrin, up and around, moving about the stage? Bored, at loose ends, noticing that discreet little wooden knob, all in black?

Silent and swift as the headless horseman's horse, Josh slalomed through the collected junk, noticing along the way there would be no escape through those smeary windows. Bars could be dimly seen on the outside, and an alley between the end of this building and the side of the first one on the cross street. Forgetting the windows, Josh angled through that side doorway into a kitchen where all the shelves were empty because the deep broad sink was *full*.

'Here we are, here we are. Sit down, Andrei, we don't stand on ceremony here, all set, ready for the drill.'

'Yes, fine.'

As Josh headed back to his listening post against the plywood, it seemed to him he could almost *hear* Levrin square his shoulders, squelch his doubts, decide to move forward no matter how strange Mitchell Robbie had turned out to be.

'You'll use your own credit card,' Levrin said, 'but of course we'll reimburse you later. Keep your receipt.'

'Keep . . . receipt.'

'Yes. A reservation has already been made in your name at All-Boro Car Rental at Eleventh Avenue and West Fifty-fourth Street.'

'. . . Fifty-fourth Street.'

'Yes. It's a weekend rental. You needn't write that down!'

'No, fine, right you are.'

'You'll get to the car rental agency at nine on Saturday morning. The car is to be a four-door sedan, seats five.'

'. . . seats five.'

'Yes. Once you have the car, drive north on Eleventh Avenue.'

'. . . Avenue.'

'Yes. At Sixty-third Street, on the southeast corner, there is a pay telephone.'

'. . pay telephone.'

'Yes. Stop there, turn on your flashers – don't write that down, just remember to turn them on.'

'Yes, certainly.'

'Stand at the payphone and soon it will ring, and you will be given your instructions.'

To proceed, Josh told himself, to Yankee Stadium.

'And that's it?'

'That's all of it. You will follow the instructions, and then your part of the operation is complete.'

'Top hole.'

'You understand, I can't speak about the rest of the operation, only your part in it.'

'Oh, quite. Need to know. Think nothing of it.'

'Well, Mitch, I'm pleased to say, I think Mr Nimrin's choice in your case was an excellent one. Excellent.'

'What, off so soon?'

'More preparations to make. You understand.'

'I could offer you a Diet Pepsi,' the idiot said. 'With or without rum.'

'Thank you, Mitch, another time.'

The two voices receded, complimenting each other. Josh waited till he could hear neither of them anymore, then very cautiously opened the thin plywood door a scant inch, to squint out at an empty stage. As he peered there, one-eyed, Robbie came hurrying back into the theater, beaming like a halogen lamp.

Josh crept out to the stage. 'Is he gone?'

Robbie stopped just short of the stage, all the empty chairs behind him. 'Forty thousand dollars!' he cried, in a stage whisper, and actually rubbed his hands together.

'Yes, I know,' Josh said. 'In the Cayman Islands. I checked, and it's real.'

'For a weekend's work, driving something or somebody somewhere. You know it really doesn't sound that awful, when you finally get to it.'

'No, not so bad,' Josh said. 'You're driving the getaway car.'

91

22

'**F**ROM WHAT?' ROBBIE asked.
'From the massacre.'

Robbie backed until his legs bumped into the first metal chair behind him. He dropped into it, making the chair squeak. 'I suppose,' he said, 'you're going to have to tell me about it.'

It was quickly told. Kamastan; Mihommed-Sinn; gypsy curse; Yankee Stadium; assassination. When Josh was finished, Robbie stared out through the upstage doorway a while, at that far-off snow-covered mountain. At last, he frowned and said, 'They want me to drive to Yankee Stadium? *After* they do it? It'll be a madhouse there.'

'I don't know,' Josh admitted. 'Mr Nimrin says, if *he* were doing it, his people on the honor guard would shoot the rest of the honor guards, release blood packets in their own uniforms, then kill the ambulance attendants on the way out. I don't think his friends are any less ruthless or bloodthirsty than he is. Whatever the details, I guess there'd be a place you were supposed to wait, they'd meet you there.'

'Seats five,' Robbie said. 'But why do they need *me*? Why do they need *us*?'

'We're local, we know how things work, we know how to drive the local roads. That's why they have sleepers in the first place.'

Josh was back on the settee by now, Robbie still in the aisle seat in the first row, but now he jumped up to start that pacing again. 'No,' he said, glaring at the floor. 'Can't be done.'

Josh watched him. 'What can't be done?'

'All this killing.' Forcefully he shook his head as he paced back and forth on the forestage. His English-spy accent was gone, but the facial tics around his mouth were strangely reminiscent of Humphrey Bogart. 'We're shhupposed to help kill one creep from a hundred thousand miles away to help some other creep a hundred thousand miles away?'

'I a hundred per cent agree with you,' Josh said. 'Believe me, uh, Mitch' – because, if Levrin could call him Mitch, then so could a fellow American ensnared with him in this mess – 'believe me, I've been staying awake nights trying to find a way to make this not happen.'

'There has to be one.'

'If we go to the police,' Josh told him, 'we don't have enough for them, but we've done enough to get ourselves killed. I told my wife we could run and hide in Canada, she told me I'm not the type.'

Robbie stopped his paces and tics to give Josh one brief intense stare, then nodded. 'She's right, you're not.'

Josh found himself vaguely insulted by that, but rather than pursue it, get caught up in a side issue, he said, 'I suppose you are the type.'

'I would be,' Robbie said, 'if that was the way to go. But that isn't the way to go.' Suddenly he turned squarely to face Josh, shoulders hunched forward, jaw grim, arms bent like an ape. 'Yeah, Tojo,' he snarled, in a more gravelly voice than ever before, 'I'm just a little guy, but that's all right, Tojo, because there's a million more little guys just like me, and they're on their way, Tojo, you hear me? You hear me? They're on their way! *Oh*-haa-haa-haa-haa-haa!'

Robbie's insane laughter slowly died away up among the lights. Josh said, 'I don't know what I'm supposed to say to that.'

Robbie cocked his head to peer at Josh. 'All right,' he said. 'Hold on.' He went over to get the metal chair he'd been sitting on, brought it closer, and sat on it to face Josh up close. 'This is why,' he said. 'Why your wife's right, but why nevertheless we've still got to do something. And can. The difference between us, you and me, is, you're the corporate type, and I'm the creative type. That's why you—'

Stiffly, Josh said, 'I'm with an advertising agency.'

'Exactly,' Robbie said, as though he thought Josh were agreeing with him. 'You don't think outside the box because you *live* in the box. Tote that bale, get that paycheck.'

'Well,' Josh said, angry with himself for feeling defensive but unable to not defend himself, 'there is *some* creativity in what I—'

'Of course,' Robbie said. 'Sell your talents to the man, because that's the only road you can *visualize*. Here you're in this situation, you say, "If I don't do exactly what they want, they'll find out and kill me. But if I *do* do exactly what they want, they'll massacre a whole lot of innocent people." '

'Yes,' Josh said.

'You look at the possibilities,' Robbie said, 'and you say, "Close the book. No more possibilities. I'll just have to feel unhappy until something bad happens." You see where I live.'

'Yes,' Josh agreed.

'Because I don't bend to reality, you see what I mean?' His eyes were more intense than ever, as though now he were channeling Svengali. 'Reality bends to *me.*'

'Sure,' Josh said. He wondered when he could get out of here, return to a real world of real-world problems.

Robbie waved an arm, to indicate the theater. 'Between productions,' he said, 'we have classes in here, and *that's* what the classes are all about. Creating our own reality, anywhere in the world. Anywhere in a hundred worlds. You wouldn't *believe* where in space and time this little room has been.'

'Uh huh,' Josh said, and gathered himself to rise. 'Well—'

'So when do I meet this con-artist Nimrin?'

23

JOSH GOT TO Harriet Linde's office at five to six. Feeling in some weird way as though he were in the position of host here, he thought he should show up early. He nodded to the doorman on the way by, with the sense he was becoming a regular here, and when he walked into the waiting room Robbie was already present, seated at attention, knees together, on the lefthand sofa, as though he'd been called to the principal's office. He was dressed now in what he must think of as proper apparel for traveling uptown: black lace-up oxfords, black chinos, and a button-down long sleeve white dress shirt, all the buttons buttoned, including collar and cuffs, except the top button at the neck. Not what anyone else in New York was wearing in July, except a few of the non-English speaking cabdrivers.

Robbie nodded at Josh as the warning bell chimed. He pointed at the closed inner door and said, 'She says she's with a patient. Not your guy Nimrin, by any chance?'

'No, he's not a patient.' Josh came around to take the other sofa. 'She didn't say there was a message?'

'She just said she was with a patient. She came out and I said, 'I'm waiting for somebody named Nimrin,' and she said, 'I'm with a patient,' and went back in.'

'Mr Nimrin didn't say for sure he'd be here,' Josh explained. 'But I figure, if there's no message, that probably means he's coming.'

'I pretty well need to talk to the guy,' Robbie said, and the outer door opened and Mr Nimrin walked in.

He stopped in the doorway when he saw Robbie. He looked alert, tense, ready for anything. Still watching Robbie, he said to Josh, 'Who's this?'

'Mitchell Robbie,' Josh said. 'You don't recognize him?'

Mr Nimrin frowned, but stepped further into the room, letting the door close. 'You're Robbie? You've lost weight. Stop drinking beer?'

'Yes, as a matter of fact,' Robbie said. He frowned at Mr Nimrin just as hard as Mr Nimrin frowned at him. 'You were the *bartender*?'

Mr Nimrin approached, stopped on the other side of the coffee table, leaned forward, looked as though he cared, and said, 'Care for another, sir?'

'Oh, my God,' Robbie said.

Coming around the coffee table to the right, Mr Nimrin made a shooing gesture at Josh. 'Sit with your friend,' he said. 'I'll take that sofa; I'm larger.'

That was true. Josh moved over and Mr Nimrin sat down, saying, 'I'm glad you found him.'

'Levrin found him, too,' Josh said.

Mr Nimrin raised an eyebrow at Robbie. 'Then you must have played your part,' he said.

'I always do,' Robbie said. 'I heard what the plan is. Kamastan and all that.'

Mr Nimrin nodded. 'Did they give you a task?'

'Rent a car. The getaway car, according to Josh.'

'Yes,' Mr Nimrin said. 'They'll need a local driver. So all you'll have to do is keep quiet, follow orders, and all will be well.'

'I don't think so,' Robbie said.

Josh had to twist halfway around on the sofa to look at Robbie, who faced Mr Nimrin with a serious unflinching look. Meanwhile, Mr Nimrin was saying, 'I thought Josh explained the situation.'

'He did,' Robbie agreed. 'We're caught up in your scam that failed. If we don't pretend you were legitimate all along, everybody will be killed, including you.'

'Exactly so,' Mr Nimrin said.

'Well, not *exactly* so,' Robbie said. There was a bluntness to him now, the private eye at the end of the movie, explaining who's guilty of what.

Mr Nimrin raised an intimidating eyebrow. 'Meaning?'

Including Josh in the conversation, if only briefly, Robbie said, 'This is part of what I meant by bending reality to your own needs. The fact is, everything in life is a plot, a story, not just this massacre here, or Nimrin's scheme before. If you can look at the events around you as part of a narrative, you can begin to get some ideas about motivation, and where the story's supposed to wind up.'

'Sure,' Josh said. He had no idea what Robbie was talking about. He could only see that this was a different Robbie, not pacing, not bouncing off the walls, not trying on different roles as though they were sports jackets. This Mitchell Robbie was insightful and to the point.

Now, turning his attention back to Mr Nimrin, Robbie said, 'Josh still doesn't see what the story's ending is, but I got it right away. And of course you know it, too.'

Mr Nimrin seemed wary, all at once. 'Do I?'

'Certainly.' Robbie showed both hands, palms up. 'Here we are in act two, scene one, I told myself. What happens in act three, scene two? At the end of the play?'

'It's over,' Mr Nimrin said. 'You have a great deal of money, a brute has been removed from a brutal part of the world, and they will never call on these particular sleepers again.

'No, they couldn't,' Robbie said. 'Because we'll be dead.'

Josh stared. Robbie had said that so calmly, and yet he seemed deadly serious.

Mr Nimrin, also calm, said, 'How so?'

'If this thing goes off,' Robbie said, 'there'll be a *huge* stink. Everybody will want to know who was responsible, so they can go teach them a lesson. So what will they find? Gee, it's home-grown, like Oklahoma City, a coupla crazy radical guys did it all on their own.' Looking again at Josh, he said, 'They're rigging the evidence on us right now. They come in, they do the dirty, they go out, and there's nothing left but you and me, face down. The perpetrators.'

24

JOSH LOOKED AT Mr Nimrin's face, and what he saw there told him that Robbie had been absolutely right. Dead right. 'You weren't going to tell me,' he said.

Mr Nimrin gave him an exasperated snort. 'Why should I? *They* have to believe that you two are authentic sleepers, or my life is ended. Painfully. As important as your life no doubt is to you, so is my life important to me.' Nodding to Robbie, he told him, 'Unfortunately, you are very good. Now that you've seen the snare hidden in the underbrush, the situation becomes more complex.'

'You need us to keep you alive,' Robbie said, 'and we need you to keep us alive.'

'True.' Mr Nimrin pursed his lips and patted his thighs in a pensive manner. 'Unfortunately, I don't see how it can be done.'

'And,' Josh said, 'stop the assassination.'

Mr Nimrin gave him a surprised glare. 'Do what?'

'We have to stop the assassination. We can't have—'

'I hope,' Mr Nimrin said, in a cold and precise way, 'that this is merely emotion speaking, and that a wiser part of your head will soon hold sway.'

Robbie said to Josh, calm but meaningful, 'He's on their side, you know.'

'But—'

Josh looked helplessly at Mr Nimrin, seeing how coiled and watchful the man had become, understanding belatedly that he, at this moment, was at the very brink of a Van Bark-level mistake. Because he and Mr Nimrin had been working in concert for more than a week, he'd settled into the comfortable conclusion that they were partners, on the same team, working together for a common goal. But that wasn't true. He said, 'You *want* the assassination.'

'Everyone in this room does,' Mr Nimrin said. 'I want that clear.'

'Well, no,' Robbie said, and Mr Nimrin turned his dangerous attention in Robbie's direction. Appearing unfazed by that laser look, Robbie said, 'Josh and I have a slightly different goal from you. You want to save your own skin, and you want the job to succeed.'

'It is *my* organization,' Mr Nimrin said. 'It is true I am no longer trusted at the highest levels, but it's still my organization. I have belonged with them my entire adult life, through changes of government, social structure and enemy. If the removal of Freddy Mihommed-Sinn is now considered vital to my organization, for whatever reason, then that is my goal, as well. And it must be yours.'

'That's where we disagree,' Robbie said.

Josh said, 'Mitch, I don't know. I don't think disagree is what we want to do here.'

'Wait for it,' Robbie told him, and said to Mr Nimrin, 'We're not in your organization. You signed us up without our knowledge or consent. So we don't care if your organization wins or loses. All we care is that we're both still alive when all you people have gone back where you came from.' He pointed an astonishingly rigid finger at Mr Nimrin. 'You got us into this. You can help to get us out.'

'How?' Mr Nimrin seemed really to be interested in the answer.

Robbie said, 'They don't trust you one hundred per cent at this organization of yours anymore, but you're still in it, you're still around those people.'

'Very much so.'

'So you can find out what their plans are for us,' Robbie said.

'You already know,' Mr Nimrin pointed out.

Robbie shook his head. 'No, their exact plans. What do they mean to do to us? And also, what evidence are they faking, to make us the bad guys? We'll have to know what it is, and where it is, so when the time comes we can get rid of it.'

'I'm not sure,' Mr Nimrin said. 'They don't tell me much these days, I'm sorry to say. I didn't even know Freddy Mihommed-Sinn was the target.'

'You're a spy,' Robbie told him. 'Act like one. Spy on them.'

Whatever Mr Nimrin might have said he didn't, because as he opened his mouth the interior door opened as well, and a man came out, short, obese, fat-faced, dressed in the world's largest pair of blue jeans and a yellow polo shirt like sunrise in the desert. In the crook of his left arm, he held a teddybear close to his chest, its nose against his heart. Tiny eyes peered out at them from inside the fat man's round pale face. If he could have showed an expression there, it would probably have been hauteur. He rolled across the room like an approaching low, and departed.

When they were alone again, and the fat man's impact had lessened, Robbie said, 'You have to help us, you know.' He waggled his pointing finger between himself and Josh. 'Because, if we disappear, your goose is cooked, and you know it.'

Mr Nimrin's attempt to scoff lacked a certain conviction. 'Disappear? How do you expect to do that?'

'Oh, come on,' Robbie said. 'Josh probably wouldn't be able to pull it off, so he's dead meat—'

'Hey.'

'—but I'm an actor. I could be somebody else in twenty minutes, stand right in front of you, you wouldn't know it was me.'

'Oh, fine,' Josh said. 'Now I've got *two* masters of disguise.'

'Not disguise,' Robbie corrected him. 'Disguise is for amateurs. What I do is character.'

Mr Nimrin clearly hadn't liked the amateur crack. 'If you could disappear so readily,' he said, sounding miffed, 'why haven't you done so?'

Robbie spread his hands. 'What – and give up show business?'

25

THEY LEFT MR Nimrin in the waiting room, looking at that interior door. The distant bell rang twice as they went out to the lobby, and Robbie said, 'Interesting character, Nimrin. Hard to play opposite, though.'

Josh frowned at his profile as they crossed the lobby. 'Play opposite?'

The doorman held open the outer door, and Robbie paused in front of him to say, 'You're doing a fine job. Excellent.'

The doorman was surprised, but not displeased. 'Thank you, sir,' he said, and even bowed a little.

Outside, Robbie said, 'Quick, we'll talk around the corner.' As he went, with long brisk steps, he unbuttoned his shirt cuffs and rolled them neatly above his elbows.

Following, Josh said, 'What do you mean, play opposite?'

'He does that exasperation bit,' Robbie said, as they made it around the corner of the building, where he stopped, back against the sandstone wall. 'But if you play into that,' he said, pulling his shirt-tail out, 'you're just reacting, you aren't creating anything.' Unbuttoning the bottom shirt button, he loosely tied the shirt-tails in front, almost but not quite creating a bare midriff. 'So you saw what I did.'

'No,' Josh admitted. 'I didn't.'

'No?' Robbie seemed surprised. 'I was afraid it was too obvious. Nimrin got it, though,' he said, and pulled a richly blue beret out of his hip pocket.

'I still don't get it,' Josh said.

Robbie shrugged. 'I played Nimrin,' he said, and placed the beret carefully on his head, a little forward, a little to the left. 'I mirrored it back at him. But a calmer Nimrin. Every scrim he puts up, I put up the same one. I think it helped. How do I look?'

He stepped back a pace and posed, arms out at the sides, palms forward, like a ballet dancer about to make his move. He seemed taller but just as thin, graceful, in his black pants and casually-tied white shirt and jaunty blue beret. Josh nodded at him. 'French,' he said.

'Almost,' Robbie said, pulling a crumpled pack of Gauloises from his pocket, 'but not quite, not yet.' He pulled one fat lumpy cigarette from the pack and frowned at it. 'I hate cigarettes,' he told the Gauloise, then looked at Josh, 'but they make such great props. Keep an eye out for him.'

Josh leaned to the side to look around the corner of the building. 'Not yet.'

'Probably be a little while with his ladyfriend,' Robbie said. 'Anyway, things are looking up.'

Josh looked back at him. The Gauloises pack was gone, the cigarette was lit and now dangled from the corner of Robbie's mouth. Josh said, 'What do you mean, things are looking up? I thought I just found out things were even worse than I knew.'

'You mean us being the late great patsies,' Robbie said, taking the cigarette from his mouth, holding it at his side. 'Well, it was a good thing for you to know that,' he said. 'And much better for it to come from Nimrin. If it just came from me, you might not believe it.'

'I still don't want to,' Josh said. 'How are things looking up?'

Robbie offered a very Gallic shrug. 'But now, Nimrin is working for *us*.' He didn't quite have a French accent, but he had something that was a reminder of a French accent.

'Working for us?'

'He'll do our spying for us, will he not?' Another Francophone shrug. 'He'll tell us where the bodies are buried.'

'Where our bodies are buried, you mean.'

'Where the *evidence* against us is buried,' Robbie corrected him. 'Very important. What do you think, should I add a little eyeliner, for that decadent look?'

Josh said, 'I don't get you. In three days from now, a bunch of professional assassins plan to kill us, *kill* us dead, and you're just bouncing along, playing games.'

'Listen, Josh,' Robbie said, dropping his Gallicisms to become the Old Trouper, explaining the mysteries of the The-ah-ter to the Kid. 'We're in a performance, you and I, we've both got a role to play. Very Bulldog Drummond. No, Scarlet Pimpernel. We *laugh* at danger! Ha-ha-*ha!*'

'I don't laugh at danger,' Josh said.

'Not *inside*. But outside, your role and my role is to be supremely self-confident, because if we falter, if we let doubt creep up on us, we're finished.'

'Then I'm finished,' Josh said.

Robbie took another step backward, to give Josh a sweeping up-and-down glance, a stern and disapproving survey. 'You know, Josh,' he said, 'I need you to play your part. It's hard for me to direct you *and* play opposite you.'

'I don't know what you want,' Josh said.

'Deliver your lines and don't bump into the furniture,' Robbie said, as though that were the easiest thing in the world. Then he cocked a hip, as though about to start a musical number, pointed at Josh, and said, 'You're going out there a scared little girl, but you're coming back a star.'

Josh said, 'Shouldn't you be quoting something about "with my shield or on it"?'

Robbie laughed. '*Now* you're getting into the spirit!'

'I am?'

Robbie suddenly looked soulful to the max. With right palm pressed to his heart, he lifted his left forefinger and the Gauloise beside his left ear, and intoned, 'Out of this nettle, danger, we pluck this flower, safety.' He dropped both hands to his sides. 'One Henry Four. I don't know how much I'll accomplish tonight, I have a curtain to make at eight-ten. But luck may be with us, who knows? You go home, and we'll talk tomorrow.'

'Fine.' Josh was ready to go home, even though he knew what was there. 'See you, uh, see you.'

'Just exit,' Robbie advised him, so Josh walked away eastward, toward Broadway. When he looked back from midblock, Robbie was standing with his back against the building, one leg bent, the foot pressed to the wall. Cigarette smoke curled upward from him, like a tiny signal fire.

Josh walked on. At the corner, he crossed to the right, then paused again, to look diagonally back down the long block just as Mr Nimrin came hurrying around that far corner, managing to move very rapidly while retaining his dignity. He rushed past the skinny Frenchman draped against the building and kept on. Coming this way.

Whoops. Not wanting an unexplainable encounter with Mr Nimrin at this point, Josh stuck out an arm and hid inside a taxi.

26

TINA PAUSTO WAS on the sofa, watching the network news. 'We'll be back in a—' the anchor said, and she offed him with the remote, then smiled at Josh and said, 'Well, my dear, how was your day?'

Surprised, he said, 'Fine,' and stood just inside the living room to look at her.

This was the warm and congenial Tina Pausto back again, dressed now in a pale blue silk blouse that draped on her like the gowns of Greek goddess statues, plus sleek black slacks and black spike heels. On the coffee table in front of her were the white ceramic ice bucket on the Tweety potholder, unopened champagne bottle thrusting up, two tall skinny champagne glasses, and a closed copy of *Vogue* magazine thick enough for a sniper to take cover behind.

He remembered last night's decision, under this same coffee table, to ingratiate himself with Tina Pausto, drink with her despite Mr Nimrin's warning, worm his way into her confidence, learn her spy secrets. Now, actually in her presence, the erect champagne bottle between them, he saw he'd been planning to open the tiger's cage and just stroll on in. Whistling, no doubt.

Not that she was caged. Not tamable, not without peril, not to be trusted.

Hoping he didn't sound as skeptical as he felt, Josh said, 'What's the occasion?'

If it were possible for a tiger to have a guileless smile, she had one. 'Why, it is your return,' she said, 'at the end of the long day, putting bread on the table for your family. Such a different life for you.'

He didn't understand. 'Different?'

'From the Rimbaud you were, once upon a time,' she explained, and while he sorted that out, deciding she hadn't said 'Rambo' after all, she went on, 'I have seen your dossier, after all, naturally I have.'

Oh, the blowhard days of Uncle Ray's; of course she'd know all about that, it was the character Mr Nimrin had made for him nine years ago – with a little help from himself, he had to admit – that had been growing in the darkness all this time, like a poisonous mushroom, now ready to eat. She'd come to this apartment expecting a slightly older version of that fellow, had been amused and dismissive when she'd seen what a domesticated boy he'd become, and now?

He said, 'Champagne at vespers? Has that become our regular routine?'

'Oh, my dear,' she said, kindly and friendly and absolutely untrustworthy, 'we shall have such a short time together. I asked myself, why should I not be amiable?'

'No reason.' But, he thought, no reason either way.

'You are, after all,' she said, 'such a hero.'

'That's not friendly,' he said. 'To make fun of me.'

She looked surprised and penitent. 'Make fun of you? But no! I mean it. You are a hero.'

'Because I'm working for . . . whoever you people are?'

'Not at all,' she said. 'I assume you are, like most of us, in it for the money. No, to make a marriage, make a family, to remain true and loyal. Loyalty is heroic, wherever we find it. And I may tell you, we find it seldom. *Please* open the champagne.'

'Oh. Yes.'

As he unbent the wire and worked the cork free, she said, 'I thought perhaps, this evening, after you receive your phone call from your wife— Her name is Eve?'

'Yes.'

'May I call her Eve?'

'Not to her face,' he said, and poured champagne as she laughed.

'No, certainly not,' she said. 'But after your Eve telephones you this evening – what nice symmetry that is – I thought we might go out to dinner together, if you felt agreeable.'

'Dinner? Oh, well, sure.'

'Just somewhere simple, here in the neighborhood,' she said. 'And perhaps a movie after. There's an espionage film playing over on Broadway.'

He handed her her glass, lifted his, they clinked, and he felt again that instant of electricity in the air, circling their arms, but less this time, the force diminished. I must be getting used to her, he thought, and said, 'An espionage film? I'd have thought you get enough of that at home.'

She laughed again, as the phone rang. 'It is unfair,' she said, 'to make me laugh and then not sleep with me. Go talk to your Eve, and then we will dine.'

'Are you all right?'

'Sure. Fine.'

'Did you meet the fellow Dick Welsh found?'

'Oh, yeah. He was there, all right.'

'What's he like?'

'Well, he's in the theater, you know. Theatrical.'

'Doesn't sound as though he'll be much help.'

'Oh, well, I don't know, maybe. He agrees with you that I'm not the type to go off and start a new life.'

'Good. Theatrical but sensible. And the other one is still there?'

'Yes. I was thinking and, you know, I can't come out there this week-end. Maybe Sunday.'

'I had the same thought. I'll miss you.'

'We'll miss each other.'

'I wish it were over.'

'Soon.'

'I thought I'd be sorry when the rental ended. Boy, was I wrong.'

'Love you.'

'Love you, too. Be careful, Josh.'

Well, it's too late for that, he thought, as he hung up, hoping an eavesdropper would not have been able to make too much of that call.

They just strolled idly in the neighborhood in the long summer evening, he and Tina Pausto, or so it seemed, but then she said, 'That place looks presentable, let's read the menu,' and it was where he'd had dinner with Eve the night before.

A coincidence? He watched her profile as she studied the menu in its frame on the wall beside the restaurant entrance, but saw nothing to suggest she might be toying with him. And it was after all merely a handy restaurant in the neighborhood, so it didn't have to be a coincidence at all.

At least they weren't shown to the same table, but one closer to the front, and the girl seating the customers tonight was different from the one last night. It was the first time Josh was in a public place with a woman whose beauty was so powerful it made a palpable stirring in the room, and he found that both heady and oddly frightening. They sat, and a different waiter from the previous night brought menus and the wine list.

'You will choose a nice chardonnay,' she told him, when the waiter left. 'In the summer, I like a chardonnay.'

'Fine.'

They ordered wine and food, he tasted and approved the wine, and when they were alone again she said, 'I'm flattered.'

He didn't get it. 'Flattered?'

'You have bought for me a more expensive wine than for your Eve last night.'

He stared at her, that pleasant smile, that clear brow, those knowing eyes. There was nothing threatening about her, which was the most threatening thing of all. 'You know about that,' he said.

'But my dear, that's my job.' She sipped, put the glass down, smiled at him. 'You wouldn't want me to be bad at my job, would you?'

'No,' he said.

Watching her long fingers toy with the stem of the wineglass, she said, 'How much have you told her about what we're doing?'

There was no point in denial. In fact, he thought, his only salvation, if there was any salvation, lay in candor. 'Some,' he said.

'If Andrei knew,' she said, still not looking directly at him, 'he would be very angry.'

'If?' Maybe there would be salvation, after all.

'He would consider it a terrible breach of security,' she went on. 'Andrei is very serious about security.'

'I'm sure he is,' Josh said, thinking about Robert Van Bark, and the waiter brought their first course, interrupting the conversation. When he had gone, Josh said, 'But Andrei doesn't know.'

'No, I have not reported this to him. This salad is delicious. The walnuts, what a lovely idea.'

'Are you going to report it?' The clenched knot his stomach had become suggested a restaurant was not perhaps the best environment for him right now. A mountaintop cabin a million miles from Tina Pausto and the security-conscious Andrei and the fumbling scammer Nimrin, *that* might be the place for Josh Redmont right now, if only he could will himself there.

She put her fork onto the salad plate and gazed at him, thoughtfully, as though she hadn't yet decided whether to report him or not. 'Again,' she said, 'that's my job.'

'Yes.'

'But,' she said, 'you could no more hide the truth from your Eve than you could fly.'

'No.'

She nodded, smiling at him. 'You would never willingly hurt your Eve, and she would never willingly hurt you. So she will keep your secret.'

'That's right.'

She picked up her fork, speared endive, and again smiled at him. 'And *I* shall keep your secret, too.'

'Thank you.'

'It will be,' she said, 'our own little secret.' The endive slipped past her lips, her teeth. Her mouth closed, and smiled at him.

Throughout the espionage movie, which Josh thought self-important, Tina Pausto kept laughing her musical laugh at inappropriate places, causing other people to swivel and glare at her, then blink at her beauty and turn back quizzically to the screen; *was* there something funny there?

Afterward, on the walk home, he asked her what she'd found to laugh at, and she laughed again, lightly, and said, 'Oh, actors, they are so winsome. I could eat them up.'

The smile on the face of the tiger.

27

A T TEN-FIFTEEN, the secretary Josh shared at the office with four
other reps buzzed him to say, 'A Mr Robbie on two.'

'I'll take it . . . Mitch?'

'You do business lunches, don't you?' Deep voice. 'We're going to have
to increase market share, gentlemen, or we're going to have to drink the
Kool-Aid.'

Josh did a smile that Robbie couldn't hear, and said, 'You want to come
uptown for lunch.'

'Strictly business. Things to report.'

They settled on one o'clock at the Tre Mafiosi, a good Italian place not
far from his office, usually full of publishing and television people, and
Josh tried to return his attention to his employer's concerns.

It was easier to keep his mind on the job, though it shouldn't have been.
The night before he'd folded a winter blanket onto the living room floor
as an additional layer of softness and pushed the coffee table even farther
away from himself, so he wouldn't wake up with his head under it. Then,
after a week and a half of troubled catnaps, he'd slept almost normally on
that floor last night, and he'd awakened knowing that, more than the
blanket underneath him, it was the dinner conversation with Tina Pausto
that had eased his mind and let him relax into slumber.

Should it have? In two days, he had met three Tina Paustos, first the
coolly seductive one, and then the impatient dismissive one, and now the
pal, keeping his little secrets. As to which of those was the real Tina
Pausto, obviously the answer was none. Everything she did was for calcu-
lation, and for her employer. If she'd decided that Josh's breach of security
with Eve hadn't endangered the current mission, then she risked nothing
if she kept her knowledge to herself. At the same time, she put Josh in her

debt. Not for any specific payback at the moment, but for insurance on down the line.

Whatever; it had worked.

Here we were at Thursday, with Premier Mihommed-Sinn due to fly in from Kamastan tomorrow, the ceremony at Yankee Stadium scheduled the day after that, and what so far had Josh done about it all? He'd kept himself alive with Tina Pausto's help, but not much more. The bad things were on their way, thundering toward the point where all the evil would meet, in the innocent open air, and here he was, still immersed in Cloudbank.

Again Robbie had arrived first, now dressed, Josh guessed, from some production of *Death of a Salesman*, in a seedy beige suit too big for him, wrinkled white shirt with plowed ruts in the collar, and a narrow stained black necktie severely knotted at the throat, as though Robbie had been considering suicide.

But he wasn't. He was, in fact, pleased with himself. Pouring himself some more Pellegrino, he said, in a Texas twang, 'Nice little place you got here.'

'We like it,' Josh said, doing his own attempt at Texas. 'It may not be much, but we call it a restaurant.'

Robbie gave him a surprised look. 'What happened to gloom and doom?'

'Oh, they're still there,' Josh said, 'one on each shoulder. But last night Tina Pausto told me she knows I've told Eve what's happening, and she'll keep my secret, so Andrei Levrin won't crush me like a kitten.'

'She's making an ally,' Robbie commented. 'Keeping side doors open.'

'I'll take it,' Josh said. 'We don't inquire into motivations.'

The usual stuff involving menus and waiters ensued, and after it Robbie said, 'Well, while you were working your wiles on Pausto—'

'Sure.'

'—I was on the commuter train to Port Washington.'

A town on the north shore of Long Island, not very far out at all; from its heights, New York City could be seen. Josh said, 'That's where Mr Nimrin went?'

'Straight there. I was glad it wasn't one of the long commuter runs, to Montauk or Port Jefferson. I didn't know what his stop was, so I had to stay with him. I stayed on the train, past all those little stations, and of course he never piped me. End of the line, Port Wash, off he gets and into the men's room at the station, and never comes out.'

'Disguising himself.'

Robbie made a disgusted face. 'I'm afraid you're probably right. I didn't really believe it of him, and whatever he does it's still a far cry from the thing I do, working from the inside, crea—'

'Mitch.'

'You're right,' Robbie said, and the food they'd ordered arrived, and the next thing Robbie said was, 'This is all really very good.'

'Yeah, it's a good place.'

'I'm astonished you don't weigh three hundred pounds.'

'Tell me about Port Washington.'

'Well,' Robbie said, 'I did have to get back to the city, I had a curtain to make, in fact barely made it, so I waited around until the next train was about to start the other way. Then I did a quick search of the men's room, and of course, no Nimrin. So home I went, and did my best for Mr Shaw, then trained back *out* to Port Wash—'

'Late at night?'

'That's what it was, yes,' Robbie agreed. 'But I felt a certain urgency.'

'Yes, sure.'

'Now, Port Wash is mostly a high-end commuter town,' Robbie said, 'quite old, the newer stuff off somewhere. There are a few heights overlooking Long Island Sound, and a few estates up in there, and it seemed to me that's where the safe house would have to be, up in Gatsby territory, to give them the room and the privacy they'd need. I cabbed up and prowled around outside some of them, looking for I don't know what, a car with diplomatic plates maybe, or a helicopter launching pad. Or a Russian name on a mailbox. Or maybe even a sentry on patrol.' He shook his head, chewed some cod, said, 'Nada. We've gotta go out there by day.'

Josh paused. 'We?'

'Four eyes are better than two.' Robbie waved his fork. 'Remember, you're the one came to me, said we have this urgent problem, and we *do* have this urgent problem. Your girl friend is keeping your secret right now, but for how long? At this moment, she thinks it's best to line up with you. Tomorrow, or later today, who knows. Josh, Mihommed-Sinn is flying in *tomorrow.*'

'I know, I've been telling myself that.'

'Do you have to call your office,' Robbie asked him, 'or can you just go?'

Josh hesitated, then shrugged. 'I have to call my office. But we can't drive out there, they know my car.'

'That,' Robbie pointed out, 'is why God gave us the trains.'

'You're right. Yes,' he told the waiter, 'I'm done. No, no dessert.'
'Coffee,' Robbie said. 'You should, too.'
'Okay, coffee,' Josh said. 'Not that I'm likely to fall asleep.'

28

ON THE TRAIN, Josh was dressed as he'd been for lunch, lightweight jacket, tan chinos, pale blue short-sleeved dress shirt; the yellow tie was now rolled and in his jacket pocket. Robbie, it turned out, had checked a black backpack at Tre Mafiosi, into which, during the trainride, he'd stowed the *Death of a Salesman* suitcoat and shirt and garroting tie, and out of which he'd brought a khaki short-sleeved shirt with pocket flaps. Wearing both this and the backpack, he looked like the den leader of a previously unknown offshoot of the Boy Scouts.

Their train pulled into its end-of-the-line berth at ten minutes to three. They'd have another six hours of July daylight, plenty of time to search an area this small, a stubby peninsula jutting northward into Long Island Sound. Robbie had alerted a standby to take over, in case he didn't get back to the theater in time tonight, so all they had to do, until the sun went down, was look for Mr Nimrin.

The town itself was all diagonals, some parts angling down toward the water and the view westward across to Kings Point and Great Neck, the Bronx beyond that, other parts twisting upward and eastward toward the heights over by the more affluent sections of Sea Cliff and Sands Point, where most of the estates and monasteries could be found.

Robbie paused at a bench on the station platform to delve into his backpack once more, bringing out a thick manila envelope scrawled with addresses and rubber stamps and postage stamps, all messily wrapped in thicknesses of clear tape, with bits of ragged envelope sticking hairily out at the corners. It looked to Josh, seeing it briefly and at an angle, that it was addressed to Ellois Nimrin at some incomprehensible location over which the ink had run or the paper worn away.

Nodding at the package, Josh said, 'What are you going to do with that?'

'There's a Mailboxes-R-Us in town,' Robbie said. 'They'll know everybody.' Slipping on the backpack, he stood and said, 'Come along. I'll be in the part, so you'll have to listen to directions, and keep an eye out for anything funny.'

Josh had no idea what Robbie meant by 'anything funny,' but didn't ask, since he suspected Robbie had no idea what he meant, either. It was simply a theatrical way to end the statement.

They walked away from the railroad station and into town, agreeing that Josh would go into the mailbox place first and stand filling out forms while Robbie came in and did his dance. The storefront itself, in squared-off red, white and blue design, was midblock, between a video rental shop and a cellular phone place, so a generation ago all three of these stores would have been something else.

Josh went inside and found there a clean and cluttered space, with cartons piled up in stacks and a wall of mailboxes and pigeonholes behind a chest-high counter. Three young employees in white smocks cheerfully carried boxes around or studied manifests. They glanced smilingly at Josh, but then went back to what they were doing when they saw him turn toward the side-counter where the forms were.

This was a chain that provided any kind of mail-related service you could think of except the actual delivery of mail. They'd serve as a convenience address, they'd do packing (and gift wrapping), they'd sell empty cartons and packing materials, they would deliver to the post office, and they offered a variety of stationery and envelopes as well.

Josh bent over a form enlisting himself – or Matt Fairlough, the first name he came up with, not that good a friend – into the ranks of those who wanted to receive their mail at this location until further notice, and behind him Robbie bustled in, looking worried, energetic, and inept.

'Oh, boy,' he told everybody. 'Oh, Jesus, I hope you people can help me.'

They hoped so, too. Two boys and a girl, they all approached Robbie as he hustled to the counter, dropping the package there like the sea captain dropping the wrapped black bird in Sam Spade's office; however, he did not fall dead immediately after.

'What is it?'

'What do you need, man?'

'Can we help?'

'I'm supposed to deliver— This is gonna cost me my job, I can't afford to lose my job in the *summer*, I can't—'

'Let's see.'

'What is this?'

'Let's just take a look.'

All three bent over the package on the counter. 'Boy, this is a mess.'

'The *name* I figured out,' Robbie told them, pointing at it. 'Eloise Nimrin. Only I think it's a guy, he's supposed to be someplace with a lot of Russians, or Polish, or Hungarian, I dunno, I just can't find the place, I don't *dare* bring this back to—'

'Russian?'

It was one of the boys who'd lit up at that clue, and now the other two plus Robbie looked at him in sudden hope while Josh reached for a second form.

'I bet,' said the boy who'd worked it out, 'it's one of the people up at Mrs Rheingold's house.'

'Rheingold?' The girl wasn't sure she knew the name. 'Who's that?'

'You know,' the boy told her. 'The old lady up by—'

Then the other boy got it. 'The hermit!'

'That's the one.'

Robbie, full of doubt, said, 'Hermit? No, this is a guy, Nimrin—'

'We don't have any dealings with her,' the first boy explained, 'because she never leaves her compound up there. But everybody knows about her, she—'

'Oh!' said the girl, catching up. 'The old lady up north by Sands Point, with the great big wall!'

'That's the one,' the first boy agreed, and told Robbie, while Josh wrote on the second form, *Mrs Rheingold, hermit, north, Sands Point*, 'I used to hear about her when I was a kid. Everybody was scared to go around there.'

The second boy said, 'She's got a bunch of staff up there, servants, you know, I think they're all Russian or something like that. They don't come to town either.'

'Well, the butler does,' the first boy said. 'He comes down and does the shopping, I've seen him in the Grand Union. He's got some kind of accent, maybe he could be Russian.'

The girl nodded, emphatically. 'That'll be it,' she said. 'You go up there, they'll know. If this man isn't there, they'll know where he is.'

'Just tell me how to find the place,' Robbie begged them.

'Go out Sands Point Road through Manorhaven,' the first boy told him, 'and take a left on Sandy Drive,' as Josh wrote it all down. 'Not Sandy Road or Sandy Lane.'

'Got it. Sandy Drive.'

'If you get to Middle Neck Road,' the girl told him, 'you've gone too far.' Josh didn't bother to write that down.

'Out Sandy Drive,' the first boy said, as Josh crumpled and threw away his first form and pocketed the second, 'you'll come to these brick gateposts and a closed gate and a big high wall and all kinds of keep out signs.'

As Josh walked to and out the shop door, the second boy added, 'Posted, No Trespassing, No Solicitors, all of—'

And so on, no doubt. Josh paused on the sidewalk to decide from the sun where north was, and turned in that direction as Robbie hurried out, shouting many thank-yous behind him.

'You got it,' he told Josh.

'I got it,' Josh agreed.

29

JOSH STARTED WALKING north, but Robbie didn't. When Josh looked back, Robbie said, 'What are you doing?'

'It's supposed to be up this way.'

'We don't *walk* there,' Robbie told him. 'It's too far to walk. You're a rich guy, we'll take a cab.' Turning away, he said, 'We'll get one back at the railroad station.'

Following in Robbie's wake, Josh said, 'Why do *I* always have to pay for the cab?'

'Because you're a capitalist lackey,' Robbie explained.

Josh was sure there was a perfect retort to that remark, but as they walked along, southward instead of northward, he didn't hear himself say it, so he never found out what it was.

There was one taxi waiting at the station, a big old gray Chrysler stationwagon. The driver was a very fat woman of probably sixty, spread over much of the front seat like melting ice cream, dressed in a green plaid flannel shirt, tan chinos, and open-toed golden sandals. She had been reading *Elle Decor*, which she put onto the seat beside her as they approached.

'Hi,' Josh said. 'You free?'

'Well, I'm reasonable,' she said. 'Hop in.'

They did, and Robbie said, 'We'd like Sandy Drive off Sands Point Road the other side of Manorhaven. Not Sandy Road or Sandy Lane.' So why had Josh made all those notes?

'Sandy Drive, I know exactly where you mean.' There was no meter in the cab. 'That's seven dollars,' she said.

Josh bet it wasn't seven dollars, not really, not for a local, but Robbie said, 'Fine,' and the woman started the Chrysler engine, which coughed a lot.

As they drove through town, stopping at a red light, the woman said,

117

'What you boys doin' up there?'

Josh was trying to think of some story to make up, but Robbie said, 'We're going up to Mrs Rheingold's place.'

Interested, the woman looked at them in her rearview mirror, then drove forward through the green light, saying, 'Really? They hirin' again up there? Been quite a while. Got all those foreigners up there.'

Robbie said, 'You know the place, do you?'

'Oh, that's just the saddest story,' she said.

Robbie slid forward to rest his forearms on the front seatback, near her large head with all the fuzzy gray hair. 'Really?' he said. 'I *love* sad stories. Tell.'

'Well, old Mrs Rheingold,' the cabby said, 'she must be ninety, maybe even more. She was one of the Caissens, old-time family around here, you know. Early settlers. Daughtered out.'

'That's tough,' Robbie said.

'She was the last. Miriam? Something like that. Her mom and dad both died in the 1917 flu epidemic, when she was just a little girl. She was brought up, in the big estate there, by some old aunts and people, kept dying off.'

'Wow,' Robbie said.

'They saw to it she had her schooling, though,' the cabby assured them. 'Bryn Mawr and all that. Then she met *him*.'

Robbie said, 'I *thought* it was gonna be like that.'

'Just like that,' the cabby said. 'Jock Rheingold. A Dartmouth man, but it seemed as though it might be all right.'

'Oh oh,' Robbie said.

'Well, they got married,' the cabby said, 'just around the time the last of her aunts expired, leaving her the absolute last Caissen, and not even a Caissen anymore but a Rheingold.'

'Daughtered out,' Robbie said, and Josh suspected Robbie had repeated that because he'd just now figured out what it meant.

'But that wasn't the worst,' the cabby said. 'There were rumors about Jock Rheingold from the beginning—'

'But she was in love,' Robbie said.

'You know it. He claimed he was a bond salesman down in New York, but there were rumors about dealings in New Jersey, whispers that bonds weren't where he made his living at all.'

'He wasn't a' – Robbie was twitching all over in his excitement – 'wasn't a *bootlegger*, was he?'

'No no, nothing like that,' the cabby said, and Josh knew he and

Robbie had both leaped ahead to a Gatsby finish. But it was to be something else.

'Well, then what?' Robbie asked her.

'A developer,' she said. 'Over there in Jersey, he was putting up all those little houses you see, all look alike, one right after the other, no idea *who* lives in those places.'

'Exactly,' Robbie said.

'Well, he wasn't doing it around *here*,' she said, 'you could say that much for him. But others were. You see what we're driving through.'

Josh said, 'I think the town planners call it "mixed use." '

'Very mixed, you ask me,' the cabby said. 'Anyway, when the truth came out, it just broke Miriam Caissen's heart, or Mrs Rheingold, as she knew she had to be known the rest of her life. How could she hold her head up ever again in the community she was born into, sharing her bed with a developer? A fellow bringing in who knows who, everybody cheek by jowl, no discrimination at all.'

'Exactly,' Robbie said.

'She had no choice, really,' the cabby said. 'She had to divorce him.'

'Absolutely,' Robbie said.

'But he brought in some very slick lawyers from New York,' she said, 'or maybe even from New Jersey.'

'Wow,' Robbie said.

'At the end of the day,' the cabby said, turning left onto Sandy Drive, 'Jock Rheingold wound up with a *huge* settlement.'

'The cad,' Robbie said.

'That's right,' the cabby agreed. 'She got to keep the big house, and the antiques, and most of the cash, but he got half the property.' Pointing off to the right, she said, 'You see what he did with it.'

Boxy Cape Cod houses in pastels marched away in rows to the right, on a squared-off grid of blacktop, like a minimum security prison. The development was old, and had not aged well. Over the years, people had put additions onto the original tiny boxes on their tiny lots, filling the eye with planned uniformity overlaid by unplanned clutter.

Robbie said, '*He* did that?' He sounded awed.

'That was all Caissen land,' the cabby said, 'the part she lost to him in the divorce. And that's what he did with it. For revenge, some say.'

'Wow,' Robbie said.

Pointing again, the cabby said, 'And that's her wall.'

A gray stone wall that had to be twelve feet high marched along beside the final row of little houses. Robbie said, '*She* did that?'

'So she'd never have to see the desecration of her land,' the cabby explained. 'And became a hermit for the rest of her life. Still up in there, ninety-something years old.'

'Wow,' Robbie said. 'What happened to *him*?'

'Died in prison,' she said.

'No!'

'Yes. Went to prison for bribing Congressmen, all about some more development over in Jersey. Got stuck with one of those homemade knives they make in prisons. Shivs, they call them.'

'That's what I've heard,' Robbie said.

'Here's where you're headed,' the cabby said, and pulled to a stop at a tall iron gate flanked by tall brick gateposts, just where that high stone wall stopped at Sandy Drive.

'What a story,' Robbie told her.

The cabby shook her head. 'Wealth,' she said. 'Greed. Property. I'm glad *I'm* not rich. That'll be seven dollars.'

30

STANDING IN FRONT of the closed gate, with the cabby's story fresh in their minds, it was easy for them to see the history of the place in the layout. These high square brick gateposts, topped by gray stone balls, were surely the original entrance markers to the Caissen estate, which would have stretched from left to right, west to east, from Sandy Drive north to Long Island Sound. Originally, the gate itself would have been much less imposing, with possibly even a gatehouse, and a simple stone wall along the road.

Once Miriam Caissen had been unlucky in love, however, and the court, using the same Solomon precedent they always do, had split the baby in half, everything to the right of the gateposts had been lost to the estate and turned into that warren of the working class. The original stone wall along the road, which was the obviously older workmanship up to about three feet, had been heightened to seven feet and topped with broken glass embedded into concrete, while the monster wall along the dividing line had been made tall enough to keep out not only interlopers but the very view itself.

The only place to see inside the estate property was through the iron bars of the gate, where a neat crushed-stone road led at an oblique angle to the left, inward through very messy underbrush and crowded-together small pine trees and scrubby bushes and interweaving vines. It all looked neglected and overgrown, and no building could be seen back in there, nor any other sign of human occupancy except the road itself.

'Let's see what's down at the other corner,' Josh said, so they started to walk along beside the glass-topped stone wall, which was, as the fellow at Mailboxes-R-Us had described, pockmarked with hostile signs: Keep Out. No Trespassing. Private Property.

121

They walked quite a while next to all this disapprobation, and then abruptly the stone wall made a right turn and streamed away north, over a gentle slope. Beyond it, along the road, was suddenly a much gentler fence, three strings of black wire stretched above a low and crumbling old stone wall. 'The neighbor,' Josh said.

'The land Mrs Caissen never did own,' Robbie said.

They walked a while beside this new fence, seeing beyond it neat parkland, specimen trees, ornamental statuary and curving blacktop paths, but no people. Then they did see someone; or actually two people. Both were middle-aged white men, seated side by side on a golf cart puttering along one of the blacktop paths at a point where it briefly angled closer to the road in order to meander around a spreading beach plum. The men were in almost identical business attire of dark suit, white shirt, dark blue figured necktie, and black oxfords. They would have looked perfectly normal, except that they were seated side by side on that traveling settee, and that both wore Day-Glo orange baseball caps with Day-Glo green *CC* emblazoned on the front.

Josh and Robbie stopped to take in this apparition, just at the moment when the two men noticed them in return. Simultaneously, they offered big smiles and big round waves; the same wave, synchronized, like Tweedledee and Tweedledum, scootering through Wonderland. Josh and Robbie waved back – what else would you do? – and then the blacktop curved the men away, and off they went, out of sight among the varied plantings.

Josh said, 'What the heck was *that?*'

'Something new under the sun,' Robbie suggested. 'Let's go see.'

They continued to walk, and as they went they saw a few other golf carts, all at a greater distance, all with their complement of two business-suited orange-topped white men aboard. Then, even farther back, they saw a group of maybe a dozen such men, strolling along in animated conversation.

And here was the entrance, a broad white concrete sculpture, ten feet high, of hands with their fingertips meeting, in the symbol of making a steeple. Between the spread-apart palms was the entrance drive, and way back in there was what looked very like the plantation from *Gone With the Wind*. An elaborate billboard on posts beside the entrance, featuring the make-a-steeple hands in all four corners, read, in large green letters on a white background, *CHRISTIAN CAPITALISM*, and in smaller green letters beneath, 'A Retreat *To*, Not *From*.'

A bright orange bar was down across the entrance, between the hands, with a guardshack containing a brown-uniformed guard just inside it to the left. The guard, air-conditioned within his glass booth, was reading a magazine, and didn't look up as they neared, since he was programmed to respond only to automobiles.

So, from east to west, this side of Sandy Drive consisted first of Revenge Estates, then the remaining half of Mrs Rheingold's property, then these beanied Capitalists in their parkland. What an odd pair of neighbors Mrs Rheingold was tucked between; if an estate, even half an estate, can be tucked.

Robbie grabbed Josh's forearm: 'We go back.'

'You've got an idea?'

'We just do it,' Robbie said.

As they walked, returning toward the more imposing wall that surrounded the Rheingold property, they saw more of the traveling pairs of orange-topped men and another group of the strollers. 'Something like a monastery,' Josh suggested.

'I bet it's tax deductible,' Robbie said. 'And the thing is, except for the hats, we could just go in there and mingle.'

'Are we going in there?'

'I think so. Let's check out the security.'

Josh didn't see any security to speak of, just the three iron wires above the old stone wall, but he walked along with Robbie, and when they got to the juncture of the two properties, where Rheingold's wall undulated north, Robbie bent to study the post holding the wires. Josh watched the sparse traffic on Sandy Drive – mostly service-related, he noticed, plumbers and furniture store vans and diaper services – and then Robbie said, ' Ah hah. I thought so.'

Josh looked at him. 'You thought what?'

'Where there are capitalists,' Robbie told him, 'even Christian capitalists, there will be paranoia.' Pointing at the post, he said, 'Electric eye; see it?'

Josh bent and did, the steady small amber light beam at just about five feet above the ground. 'That wouldn't be easy to step over,' he said.

'Under,' Robbie told him. 'There's room between the beam and the top of the stone.'

Josh looked out at the road; no delivery trucks, no repairmen. 'Try it,' he said. 'I'll watch your back.'

'You don't have to get melodramatic about it,' Robbie told him, as though *he* didn't.

Pretending patience, Josh said, 'What I meant was, I'll watch to see if the light shows up on your back.'

'Oh, sorry.' Robbie grinned. 'Good idea. I'll do the same for you.' And he dropped to his knees like a penitent, to crawl through.

Neither of them broke the beam.

31

THE MEANDERING BLACKTOP paths where the golf carts roamed didn't extend to this extreme end of the Christian capitalists' land, so they were alone as they walked beside Mrs Rheingold's wall, which remained too tall to look over, but with continuing glints of broken glass along the top. After a minute, Robbie said, 'You know, the law is, private property owners can't block a beach, so this wall has to stop before it gets there.'

'If there's a beach,' Josh said.

'Well, a waterline,' Robbie said. 'The point is, the wall has to stop before it reaches the water, so then we can just walk around the end of it. What do you think of that?'

'I think it sounds too easy,' Josh said.

'Me, too,' Robbie said, and stopped. 'I just have to see in there. Give me a boost, will you?'

'You can't go over, not with that glass.'

'Not over, just up. So I can see inside.'

'Fine.'

So Josh stooped and made a stirrup of his cupped hands. Robbie put a foot in the stirrup, a bracing hand on Josh's shoulder, and Josh straightened, lifting Robbie high enough to rest his forearms carefully on the top of the wall and look at Mrs Rheingold's hermitage.

Josh waited a while, bearing most of Robbie's weight, seeing nothing but stone wall two inches from his nose, and then he said, 'What do you see?'

'Well, not much. Let me down, you can take a look for yourself.'

They switched positions, and when Josh rose up he saw a much messier landscape than that created by the Christian capitalists. Weedy scrub growth was everywhere, much of it old fallen trunks and branches from years of windstorms. Some distance away, a gray stone pile of a house was visible, its bay windows gleaming copper, its black roof sagging, the whole structure seeming to be in a long slow process of sinking completely into the ground. A small slice of driveway was visible leading away from the house, and here and there were cleared rectangles of land that might once have been gardens or vegetable patches, long overgrown but retaining something of their shapes. A look of abandonment and decay was everywhere, as though the house hadn't been lived in for more than a century.

Off to the left, northward toward the Sound, he could just make out some more stone wall, at right angles to this one, with more glinting of shards of glass. So the wall made a turn before the waterline in order to continue across the rear of the property, which meant the idea of wading a bit to get around the end of the wall was, as they'd supposed, too easy.

Josh was about to tell Robbie he was ready to come down when movement over by the house caught his eye. Some people had come out, and were moving through the scrubby woods in this direction, though not as though they'd seen the eavesdroppers. They seemed to have something else in mind.

Josh squinted, trying to see them, since even in full daylight there was a kind of evening vagueness inside there, and as the group came nearer he saw they were four men, young, with thick black hair and full black beards. They were dressed alike in elaborate sneakers, dark green shorts, and white T-shirts. They picked their way through the undergrowth at a diagonal to Josh until they reached one of the once-cleared sections. There they stopped, conferred briefly, and then formed a line, standing at attention side by side, shoulder to shoulder, their right profiles toward Josh.

'You're getting heavy up there.'

'Hold on a second, there's people. I'll come right down.'

Apparently, one of the four men gave orders, though quietly, so that Josh couldn't hear him. The four made a snappy left turn, then began to march, left arms swinging in an exaggerated manner, right arms held bent upward, forearms parallel to the ground, as though they carried rifles on their shoulders.

Josh stared, fascinated and appalled. They marched five paces across the semi-clearing, rigidly together, then one by one made a sharp left, then another.

'Josh. Enough already.'

'Right. Here I come.'

Josh lowered himself, then made a stirrup again and said, 'You have to see them.'

'Who are they?'

'The assassination team.'

'Really?' Up he went, and studied the assassination team for a minute, then came down again and said, 'They're rehearsing.'

'They're drilling,' Josh told him.

'It's the same thing.' Robbie shook his head. 'In any profession,' he said, 'to be good at it, you have to keep doing it. They don't want to look like rusty amateurs when they slip into that honor guard.'

'Okay,' Josh said. 'Now that you've seen them, how do we stop them?'

'We'll talk on the way back,' Robbie said.

Josh gestured at the wall. 'You don't want to try to get in there?'

'Why? There's probably a door on the waterside, people always leave one exit to the sea, but it'll be locked solid. And we don't want to be in there anyway, Josh, not with those people.'

'No, I don't,' Josh agreed.

'Come on.'

They walked back along the wall, headed for Sandy Drive. Josh said, 'Do you suppose she has any idea what's going on?'

'Mrs Rheingold? No,' Robbie said. 'Not for seventy years.'

They made it back to the road, slid out of the Christian capitalists' property between low stone wall and high electric eye, and turned to walk back to town.

'Too bad we can't call a cab,' Josh said, not meaning it.

Robbie gave him a look. 'I'm surprised you don't carry a cellphone.'

'Too many people reach me as it is.'

They walked past the iron gates closed over the entrance to Mrs Rheingold's property, and looked in at the same nothing as before. That moldy old pile of a house couldn't be seen from here, nor could the marching men. They walked on, Revenge Estates now on their left, schoolbuses stitching through it, returning the summer-schoolers to their cookie-cutter homes.

As they walked Josh shook his head. 'I wish I'd brought a camera.'

'Why?'

'To take pictures of those guys drilling.'

Robbie frowned at him. 'What good is that gonna do?'

'Well, look. There's nobody following us now. Nobody knows where we are. If we had something to *show* the police, we could go to them, and end this thing.'

'Show them what? Pictures of four guys walking around in the woods?'

'Drilling.'

'Who says? *We* say they're walking with pretend rifles. Prove it.'

Josh shook his head. He felt hemmed-in on every side. 'You know,' he said, 'our Fire Island rental is over on Monday, I was supposed to go out there tomorrow to help pack. Eve and I talked about it, and it seemed as though I should stay in the city, try to *do* something to make this horrible thing stop. But what am I accomplishing? What are *we* accomplishing? Nothing.'

'We're working on it,' Robbie said, but he sounded defensive.

Frustrated, Josh said, 'God damn it, Mitch, it should be so *easy*. Just go to the police, that's what they're for.'

'Sure,' Robbie said. 'Turn ourselves in as spies. Show the evidence, the checks over the years and the bank accounts down there, wherever it is.'

'Cayman Islands.'

'I don't really care. The point is, the only evidence we could show the police is evidence of *our* guilt. Nobody's plans to kill anybody, no nothing except us. Sleepers. Moles. Traitors, with the big T.'

Frowning deeply, Josh walked along next to the rows of little anonymous houses, trying to think. 'What if – what if, when we get back to town, I go to the police, tell them everything, tell them to go to my apartment, they'll find all those guns and uniforms there, and probably Tina Pausto, too.'

'They'll kill your wife and child,' Robbie told him. 'And my old mother in Hartford, I have no doubt. Any security lapse, our families get killed.'

'All right, all right, what if . . . What if, when we get to town, I first call Eve, I tell her to take Jeremy and go to her mother in New Jersey, and you—'

'That's a great hideout.'

Josh stopped on the roadside, occasional traffic whipping by as he stared in agony into space. 'There's no place to hide, is there?'

'Either we get the goods on these guys,' Robbie said, 'or they do their thing. And if they do their thing, it's our job to be the dead perps.'

Josh moaned. 'I thought you were somebody who thought outside the box.'

'I do.'

'And?'

'Well . . . I don't see anything out there yet.'

They walked along in silence another minute, not companionable, and then Josh said, 'What if . . .' and again, 'What if . . .'

'Go ahead, Josh,' Robbie encouraged him. 'We can't know it's a bad idea until you come out with it.'

'All right,' Josh said. 'What if I call Eve and tell her not to go to her parents, but to go someplace else and not tell me where.'

'You've got a kid.'

'I know,' Josh said. 'It wouldn't be easy.'

'For my mother in Hartford,' Robbie told him, 'forget it. She won't even take the *train*.'

Josh plodded along, hemmed in, confined, hopeless, doomed. 'Mitch,' he said.

'Yes, Josh?'

'It's all slipping away from us. Here we are, we know so much, we found out so much, and none of it means a thing.'

'You're right,' Robbie said.

'I don't want to be right,' Josh told him.

They walked along another minute, ignoring the summer sun, the schoolbuses, the little houses. Then, abruptly, Robbie stopped and said, 'All right, what about this?'

Josh stopped and looked back at him, waiting.

Robbie spread his hands, and offered a shaky grin. 'It's a crazy idea,' he said, 'but it just might work.'

Josh nodded. 'Yeah?'

'Have you got sleeping pills at your place?'

'No. Lately, I wish I did.'

Robbie started walking again, and Josh kept pace with him. 'I'll give you a couple, when we get back to town,' he said. 'Then, tonight, you slip them to this Tina, but *you* stay awake.'

'No problem.'

'You can give me a set of keys to your place.'

Josh gave him a quizzical look. 'Yeah?'

'About two in the morning, I'll come up there, and we'll steal the uniforms.'

Josh stared at him. 'Do *what*?'

'Believe me,' Robbie assured him, 'I could use them down at the theater.'

Josh couldn't believe this. 'Steal the uniforms?'

'You get up Saturday morning,' Robbie told him, 'they're gone, you have no idea what happened. *You* didn't take them, you're still there. The corps de ballet shows up, no costumes. They can't infiltrate any honor guard in green shorts.'

'No, they'll find some . . . There have to be more uniforms.'

'That *they* can get? On short notice? The motorcade's on the *way*, man, those guys are standing around in their jocks.'

Josh nodded, slowly, like a metronome. 'Jesus, Mitch,' he said, 'it *is* a crazy idea, and it *just* might work.'

'We'll give it a try, okay?' Robbie shrugged. 'At least it's something to do. When we get back to the city, we'll do an exchange. Sleeping pills for apartment keys.'

'They'll be really mad,' Josh pointed out. 'You know, they might want to kill me just out of meanness.'

Robbie stared at him in astonishment. 'But *you're* as upset as they are!' Clutching Josh's forearm, he said, 'Listen, Josh, the time has come for you to learn the Method. *Think* into the part. You *wanted* this caper to go down, you *wanted* to earn that forty G and more. You're so pissed off you can't think straight. You blame *Levrin, he's* the one you gave the keys to, he must have given copies to too many people, some double agent in their midst.'

Josh contemplated these histrionics. 'You really think I could—'

'I *know* you could!' Robbie was increasingly excited, bobbing along on the balls of his feet. 'You've got your sides now,' he said, 'I just gave you your character, your story line. *Think* it through, between now and Saturday, *believe* in it, make it *part* of you. When it's showtime, *hit* your mark! You can do it. I've watched you, Josh, and you have talent.'

That was a secret belief of Josh's, but he'd never told anybody. He said, as though in disbelief, 'I do?'

'Absolutely,' Robbie assured him. 'Almost forty-eight hours to prepare? As smart as you are? You're gonna go out there, and you're gonna give an Obie-level performance. And you know *why* you are?'

'Why?'

'Because you're thinking about the alternative.'

That was a bucket of cold water. 'Oh,' Josh said. 'You're right.'

'Think about it,' Robbie told him. 'Get into it. You can do it.'

Josh nodded and, as they walked along, he thought about it. *What?* The *uniforms* are stolen? What? The uniforms are *stolen?* What son of a bitch— It was *Levrin! He's* the one tossing around my keys like jellybeans!

They'd almost reached the intersection with Sands Point Road, Josh working himself ever deeper into the part, when a big old Marathon sedan, the onetime New York City taxicab with so much room in the back it had an extra pair of bucket seats, swerved to a stop beside them. At least thirty years old, this vehicle was black with a huge toothy chrome grill and a boxy look that was, in fact, coming back into style. The right front window slid down. They stooped to look in and Mr

Nimrin, alone in there, had leaned over from the wheel to turn the window crank. He was furious. '*You* two! Are you insane? Get into the car!'

32

WHY DO I feel guilty, Josh asked himself. *I'm* the innocent one! And yet, unable to help himself, he did feel like a wayward teenager caught roving by a stern father after he'd been grounded. For that reason, and because he was shaken and scared, and also because he had nothing to say, he said nothing, as Mr Nimrin put the Marathon into gear and angrily accelerated.

Josh and Robbie had both slid into the big backseat (like naughty children!), Josh on the right, Robbie on the left with a couple of grocery sacks on the floor in front of him. Josh took the opportunity of his position to lean rightward against the window, so he'd be out of range of Mr Nimrin's rearview mirror, and could study the man.

Well. He was oddly dressed, actually. He was in some sort of black formal suit, not a tux but something else, and a white shirt and black bowtie. The Marathon's labored air-conditioning was on, giving the interior of the car a frosty ambiance, but Mr Nimrin still looked hot in that getup, and Josh wasted a minute trying to figure out what the man was disguised as this time when he realized, of course!

The guy at Mailboxes-R-Us had said Mrs Rheingold's butler was the one servant to come out of the compound, to do the shopping at the Grand Union. And those grocery bags at Robbie's feet were emblazoned *Grand Union*.

That Mr Nimrin was not merely posing as the butler, but for all intents and purposes actually *was* the butler, should have diminished him in Josh's eyes, but it did not. He understood now how Mr Nimrin could be under what he had described as more or less house arrest, and yet be able to show up in the city any time he wanted. He'd spent the last seven years, obviously, being obsequious and devoted and circumspect, the perfect butler, so that when it was time to act, his watchers would have been lulled into inattention.

Mr Nimrin had taken the first available right turn into Revenge Estates, and now drove northward through it, hunched over the wheel, glaring frequently at the rearview mirror; not at Josh and Robbie, but at his backtrail. He knew how dangerous his friends were.

The development sprawled like a casbah carpet across the land, ending at a chainlink fence, beyond which was rocky shoreline, Long Island Sound, and Connecticut up there to the north. Mr Nimrin turned right, drove several blocks, and then turned left again, found an empty spot, and parked.

Ahead of them along the shore was the development's beach, a narrow sandy strip with a lifeguard on his high white chair and a hotdog stand where the path led to the sand from this parking area. The beach and shallow water were full of kids of all ages; their squeals penetrated the closed windows to make a disturbing background sound, as though a drive-in movie next door were showing a horror film.

Mr Nimrin, leaving the engine on for the air conditioning, twisted himself around halfway on the seat to glare at them; mostly at Josh. 'Mitchell,' he said, 'move to the jumpseat in front of Josh, so I can see you without injuring my neck.'

'Sure.'

Josh got his feet out of the way as Robbie unfolded the seat and slid into it, resting a forearm on the front seatback as he smiled pleasantly at Mr Nimrin and said, 'Nice outfit.'

'We will dispense with the pleasantries,' Mr Nimrin informed him. 'We will discuss my not injuring my neck. No, we will discuss *you* not injuring my neck.'

'Ah, right,' Robbie said. He had become reflective all at once, a professor here to discuss situations in the abstract.

Mr Nimrin glared from Robbie to Josh. 'Why won't you two stay *still*?' he demanded.

Since he was glaring at Josh at this moment, Josh felt it was up to him to answer. 'Because we're worried about our necks, too,' he said.

'Which you've informed us,' the academic Robbie added, 'are in some serious danger.'

'But you make it worse,' Mr Nimrin insisted. 'If you persist in doing things that a committed and reliable mole would *not* do, you can only arouse suspicion. And to arouse suspicion, my friends, is to mark finis for all of us.'

'Whereas,' Robbie said, with such a slow nodding movement that Josh could almost see the pipe clenched in his teeth, 'if we behave exclusively in anticipated and acceptable ways, only *we* are marked finis, while you get out free and clear.'

'But still without my money,' Mr Nimrin said, sounding bitter.

'Well,' the judicious Robbie said, 'that's hardly our concern.'

'But it is,' Josh said, because he'd suddenly, finally, got it.

Robbie gave him a surprised look, out of character. 'What?'

'Mr Nimrin,' Josh said, 'we were both given Cayman Islands bankbooks when we were activated.'

'Yes, of course,' Mr Nimrin said, as though indifferent; but he was watching Josh keenly. 'That would have been part of the original agreement.'

'If we get out of this alive,' Josh told him, 'and not under arrest, it will only be because you helped us. We'd have to show our gratitude.'

Robbie, his mobile face flickering with wild surmise, stared at Josh. He said, 'Josh?'

Ignoring him, Josh said to Mr Nimrin, 'If, on Monday, all three of us are free and clear, we'll both sign over those bank accounts to you.'

Robbie, extremely dubious, said, 'We will?' Then he turned to look at Mr Nimrin, whose face was also undergoing several emotions, all of which he was trying to conceal, and smiled. 'Of course we will!'

'We'll write out a paper now,' Josh offered, 'the two of us, and sign it, saying, If nothing has changed on Monday, August 1st, we'll give you the eighty thousand. Now I know,' he added, 'that's a long way from the couple million you set up the scheme for, but it's also eighty thousand more than you have now.'

'Yes, it is,' Mr Nimrin said. He still sounded bitter. Looking away at the cavorting beachgoers, he said, 'Seven years, and I have been unable to get even a farthing of the Rheingold wealth. The old woman's mad as a commissar, but she's surrounded by lawyers and accountants and guardians, a manpower larger than the Hungarian army. *They're* making a nice thing of it, I have no doubt of that, but there isn't a kopek in it for me.'

'I'm sorry,' Josh said.

Mr Nimrin nodded at him. He seemed to have gotten over his earlier fury. 'Thank you.' He was still bitter, though. 'Even the tradespeople are no good to me,' he said.

Robbie, trying very hard to get on the same page as the other two, said, 'Tradespeople?'

'An enterprising independent local grocer, for instance,' Mr Nimrin explained, 'I could deal with, pad the account a bit here, a bit there, split the difference. But the *Grand Union!*' he snorted, with an angry dismissive wave at the grocery sacks beside them. 'They're all *employees*. Cowards to a man – and woman – and they wouldn't get the profit anyway, it would go to their corporate masters. Oh, *why* couldn't Marx have been right?'

Robbie, sounding honestly bewildered, said, 'I don't know. Why?'

'Socialism, for a clever man,' Mr Nimrin told him, 'is a license to steal. Capitalism is a license for capitalists to steal. As the name suggests, you first need capital.'

'Eighty thousand dollars is a start,' Josh told him, to get the conversation back on track.

Mr Nimrin considered him, and his proposition. 'I will make an agreement with you,' he decided. 'If you will *stay* in your places, if you will do nothing to cause suspicion and nothing to interfere with the mission, I will do my very best – now that you have so kindly motivated me – my very best to keep you both alive and unscathed through the operation and beyond. But, if you do one thing more to put me or yourselves or the mission at risk, I will simply take Mrs Rheingold's silver, packed into this capacious vehicle, which has a surprising resale value for collectors, and disappear into the west, leaving you to explain to your friend Andrei Levrin why I departed and why you shouldn't be terminated at once.'

'It's a deal,' Josh said. 'Mitch? Tell him it's a deal.'

'Oh, absolutely!' Robbie said, and stuck his hand out in Mr Nimrin's direction. 'It's a definite deal!'

Mr Nimrin gazed on that hand as though he didn't want to guess where it had been. 'This is not a handshake transaction,' he said. 'A written statement was offered.'

'That's right,' Josh said, as Robbie withdrew the offending hand. Looking around, Josh said, 'What do I write it on? One of these grocery bags?'

'If you will look *into* the grocery bags,' Mr Nimrin told him, 'you will find a package of stationery.'

'Oh. Okay.'

While Josh rooted around among onions and frozen orange juice cans, Robbie said, 'Stationery? Why's that?'

'Mrs Rheingold writes letters to the editor,' Mr Nimrin said, 'and prefers not to use letterhead, to appear more democratic.'

Josh came up with it, a plastic-wrapped package of lilac-colored stationery and matching envelopes, as Robbie said, 'Do any of them get published?'

'As Mrs Rheingold tends to write letters to no-longer-existing periodicals,' Mr Nimrin said, '*Collier's,* the *American Mercury, Godey's Lady's Book,* the question of publication never actually arises.'

'Here it is,' Josh said.

'I have a pen,' Mr Nimrin said, producing it from his inner jacket pocket.

Josh went first. It took a little while to agree on phrasing, but at last he finished writing it, having used half the packet of paper. He signed it and handed it to Robbie, who copied it over onto another lilac page, put his own name at the bottom, and both pages were handed to Mr Nimrin, who studied them moodily before folding them and putting them and the pen away in the same pocket.

'You know,' Robbie said, 'we'd like a lift back to the station, if that's okay.'

Mr Nimrin glowered at him. 'A lift?'

'I don't think you want us wandering around this neighborhood,' Robbie pointed out, 'so it's better for everybody if you drive us there.'

Mr Nimrin didn't like it, but clearly he could see Robbie's point. 'Oh, very well,' he said, and faced front.

'Just let me get back to my seat,' Robbie said, but Mr Nimrin didn't, jerking them forward on purpose, Josh was sure. He unpeeled Robbie from himself, Robbie made it to the left side of the seat, and Mr Nimrin drove them back through the distressing development toward Sandy Road.

Along the way, Robbie said, 'This is really a pretty good car. I'm not surprised collectors want it.'

Josh said, 'They used to use them as taxis.'

'Apparently,' Mr Nimrin said, 'they still do.'

33

IN THE TRAIN, Robbie said, 'That was brilliant of you.'
Robbie had never complimented Josh before. Pleased, Josh said, 'No, it wasn't. It was obvious, after a while.'

'To *bribe* him?'

'Sure. He got us all into this in the first place, remember, because he was trying to scam some extra profits for himself. And he sounds bitter every time he talks about money.'

'Well, I still think it was brilliant,' Robbie said. 'I would never have thought of that in a million years. You know, once, a bunch of years ago, there was one city inspector, he kept coming around, coming around, driving me *nuts*, I couldn't figure out what he was all about. "Oh, dear, I'm afraid you got a problem here, Mitch." We were on a first name-last name basis. I was Mitch, he was Mr Pomeraw. "Got a problem there, Mitch!" Sprinklers, signs, wheelchair access, posted prices, you name it. "Got a problem there." And we never *did*, not one violation, because you can't work at the kind of margin we've got and afford to pay fines. But he was distracting me, taking up all my time, driving me crazy. And finally I told a friend of mine about it, and he said, "Give him twenty bucks," and I said, "No, that's not what he wants," and he said, "Sure it is," and I said, "*I* can't offer the man money, he'd be insulted," and he said, "Give me twenty bucks and let me talk to him," so I did, you know, just out of desperation, and a few days later my friend said, "Taken care of," and I never saw Mr Pomeraw again. Years ago, never once.' Robbie shook his head. 'Amazing what twenty dollars will buy.'

'Then think what eighty thousand dollars will buy,' Josh said. 'I think Mr Nimrin's good at scamming and scheming—'

'We better hope he is.'

'That's right. Because he's the only thing between us and a posthumous life of crime.'

'You know,' Robbie said, and turned away, apparently uneasy, to gaze out the train window at a section of Queens with lumps in it. He seemed awkward, almost embarrassed.

Josh said, 'I know what?'

'Part of the deal is,' Robbie said, 'we don't do anything else. We just mind our own business, let things go however they go. He made us put that in writing, too.'

Josh nodded, but quizzically. 'So?'

'Stealing the uniforms,' Robbie said, 'is doing something. In fact, it's trying to queer the deal. Abort the mission. Give the organization a black eye.'

'Mitch,' Josh said, 'we can't let the *mission* happen. The mission is killing a lot of innocent people at Yankee Stadium.'

'I'm just pointing out,' Robbie said. 'We made a deal with Nimrin, and from the beginning, we don't mean to keep our side of the bargain.'

'We *can't*, Mitch.'

'Fine,' Robbie said. 'It just makes me wonder, you know, does Nimrin mean to keep his. Are we the only ones lying?'

'He wants the eighty thousand dollars.'

'He did seem eager,' Robbie admitted. 'But I wish we had some other little way out. You know, in case old Nimrin's fooling with us, stringing us along.'

'I'd love to find another little way out,' Josh told him. 'Any ideas?'

'Not at this particular instant, no.'

34

JOSH HAD LEARNED he could never be sure what would be waiting for him in the apartment when he got home. This time, when he walked into the living room a little after six, a twist of tinfoil in his pocket holding two sleeping pills from Robbie, the place was absolutely full. Tina was there, as expected, leafing inevitably through a *New Yorker*, but so was Levrin, beside her on the sofa, doing a crossword puzzle in a crossword puzzle magazine in Russian; Cyrillic, anyway. And in the other two armchairs were a pair of thugs, guys with wide necks, wide shoulders, low foreheads and little mean eyes. Also stubble on their jaws you could strike a match on, if you felt suicidal.

'The gang's all here,' Josh said, shutting the door.

Surprised, Levrin put his magazine and pencil down and said, 'Not at all.'

Leaning toward Levrin, Tina murmured, 'It is an idiom.'

'Oh, damn. Another. Well, come in, Josh, how was your workday? Do have a seat. It is, after all, your own living room.

Josh looked around. 'Where?'

Levrin abruptly barked at the thugs in some unpleasant language, and one of them immediately hopped to his feet, stepped to the side, put a ghastly smile on his face, and offered his chair to Josh with a sweeping gesture and a bow.

'There's chairs in the bedroom,' Josh said, as he went over to take the one offered.

'He can stand,' Levrin said, and barked again at the standing thug, who obediently backed to the wall, leaned against it, folded his arms, and went inert.

Josh said, 'What's the occasion? I didn't expect a crowd.'

'Ah,' Levrin said, with his most self-satisfied smile. He even rubbed his hands together. 'It is because I have good news.'

'Good,' Josh said.

'The operation that has brought us all together,' Levrin told him, 'is about to become accomplished.'

'Oh, that's good,' Josh said, and managed his own smile.

Tapping a fingertip to the side of his nose, looking roguish, Levrin said, 'You understand, I still can't share with you the details.'

'No, I know,' Josh agreed. 'Security.'

'Exactly. And that is why,' Levrin said, 'the other good news is, you will not have to go to Fire Island this weekend.'

Not a good idea to say he'd already planned to stay in town, for the massacre. 'Well, the rental's ending,' he said. 'I'll have to get out there eventually, help pack—'

'Done,' Levrin said, and spread his hands, offering this gift. 'All taken care of, no trouble to yourself at all.'

'What do you mean, done?' A sudden horrible suspicion was drying Josh's throat, making him blink a lot.

'The packing, done,' Levrin told him. 'The closing of the house, done. The transit of the family from the rental property, done.'

'Transit?' Josh found himself on his feet, not knowing how he got there. 'What do you mean, transit?'

'Do sit down, Josh,' Levrin said, still pleasant.

'What do you mean, *transit*?'

Levrin looked stern, but as though he were reluctant to look stern. 'Hugo has given you his seat,' he said. 'He would not like it if you didn't use it.'

Josh looked around at Hugo, who was less inert, arms at his sides, little mean eyes looking without expression at Josh. Needing the answer to his question more than he needed a confrontation, particularly with Hugo, Josh sat and looked back at Levrin. 'I need to know,' he said, being quiet and reasonable. 'What do you mean when you say "transit"?'

Levrin looked confused. Turning to Tina, he said, 'But that is the word, is it not, in English? To move from this place to that place. Transit.'

Rather than answer him, Tina looked at Josh, smiled in a reassuring way, and said, 'They are safe, my dear.'

Levrin said, 'Safe? Safe? Of *course* they're safe!' With a big jovial smile at Josh, he said, 'The whole purpose of this transit – transit? yes, transit – the whole purpose is to *keep* them safe. Keep you safe. Free you from this housekeeping details, packing, moving, free your mind from worry about your family, where is your family while the operation is going on, are they safe; yes. In a word, that's what they are. Safe.'

'Where?'

'Oh, well, Josh, you see,' Levrin said, awkward but firm, 'this is the matter of security again. Until the operation is completed, it would be better if you did not know some of these locations.'

Almost unable to form the words, Josh said, 'I need to know . . . are they . . .'

'Josh,' Tina said. When he looked at her, knowing his face must show how scared he felt, she said, 'We did not know when you would be home from your offices, so we could not make a good time when your Eve could telephone you here, so it is arranged, you will telephone to her.'

Feeling astonishing relief, even greater relief than he'd expected, he said, 'I can talk to her?'

'Of course,' Tina said. 'You may reassure her, and she may reassure you.'

'Of course,' Levrin added, 'you understand there are certain guidelines.'

'Guidelines.'

'What you may discuss, and what you perhaps should not.' Levrin shrugged. 'Your wife is being told she should not talk about where she is, and I must know that you will not ask her to violate that.'

'Of course,' Josh said. Just so Eve and Jeremy were all right, it hardly mattered where they were being kept.

Turning to the phone, at his end of the sofa, Levrin said, 'I'll dial, shall I? And then you and I may trade seats.'

'All right.'

Tossing one more smile in Josh's direction, Levrin turned to the phone, angled it so the dialpad would not be visible to Josh, and dialed a long distance number, at which point Josh knew where Eve and Jeremy were. At Mrs Rheingold's.

If only he could ask her if she'd met Mr Nimrin.

Levrin spoke a few words of that other language into the phone, then smiled at Josh as he heaved himself out of the sofa. 'They summon her.'

'Fine.'

Josh stood, and accepted the phone as he and Levrin switched seats. Next to Tina, interestedly watching him, tense, on the edge of the sofa cushion, he put the phone to his ear and heard breathing. He said, 'Eve?'

'It will be a moment,' Levrin cautioned from across the room, and the breathing continued in Josh's ear. It was repellent, warm and moist and hairy.

Then it went away. And then he heard the familiar voice, shaky but strong: 'Josh?'

'Eve! How are you? '

'Well . . .' She sounded unsure how to answer that. 'I'm all right,' she said, uncertainly. 'I mean, these people came and said they were from you, and they knew I knew, you know, all about it, and they were there to help me pack. Josh, they weren't mean or anything, but they made it very clear, they weren't taking no for an answer.' She sounded indignant at the memory.

'No, that's right,' Josh told her. 'Go along with them, just go along with them.'

'I did,' she said. 'And here I – I'm not telling him where!' she snapped, away from the phone.

'Eve,' Josh said, frightened for her, 'don't argue with them.'

'I *know* the agreement,' she said, mulishly, either to him or to 'them.' 'I'm just allowed to tell you Jeremy and I are all right, and we're glad you're all right, and we're looking forward to seeing you back in New York.' Her voice didn't quite break. 'I *am* looking forward to seeing you back in New York.'

'Oh, me, too,' Josh said. 'When this is over, as soon as—'

'Ah-*ahh!*' Levrin said, fake jolly, getting to his feet. 'I think you've had your nice chat now,' he said, standing there, not approaching. 'Don't you agree?'

'But—'

'What *long* chats you'll have,' Levrin assured him. 'When this is all behind us. Tell your darling goodbye, Josh.'

'I'm supposed to say goodbye now.'

'I'm getting the same message,' she said.

'I'll – I'll see you soon. I'm sorry.'

'Don't be. See you soon. Love you.'

'Love you,' Josh said, aware of all those eyes in the room. He waited till he heard the click, then hung up.

Levrin had advanced to the middle of the room, happy, buoyant, clapping his hands together. 'Now!' he announced. 'What do you say we order out? Pizza!'

Were they never going to leave? While waiting for the pizza, they all sat around laughing at the network news; while eating the pizza, they glumly watched a sitcom; after the pizza, they spent the evening laughing at hospital and police shows. And through it all, Josh kept thinking: Robbie.

Originally, he'd thought he and Tina might have dinner again, where he could dissolve the sleeping pills into her chardonnay at some point while she was in the ladies. Or, if that wouldn't work out, he could have a drink with her later in the evening and slip her the Mickey Finn then.

But nothing was possible in this crowd. They had beer with the pizza, out of cans, Hugo and the other thug belching after every swallow. Tina barely sipped from her beer at all, looking completely out of place doing so, and in any case she and her beercan were too far away beyond Levrin and there were far too many eyes in the room, not sufficiently occupied by what they were seeing on the television screen.

Robbie. No way to get in touch with him, warn him not to come, the scheme wasn't going to work. In the middle of the night, he'd show up – two o'clock, they'd agreed – and Tina would not be drugged. For all he knew, the entire crowd would still be here, in the living room. A key turns in the lock; all eyes turn to the door; Robbie makes the most dramatic entrance of his career; Robbie and Josh both exit, with prejudice.

How could he make this not happen, how could he intercept Robbie somewhere along the way? He couldn't make a phone call. Put a sign on the outside of the apartment door? 'GO AWAY.' But how could he move even that far, without being seen?

The local news at eleven, particularly the apartment fires, were really rib-tickling for this crowd. They sobered for the weather, though, showing a great deal of interest in the weekend weather report, and then, just as an unnecessarily cheerful roundfaced man threatened to give them a complete recap of the day's sports, the phone rang.

Josh stared at it, in sudden unreasonable hope. Could it possibly be Robbie, checking that the coast was clear? No, it couldn't; but could it?

'Answer it, Josh,' Levrin said, and Josh saw that Levrin was beaming, like a generous uncle on Christmas morning.

Josh said, 'You know what it is?' as the phone rang again, and Tina wielded the remote to remove the sportsman from the room.

'But it's your Eve,' Levrin told him. 'We knew you would both sleep more peacefully if you were to speak one more time this evening, so on this occasion *she* is phoning to *you*. Answer it, Josh.'

So he did, on the third ring: 'Eve?'

'Josh.' It was her, as promised. 'They said I should call you again before bedtime, so you wouldn't worry.'

'Yes, they just told me that, too. So I guess I shouldn't worry.'

'I guess.'

'Last time,' he said, 'I didn't get to ask you about Jeremy. I know you

143

said he's all right, but—'

'He's asleep,' she told him. 'They have a crib for him, he's really too old for it, but it's amazing, Josh, it's an *antique*, I've never seen anything like it.'

Mrs Rheingold's crib, Josh thought, and said, 'So he didn't mind the change.'

'No, not a bit. There's toys they bought for him, and you know he likes new people, new places. Oh.' Exasperated, she said, 'They're afraid I'm going to tell you where we are.'

'I don't even want to know,' Josh said. 'We'll talk next week. When it's over.'

'Ah *ah-ah*,' warned Levrin.

'Whenever it's over,' Josh amended.

Eve said, 'They want me to say goodbye now.'

If only, Josh thought, I had a secret code with Eve. We've been married for years, why don't we have a secret code? Why can't I tell her, 'Blue sails are the most beautiful in the moonlight,' and she'll know I mean, 'Call Mitchell Robbie and tell him not to come here.' Why did we waste all this time together? He said, 'I love you, Eve.'

'Love you, too. Bye.'

'Bye,' he told the dead phone. He hung up, and all the others were on their feet, so he stood, too. 'What now?'

'Well,' Levrin said, at his most amiable, 'now we leave. You stay, we leave. We wanted to be here for your phone call, but now we want to leave.'

'Oh. All right.'

'But first,' he said, 'I wish to see the matériel. What you are holding for us. You understand, I have never seen it.'

Tina, the hostess, said, 'Come with me, Andrei, I'll show you.'

'Yes. Come along, Josh.'

They left the thugs in the living room and walked to the bedroom, where Tina opened the closet door and Levrin admired the uniforms hanging there while Josh could comfort himself with the thought that at least they hadn't stolen them *last* night.

'Beautiful,' Levrin pronounced the uniforms, and told Josh, 'They are legitimate, you know. Government issue. They come from a friend in the army.'

'That's nice.'

Levrin was less interested in the guns and not at all interested in the ammunition next door in Jeremy's room. He gave a few amused smiles when looking from Josh and Tina to the bed and back, but said nothing until they returned to the living room, where he gave Tina what might have been an ironic bow, as he said, 'Good night, Tina.'

'Good night,' she said, and yawned.

Levrin's smile at Josh was definitely ironic. With a little glance at the sofa, he said, 'And you have a good night, too, Josh.'

'Thank you,' Josh said.

35

TINA WOULD NOT have a drink with him. 'But I am so *sleepy*,' she said, and yawned again for emphasis. 'It is that Andrei. Being around him makes me exhausted. Time goes, and he is more and more and *more* relaxed, and the very air around him drags down with weariness.'

Levrin made Josh feel the same way. He was surprised and pleased that Tina shared his reaction, but that wasn't the issue here. The issue here was Robbie. 'Just one nightcap,' he said. 'Or a glass of champagne.'

'Oh, but so wasteful,' she said.

'Not at all. I know a way to keep champagne until the next day, and it doesn't go flat.'

'No, impossible,' she said, and yawned. 'Excuse me. What is this way?'

'I'll show you,' he said, and turned toward the kitchen.

But she waggled a finger to make him stop. 'No, *tell* it to me,' she said.

'All right.' If I can keep the conversation going, he thought, maybe I can get her to take a drink after all. 'You put the handle of a silver or silver plate spoon into the top,' he said, 'hanging down toward the champagne. The bowl of the spoon is too large to fit into the neck, so it just hangs there. Put the champagne in the refrigerator, and the next day it's still bubbly.'

'Impossible,' she said.

'Let me show you,' he said, and turned again toward the kitchen.

'Another *time*, Josh,' she said, almost pleading. 'I am really too weary to go on. We will have a drink another time, and you may show me this spoon trick.'

There was no hope. 'If you insist,' he said. 'Another time.'

'Good night, Josh.'

'Good night, Tina.'

She turned toward the bedroom, then looked back, with a little seductive smile. 'If I didn't know better,' she said, 'I would think you were trying to get me into bed.'

'Ha ha,' he said, and thought, but that is what I'm trying to do. And not succeeding.

Nervousness kept him awake. For a little while after they said good night, he heard Tina moving around the apartment, then saw the bedroom lights go out, and heard nothing more.

Was Andrei Levrin as good as a sleeping pill? Would his presence all evening have enough power to keep Tina Pausto asleep even without chemical assistance? He could only hope so, and fret.

He wasn't on the floor tonight, since he didn't want to sleep, but sat on the sofa, where he watched two hours go by with glacial slowness on the red LED readout of his alarm clock. He actually did nod off a few times – when a *:27*, for instance, would become a *:32* with no intervening numbers – but always some sound from the outside world would carom into his head and whisper, 'Robbie,' and his eyes would pop open.

1:57. A faint scratching at the door. Robbie trying to fit the key into the lock. Josh rose to cross toward the door, which opened before he got there, letting in lightspill from the hallway and the silhouette of Robbie. 'Ssshh,' Josh whispered. 'Come in,' he whispered. 'Close the *door*,' he whispered, afraid the light would draw the undrugged Tina to consciousness.

Robbie obeyed everything, whispering, 'What's up?'

'I didn't get to give her the pills.'

'Oh, boy. I've got everything ready, I've got guys from the cast to help carry, I've got a van. Is she asleep?'

'Yes, but not drugged. And she's in there with the uniforms. That's the closet they're in.'

'Maybe we could tip—'

The living room lights flared on, blinding everybody. Josh, squinting like mad, hand up to his forehead like the lookout searching for land, turned to the inner doorway to see Tina standing there, in a long translucent violet nightgown, draped in more or less strategic folds. Her hand was still on the lightswitch, her eyes blinked around blearily. 'Something woke me,' she said.

'And am I glad it did,' Robbie said, advancing toward her, beaming like a lighthouse. 'You must be Tina Pausto.'

Josh, in panic, had been desperately trying to think of a story to tell, but it would not have included Robbie saying, 'You must be Tina Pausto.' He stared, at Robbie's cheerful self-confidence, at Tina's growing confusion, and all he could do was hope against hope that Robbie knew what he was about.

Tina frowned. 'You know me?' Her expression might become dangerous.

'Well, I recognize you from old Nimrin's description, years ago,' Robbie said, digging the hole ever deeper.

Now the expression she leveled on him *was* dangerous. 'Ellois Nimrin?'

'What other is there?' Robbie took a stance. 'Poppycock!' he announced. 'I don't want another word out of you. I know what I know and that's what I know.'

'But that was perfect,' Tina said, with a sudden happy smile, and Josh realized what Robbie had just done was a dead-on Ellois Nimrin imitation.

'I can do Andrei Levrin, too,' Robbie told her, 'but let's not make ourselves sad.' To Tina's laugh of girlish glee, he said, 'I am Mitchell Robbie. I hope I will be Mitch to you, and I hope you will be Tina.'

'I'm sure we shall be,' she said, and permitted him to take her hand and bow his head over it. She looked pleased, then surprised, and looked at her hand doubtfully when he straightened. 'But you—'

'The original air kiss,' he told her. 'In the old days, when that was a more common greeting, the gentleman would actually kiss his own thumb, rather than permit his lips to touch her flesh, unless he knew her considerably better than you and I know one another. So far.'

'So far,' she said, with a flirtatious nod. She was a foot taller than him, but she almost managed to appear as though she were looking up at him. So I finally get to see a courtesan at work, Josh realized.

'But I had no idea you two knew each other,' she said.

'Oh, sure,' Robbie said. 'Old Nimrin recruited us together, years ago.' With a guileless smile at Josh, he said, 'Down at Uncle Ray's, wasn't it?'

'Right,' Josh said.

Now she was blinking in confusion at the living room. 'But it's so late,' she said, 'and you are—'

'I'm going to help Josh with the move from Fire Island tomorrow,' Robbie said, 'so I'm here to discuss it. I'm in a play downtown, you may have heard of us, so I couldn't get here till after the show. I know I should be sorry I disturbed your rest, but in fact I'm not.'

'I'm not going to Fire Island,' Josh told him. 'The plans are changed.'

Surprised, he lifted an eyebrow. 'Oh?'

'And I am not really resting,' she said, sounding fretful now that she was reminded. 'It always happens, when I go to bed too early. When I go to *sleep* too early. I wake up in the middle of the night, *so* restless. If only I had a sleeping draught.'

Josh opened his mouth, but Robbie got there first. 'I'm sure Josh has some sleeping pills. Haven't you, Josh?'

Josh was still in his clothing, the twist of aluminum foil with the sleeping pills still in his pants pocket. 'Sure,' he said. 'In the bathroom. Wait here, Tina, chat with Mitch, I'll get you a couple and a glass of water.'

He raced into the bathroom, paused to gaze in wonder at the rictus-faced maniac in the mirror there, undressed the sleeping pills, filled a glass with water, and hurried back to the living room, where Tina was saying, 'It's rather too bad, really, that I wasn't assigned to you, rather than— Oh, there you are, Josh.'

'And here are the pills. And I heard that.'

She took them, swallowed them with water, and said, 'Thank you. But you must admit, Josh, for me, you are not that ... stimulating.'

'I know,' Josh said. 'Sorry.'

'We have world enough and time, lady,' Robbie assured her. 'Come see the show tomorrow night, I'll leave passes at the box office.' Pointing to Josh, he said, 'Bring your wooden indian.'

She laughed. 'What a delightful idea. But I must not waste these pills.'

'No,' Josh agreed.

'Good night to you both,' she said, and departed, with the waterglass.

Josh walked to the door with Robbie. 'I couldn't believe that,' he whispered. 'Jesus, you took a chance.'

'Not really.' Then, 'I don't care about your past, darling,' he whispered. 'It's your future that interests me.' With a grin and a wink at Josh, he whispered, 'A week or two of your future, anyway. See you in half an hour.'

36

TINA SNORED. JOSH could only assume she didn't snore as a general rule – it would be a negative quality in a femme fatale – but that it was a side effect of the sleeping pills. Nevertheless, he felt embarrassed for her, and guilty for himself, having brought four men into the bedroom to listen to Tina saw wood.

The three new ones were Robbie's castmates in the play, introduced in whispers in the dark living room as Nicola, Petkoff, and Bluntschli, which made them sound more like Levrin's friends than Robbie's. But then Petkoff whispered, 'Mitch, I'm not Petkoff now,' and whispered to Josh, 'I'm Tom, that's Dick, and that's Harry.'

'No jokes,' Harry/Bluntschli whispered.

Robbie whispered, 'That's why I told him your character names, but whatever you want. Let's do it.'

So they went into the bedroom, where Tina snored in long grumbling rollers, and Josh opened the closet door. No room in Manhattan is ever entirely dark, the halo over the city seeping in everywhere, so they had no trouble finding the uniforms. They took it all, hats and boots as well, filling their arms and shoulders, all four staggering with the weight of it when they left the room. Josh closed the door behind them, then hurried ahead to open the hall door.

On his way out, Robbie whispered, 'Come to the show tomorrow night. Be sure to bring Tina.'

'What part am I supposed to be playing?' Josh asked him. 'Pander?'

Robbie was amused by that. 'Certainly not. You are the Nurse, the good Nurse. See you tomorrow.'

Nearly three o'clock, and he still wasn't asleep, though he was now stretched on his substitute bed on the floor. Removing the uniforms from this apartment had almost seemed like a lark ahead of time, until it was done. Only now did he really stop to think how dangerous it was.

It was true that Tina was unlikely to find the uniforms missing. Since the closet had been so full of Josh and Eve's clothing, plus the uniforms, she was using the smaller closet in Jeremy's room, plus the small suitcase in there that had so upset Eve. Still, Levrin had wanted to look at them tonight, and who knew who else might want to see those props before showtime?

Josh remembered the pose of outraged innocence Robbie expected him to perform when the discovery was eventually made, and the more he thought about it, the more sure he was he wouldn't be able to bring it off. *Robbie* could do it, that was the sort of thing he did all his life anyway, but Josh was not a great pretender.

Levrin and his goons, Josh knew, wouldn't even have to actually torture him to make him tell the truth. All Hugo would have to do was turn those little mean eyes in Josh's direction, and Josh would spill every bean he had. He'd spray like a fountain. Then they would squeeze him like a pimple, race down to Good Rep, squeeze Robbie like a pimple, get their uniforms back, and be off to Yankee Stadium.

With a side trip to punish Eve and Jeremy.

But what else could they have done, he and Robbie? What else could they do? I'm going out there a scared little boy, Josh told himself, and I have no idea what I'll be when I come back. If I come back. But I had to try it, didn't I?

2:56. It had been *2:56* an awfully long time, hadn't it? Was the clock stuck? It shouldn't be—

2:57. Well, all right, but when am I going to get some sleep? *2:57. 2:57. 2:57. 9:23.* What was that?

'Rouse *up*, sleepyhead!' called the cheerful voice of the well-rested Tina. 'It's a new day!'

37

THE NEW DAY was the worst day of Josh's life. Friday, and he'd originally expected to be on his way to Fire Island, to spend a weekend with his family, packing and fretting, with Eve to lend him support. Instead of which, he was alone in the apartment in New York, just fretting. No distractions. No support.

Would Premier Mihommed-Sinn's arrival in the city today get live coverage from any of the local stations? No; not the stations he could get without cable, anyway.

After a glum breakfast, he went out to get the *Times*, and at least the *Times* knew the Premier was to arrive today. Some background was given in the piece, though not the gypsy curse, and a rundown on tomorrow's events at Yankee Stadium, in which Premier Mihommed-Sinn and his Olympic sprinter, Drogdrd Ozak, while important, were far from the only principals. A number of worthy athletes from around the world were being honored, all of this in connection, apparently, with some important gathering at the United Nations. Notable names would be present at the stadium to receive awards, to present awards, or merely to stand around being important. Of honor guards there would be several, of ceremonies many, but of slaughter? None was mentioned.

A little before eleven, Tina appeared, in a fitted short white dress and amazingly tall red heels, so that now she had to stoop to get through doorways. Over her shoulder and bouncing on her hip was a shiny red bag that matched the shoes . . . and, come to notice, her lipstick. She seemed energized, happy, charged-up, particularly in contrast to Josh's condition of funk.

'My dear,' she announced, 'I must be leaving New York in just a very short while. Before I go, I must stop in at one or two shops. Are we to attend this theater tonight?'

'I guess so.'

'I shall buy something to wear. Off-Broadway, is it not?'

'Very off-Broadway.'

'I shall be found,' she told him, 'in better stores everywhere.' And off she sailed, leaving Josh more morose than ever.

Afterward, he could never remember how he got through that Friday, alone in the apartment, not knowing if he was going to be responsible for mass murder, not knowing if he was going to be tortured and murdered himself for betraying Andrei Levrin's cause, whatever it was, not knowing what would happen to Eve and Jeremy over this horrible weekend.

He sat through it, he got through it. He knew enough not to look at the clock, but he couldn't keep from thinking about all those checks. United States Agent. How could he have kept them? If United States Agent were truly impossible to reach, how could he have risked taking their money?

It all seemed so stupid now. He'd never needed the money that badly, not even at the beginning. It had just been easier to take it, that's all. Easier for him, easier for Mitchell Robbie, easier for poor Robert Van Bark.

Three others had not taken the money, not cashed the checks. What moral fiber did they have that Josh lacked? Or what wisdom? What was it inside *their* heads that had told them, 'Don't go there, don't have anything to do with that,' that was not in *his* head? Was he a moral weakling? Was he simply a fool?

Never in his life had he felt such self-doubt, nor ever had he had such leisure to nurse it.

Black Friday.

38

WHEN TINA SWEPT back in at about five-thirty, she was as radiant and invigorated as ever, though now burdened with any number of bright shopping bags. She dropped them on the coffee table in front of the lumpish Josh and on the sofa next to him, surrounding him with intimations of a more gladsome world. The names he could see on the shopping bags were Ferragamo, Prada, Bergdorf-Goodman, Henri Bendel. Femme fatality must pay well.

She stood, long and lean in her snug white dress, one hand on one cocked hip, and studied him, half in concern and half in mock-concern. 'But my dear,' she said, 'why such a long face?'

'Because I'm sorry I got into this,' he told her, too low to care anymore what any of these people thought of him.

'Oh, my poor dear,' she said, and sat in the chair beyond the coffee table, the better to consider his case. 'It's because of your Eve, isn't it?'

'That's part of it.'

'I know,' she told him. 'There were many discussions about that action. There was a fear – I must tell you, *I* expressed it – a fear that it would harm your morale.'

'Looks like you were right.'

'But security remained paramount. That Andrei,' she said, as though he were just some naughty child, 'he does not explain himself well, and he does not give consideration to other people's feelings.'

That was a big enough surprise to make Josh look at her more closely. Other people's feelings? These assassins, these spies, agents, whatever to call them, did any of them ever consider other people's feelings, except as tools to manipulate?

And what was Tina Pausto doing now? Cooling him down, keeping him calm enough to go on being useful to the scheme. But it didn't matter if he knew that. She was very good at her fakery, as of course she would be, and it was succeeding. He could see through her, and yet the simulation of fellow-feeling worked just as well as the real thing. He found himself responding, wanting to be soothed. He said, 'I don't see why they had to do it. Why not let Eve and Jeremy stay where they were? Come back on Sunday, when it's all over.'

The look she gave him now was a keen one. 'Josh, what do you know of our operation?'

'Everything,' he said, and shrugged. What did anything matter? It was too much effort to go on lying.

Watching him, she said, 'Everything?'

'I know what the honor guard is going to do at Yankee Stadium tomorrow. I know about Premier Mihommed-Sinn. And I know you're keeping Eve and Jeremy out at Mrs Rheingold's. All right?'

She sat back, astonished. 'But, my dear, you are amazing! You learned all this— Not from *me*. And I know not from Andrei.'

Something kept him from mentioning Mr Nimrin, though why he should go on thinking of Mr Nimrin as being worthy of protection he couldn't think. Maybe it was just perversity, the gloomy pleasure of being able to say, 'I'll keep my sources to myself, if you don't mind.'

'Why should I mind?' She offered him one of her sunniest smiles. 'You must know, I am not always absolutely completely open with you, either, my dear.'

'I suspected that.'

She laughed, then patted her knees with her long fingers. 'So you see,' she said, 'you have no reason for these sad looks. You know everything that will occur, you know your own so-minor part in it, you know that your family are safe and well cared for in Mrs Rheingold's very lovely estate, with its incomparable views of Long Island Sound. You even know when this will all be over, so that you may return to your normal life. Though I would suggest,' she said, leaning forward, very confidential, 'that you do something about getting cable. Particularly with a small child in the house, you do not want only these networks.'

He couldn't help it; he laughed. 'All right,' he said. 'I'll get cable. After all this is over.'

'Tomorrow,' she assured him. 'It's just that little more, and then it's over, and you need never see any of us again. I know you'll like that.'

'I'll like it more with Andrei than with you,' he said.

She was delighted with him. '*Now* you're better,' she said, and jumped to her feet. Gathering up her shopping bags, she said, 'I will change and— It is an eight o'clock curtain?'

'Yes.'

'Very good. I will change,' she said, and stood there holding all those bag handles while she considered him. 'And you will change also,' she informed him. 'Change into more festive garments, and into a more festive face.'

'I'll try.'

'We shall have a light snack in this neighborhood,' she said, 'but not too much, because we don't want to fall asleep in the theater. The actors would be so insulted.'

'I'm sure they would.'

'After the play we'll have our real dinner.' Bright-eyed, she said, 'Perhaps your friend Mitchell will join us.'

'I wouldn't be surprised,' Josh said.

39

TINA PAUSTO COULD create a stir at the Academy Awards. At the Good Rep theater, she caused more than one patron to walk into a wall. So tall, so sleek, so slender, poured into a basic little black dress from which her completely admirable silvery legs emerged and emerged and emerged. Josh, next to her, felt it must be like this to walk your pet cheetah.

The cab, which they'd had no trouble capturing (those legs), debouched them in front of Good Rep at five to eight, to find a little cluster of smokers making a miasma in the forecourt. They went through, smokers staggering back from Tina's abrupt presence, and in the little black lobby they waited briefly while another patron had dealings with the young man now on duty at the saleswindow. That patron having cleared, Josh moved forward and said, 'Tickets are being held for me. Redmont.'

The clerk riffled through several envelopes in a small wooden box whose tilted-back top said *recipes*. He riffled again. 'Spell?'

Josh spelled his name. The clerk riffled again, looked at Josh, shook his head. 'Not here.'

'But Mitchell Robbie said they'd be here. He invited us.'

'Not here.'

Was this some sort of practical joke? Stymied, Josh just stood there and blinked at the clerk.

Tina leaned down past Josh's shoulder to say, in honeyed tones, 'Look under *Tina*.'

Josh said, disbelieving, 'Tina?'

'Here it is,' the clerk said, and pushed the little envelope forward, his knuckles bumping painfully into Josh's knuckles because he was looking at Tina. 'Enjoy the show,' he told her.

Arms and the Man is a comedy set in a small town in Bulgaria in 1885. There's a war going on, Bulgarians led by Austrian officers versus Serbs led by Russian officers. In the first act, a Serb soldier, who later turns out to be Swiss for some reason (Bluntschli, played by Harry), hides from Bulgarian troops in the bedroom of Raina, the daughter of a Bulgarian major. She finds him, but he and his pistol talk her into covering for him. She gives him a coat of her father's, who's away at the war, and he leaves.

The next spring, out in the garden (an even more minimal set), there's some rustic comedy of the rural-lout sort, including the servant Nicola (Dick, with smudged cheeks). The father, Major Petkoff (Tom, with a pillow stomach), is back from the war, and so is his daughter's betrothed, the war hero Sergius (Robbie, looking not like just any doorman, but the doorman at Trump Tower). Sergius and Raina are both devotees of the higher emotions, full of melodramatic gestures and proud stances (a dig at romantic novels peers wanly out of the past).

Bluntschli, the Serb/Swiss, now that the war is over, shows up to return the coat. It takes another act and a half for everybody to understand that Raina doesn't really want to be a romantic ninny and that she belongs with the realist Bluntschli rather than the preening hero, Sergius. A nice round of applause, and out to dinner.

Josh was not having a good time. He and Tina and the cast, plus some others of varying significance, trooped through the night-streets after the show, loud and boisterous, across portions of the Lower East Side, where most of them were known at the bar where they filled most of the tables at the back and demanded cheeseburgers and pitchers of beer. Everyone was having a good time, caught up in the exhilaration of another performance, except Josh, who knew he didn't belong here but was afraid to think where he *did* belong. No matter what he or anyone else did, and despite the best efforts of George Bernard Shaw, all he could think about was Yankee Stadium, tomorrow. *Tomorrow.*

Could they get other uniforms, at the last minute, that assassination team? Would they believe his denials? He couldn't just go off to the police, not with Eve and Jeremy out at Mrs Rheingold's place. If he ran away, but didn't tell anybody anything, would that be enough to spare Eve and Jeremy?

Tina was describing to the enthralled group her own amateur acting experiences in the 'gim-nah-sium,' and they were all assuring her she was a natural, she could own the stage if she ever decided to turn her attentions in that direction. Not Tina, he wanted to tell them, her interests are rather gorier than the theater could provide. But he didn't say that, or anything else, until, at a lull in the conversation – or in Tina's part of it – he leaned over to her to say, 'I have to go home.'

'Oh, darling,' she said, with great concern. 'We are all so enjoying ourselves. Do stay.'

'You stay,' he said. 'Why not? Have fun.'

She wanted to, he could see that. She said, 'Will you be all right?'

'Of course.'

She pointed a nanny's admonishing finger at him. 'Go straight home,' she said, 'and do not fret.'

'I will,' he promised, 'and I won't.'

'I'll be along after a while.'

'Enjoy yourself,' he told her, and left the bar and walked several blocks before he found a cab. He went straight home, as promised, but he did fret. In his living room, laying the blanket once again on the floor, he stopped and said aloud, 'What am I doing? She isn't coming back tonight.'

So, for the first time since Monday, he slept in his own bed, fretful but exhausted, so that he did sleep, and she did not come back, and he was still asleep at nine the next morning when the phone rang, and it was Levrin: 'Can you still be asleep? What nerves of steel you have!'

'Oh, God,' he said. He could taste the beer *and* he could taste the cheeseburgers.

'I need you to drive me,' Levrin said.

'Drive you.'

'Yes, to the airport. Kennedy airport.'

Bewildered, still waking up, Josh said, 'You want me to drive you to Kennedy airport? Now?'

'Yes, of course, who else? I am going now to the place where you keep your car.'

'My car?'

'On Eleventh Avenue. It is a Toyota Land Cruiser, very nice car. Surely you remember it. I will meet you there at ten.'

40

TEN-FIFTEEN; BUT Levrin didn't seem to mind. He and Hugo and the nameless thug leaned comfortably against Josh's car, arms folded, gazing out over coastal New Jersey, enjoying the sunny warmth of the end of July. Hurrying toward them through the rows of parked cars, Josh called, 'Sorry. I couldn't get moving this morning.'

'Not a problem,' Levrin assured him. He was in an amiable mood, probably because his plans for mass murder were about to come to fruition, in just a few hours, uptown. 'As always with airports,' he went on, 'I have left us extra time.'

'Good.'

Josh unlocked the Land Cruiser and got into the front seat, which wasn't exactly an oven; more a crockpot. Leaving the door open, he quickly started the engine, and told Levrin, sliding in on the passenger seat next to him, 'The air conditioner will kick in in a minute.'

'Briefly, we shall open the windows,' Levrin told him, and said something in that other language to the two thugs, who'd climbed into the back. Josh shut his door, they opened all the windows, and he drove out of there, pausing at the farebooth for the clerk to see his monthly pass on the dashboard and to lift the bar out of the way.

Walking hurriedly down from the apartment – it usually wasn't too far to walk – Josh had told himself that the good thing about this new assignment was that it meant he would be away from home around eleven or twelve, when the assassination team could be expected to arrive, in search of their uniforms. All in all, it would be better not to be there for that moment.

In fact, if Levrin didn't need a roundtrip, if he wanted to be left at the

160

airport, Josh might drive on up to Port Washington, just to see if it were at all possible to get into Mrs Rheingold's estate, and possibly get Eve and Jeremy out. The assassination team would be gone from there, after all, and everybody's attention distracted by the planned events of the day. He wouldn't do anything dangerous – at least, he'd try not to – but just maybe he could get himself and his family out from under this thing at last.

Anonymous phone call to the authorities? Also a possibility.

As they drove east across Manhattan, headed for the Midtown Tunnel, Josh said, 'Are we picking somebody up out there, or am I dropping you off?'

'Well, both, in a way,' Levrin told him, and apparently found that funny. Then he sobered and said, 'Yes, we will be picking someone up.'

So it would be a roundtrip. Well, there might still be time, afterward.

Saturday traffic was lighter in Manhattan, heavier east of it. It was 11:17 by the dashboard clock when they swept around the curving entrance to Kennedy Airport. Josh said, 'Where am I headed?'

'You will want the long-term parking.'

'Long-term parking? I thought we were picking someone up.'

'That is where,' Levrin told him, 'we are going to meet the people we are going to meet.' He was still pleasant, but somehow with Levrin there was always the sense that he expected full and immediate compliance with his instructions, without a lot of chitchat.

So if he wanted long-term parking, to pick someone up, that's what he would get. 'Fine,' Josh said, and followed the signs, and eventually got a claim ticket from the clerk on duty at the entrance there. As he drove out onto the pale concrete, he said, 'Just anywhere?'

'No, no, we must go where the people we are going to meet will go. You will drive all the way back to the fence.'

So he did, soon passing more and more empty spaces, then an area with almost no cars in it at all, and all of them empty. 'Somewhere around here?'

Pointing, Levrin said, 'At the fence there, go to the right a little, and then we will stop. Yes, like that. Yes, this is good, stop here. So. We open the windows, and then you turn the motor off, and we get out of the car.'

'It's going to be hot out there,' Josh said.

'We don't know how long we shall be waiting. Out you go.'

They all got out of the car, Josh on the side next to the chainlink fence, with raw fields beyond it. Bus stops dotted the broad expanse of the parking area, and a bus far away could be seen moving slowly from stop to stop, but no one was anywhere near this place.

The nameless thug had gotten out on the same side as Josh. Now Levrin and Hugo came around the front of the car, Levrin smiling, saying, 'And now, our very pleasant association must come to an end.'

Josh didn't understand. The nameless thug was behind him, the other two in front. He was distracted by seeing Hugo pull from his pants pocket a pair of white rubberized gloves, the kind worn when cleaning the kitchen. He said, 'What?'

As Hugo pulled the stretchy gloves onto his big hands, Levrin said, 'You have been very helpful, Josh, and very useful, and I want you to know I appreciate it and I thank you for it. But now, you see, your helpfulness and your usefulness are over.'

'But why come—' Josh started, and Hugo took from his other pants pocket a pistol. It was small, but looked efficient. He pointed it at Josh, who said, 'No!'

'All relationships must end, Josh,' Levrin said. 'Hugo.'

Hugo took a shooter's stance, knees bent, both hands on the pistol, almost hiding it with rubberized white plastic. Josh flinched uselessly away, realizing too late what a fool he'd been, how they'd played him from the beginning, how they'd always meant it to end this way, and then, astonishingly, the other thug pushed forward past Josh, saying something angry in their different language.

Hugo couldn't believe it. His own man was blocking his shot, walking into the line of fire. And Levrin was outraged. He yelled at the nameless thug, waved a fist at him, actually stamped a foot. The thug didn't care. He yelled back, pointed at the far-distant entrance shack, at the bus still visible across the sea of concrete and cars.

What was he saying? Don't do it here, it's stupid to do it here, someone will hear, someone will see. Take him someplace private, for God's sake.

Levrin did *not* like being argued with, and neither did Hugo. They both railed at the nameless thug, who then stepped forward and gave Hugo an angry push on the chest. Hugo, even angrier, pushed him back. The nameless thug punched at him, mostly missing. Levrin kept shouting, and Hugo slapped the pistol down onto the Land Cruiser hood to punch back. The nameless thug grabbed him in a bearhug, and they scuffled, Hugo forced back step by step.

Run, Josh told himself. While they argue, run like hell. Except they'd catch him, and even if they didn't catch him they could still shoot him while he ran.

The gun! It was right *there*. Grab it, turn, run around the back of the car, away from the fighting, then run as fast as he could for the exit.

Do it *now*. No time to be frightened, no time to forget how to breathe. *Do* it.

Josh jumped forward and grabbed the gun. It was heavier than it looked, and he lost his balance for just a second, before spinning away, the gun pressed with both hands to his chest.

Shouting behind him. He ran around the back of the car, but Levrin was already there, arms wide, blocking him, the nameless thug right behind him.

Josh spun back, and there was Hugo, coming toward him between the left side of the Land Cruiser and the fence, gloved hands spread to scoop him in.

No choice, no chance, nothing. Fumbling, he turned the gun, held it in both hands the way Hugo had held it, pointed it more or less at Hugo's body. He was terrified, trembling all over, the gun waving in his grip like a sapling in a storm, but he was so close, how could he miss from this close?

'Stop!' he shrieked. 'Stop, I'll shoot! I will! I will!'

'Weakling,' Hugo said, and stepped forward, and Josh's finger spasmed on the trigger.

It shot. The gun shot, it bounced a tremor of recoil all up his arm to his shoulder, it made a flat smack in the air like a faroff small firecracker.

The gun shot, and Hugo stopped. A dark smudge appeared on his white shirtfront. Then he smiled, and came forward again.

No! Stop it! Josh pulled the trigger a second time, but now all the gun did was say *click*, and Hugo came forward to pluck it out of his hands.

'What,' Josh said. 'What.'

Levrin, no longer angry at anybody, had come up behind Josh. 'Excuse me,' he said.

Josh, stunned, moved over and Levrin went by him to open the driver's door, reach in, and take the key out of the ignition. Then he said, 'Thank you, Josh, you may get behind the wheel now.'

'But – what happened? What happened?'

'You don't understand?' Levrin smiled in comradely fashion. 'That was a blank, of course.'

'But, *why?*'

Levrin pointed at Josh's right hand. 'Now, you see,' he said, 'there is no question, is there, that you fired that pistol today. Your fingerprints on the pistol, the chemicals from the firing of the pistol on your hand.' With a little bow, 'Get into your nice car now, Josh,' he said, 'while we wait a little.'

41

JOSH SAT AT the wheel of his Land Cruiser, hands in his lap. A warm breeze blew through the car, from right to left. Outside, while the three chatted amiably in that language of theirs that was all gutturals and throat-clearings, Hugo emptied the spent blank cartridge from the pistol and put it in his pocket. Then he took actual bullets from his other pocket and loaded them into the merry-go-round of the bent-open pistol. Then he snapped the pistol shut, clicked a button on its side that must be the safety, and put it away in the pants pocket the bullets had come from. Then he stripped off the gloves, made a joke about the gloves to the others – something, probably, about how hot his hands got while he was wearing them – and put them in the blank-cartridge pocket while the others laughed. Then he waved both hands to air them and laughed again, this time alone.

During all of this, Josh thought. Or tried to think. Or tried to think useful thoughts instead of the merely despairing and self-despising thoughts that insisted on crowding his mind.

What could he have done differently? Aside from never taking the money, what could he have done *recently* other than what he'd done? He and Mitch Robbie had played along with the program, which meant they'd both gotten to live a little longer. Robert Van Bark had chosen or stumbled upon the only possible alternative, which meant he'd gotten to live a little shorter. But once they'd decided to take the money – no, once United States Agent had decided to awaken their sleepers – the ending was already determined.

Fire the gun or not fire the gun; no difference. They had surely already worked out some other way, if he hadn't fallen for that trick, to create a stage set more realistic than anything Good Rep had ever contemplated. From the instant Andrei Levrin had first approached Josh on the ferry dock in Bay Shore, this final scene had already been determined.

Which made him at last stop gnawing at the past and start to think instead about this final scene. It was inevitable, had been from the beginning – yes, yes, we know that – but it was being prolonged.

Once they had his prints on the gun and the evidence on his hand, why had they delayed? Why not kill him now? He was in the position of the lobster who has been brought into a kitchen, but then for a while it seems to the lobster that nothing is happening.

What water was Levrin boiling?

Maybe Levrin had been telling the truth when he'd said they were to meet someone else here. Maybe they had some reason they didn't want to kill him until some other person, or some other piece of evidence, had been brought here.

So now at last he was thinking more productively. If he wanted to have a future, he had to think about the future, and leave the past alone. Think about the immediate future, between now and when Hugo would put his gloves back on. What was there in this final interval that he could somehow turn to his own advantage?

And why, come to think of it, couldn't he have a spare ignition key in the glove compartment?

Well, he didn't have a spare ignition key there, no one keeps a spare ignition key there, that's regretting the past again. Think about the future.

Who or what are Levrin and the others waiting for? Could they be bringing Robbie here, so they could both be killed together, and left with the 'evidence' of their monstrous crimes?

Then he knew. In an instant he knew, and in the same instant he understood why he hadn't wanted to know. Why he had wanted to shield himself as long as possible from the ending.

They were waiting for Eve and Jeremy.

42

FIFTEEN MINUTES OF silent horror. Fifteen minutes of begging for this not to be true, but knowing it was. Fifteen minutes while the rest of the globe rolled on but he stayed fixed on the spike of that knowledge.

Seeing the result. The three bodies in the car, in the sun, to be found ... when? There would be no anonymous phone call, nothing to muddy the waters, nothing to take from the clarity of the story Levrin and the others would leave behind.

Josh Redmont, traitor, in despair over what he had been part of, had murdered his wife and child and had then taken his own life. The proof would be clear and indisputable, and the fact of his having murdered his family and then killed himself would be the proof that he had indeed been part of the massacre at Yankee Stadium. He and Mitch Robbie, and whoever else they had gulled into this enterprise. The fall guys, the scapegoats.

What could he do? What could he do? He couldn't even get out of the car; they'd stop him, not brutally, but firmly. No unnecessary extra bruises on his body.

Meanwhile, those three stood beside the car, up near the front on his side, talking together, easy, calm in their manner and calm in their minds. How could they do this? How could such people exist? To murder an innocent inoffensive family, for some ... what?

For some temporary geopolitical advantage, to somebody somewhere, which would probably, given the history of such things, not even accomplish anything. If all the schemes and machinations of these realist political tough guys were any damn good, the world would be sorted out by now, wouldn't it? For good or for ill, somebody would have won.

But they don't care, they're pragmatists, they ride roughshod over real human beings for ephemeral advantages in a contest that never ends. They've traded in their humanity for something they think is better. They don't smell their own stink.

Do they always have to win? Do they make their messes and just move on, untouchable, full of their rotten expertise? Was there nothing for him to do but play the part of mouse, among these cats?

Think outside the box, Robbie had said. No, he'd said *he* could think outside the box, but Josh couldn't. Are you thinking outside the box now, Mitch? For how long?

Some craven corner of his mind wanted to beg, to plead for mercy, if not for himself at least for Eve and Jeremy, but he wouldn't give in, he wouldn't give them *that*. If there was some escape from this (no, there wasn't), it wouldn't come from their compassion.

Then, after a full quarter of an hour, his mind jolted forward with a new thought at last, but an odd one, so odd he didn't even question it, just leaned his head leftward out the car window and said, 'Andrei?'

Levrin, pleasant as ever, turned to raise an inquiring brow. 'Yes, Josh?' There was a faint smile on his lips; maybe he was anticipating the plea for mercy now.

Josh said, 'Could I see the note?'

That surprised him. He took a step closer, away from the other two. 'What was that?'

'You've done a suicide note, haven't you? Could I see it?'

Now the smile was broader. 'To rip it up, Josh? I don't think so.'

'I don't want to rip it up,' Josh told him. 'I just want to see it.'

'If there is such a note, Josh,' Levrin said, 'it might contain items you wouldn't want to see.'

'I already know who we're waiting for.'

'Ah.' Levrin nodded. He did not, Josh noted, look the least embarrassed. 'Still, it would be better not, I think.'

'If you don't want me to touch it,' Josh said, 'put it against the windshield. Let me read it through the glass.'

Surprised, Levrin considered that. 'You really feel the need to see this document?'

'I'd like to.'

Levrin pondered, then shrugged. 'If you wish.' And he turned and spoke to Hugo.

Here came the gloves again, and out of Hugo's hip pocket a folded sheet of paper. Levrin stepped out of the way, and Hugo came forward, unfolding the paper, to press it against the windshield in front of Josh.

Sewell-McConnell letterhead. They even had that detail. And a handwritten note that actually did look something like his own writing;

possibly his own writing under stress.

> We were wrong. We thought we could help the world if we rid it of
> its monsters. We just became monsters ourselves. I can't stand this
> pain. I'm going to a better place, with my family. I beg forgiveness.

'I certainly sound self-pitying,' Josh said.

'Finished?'

'Yes.'

Hugo took the paper away, folded it, put it back in his hip pocket, removed the gloves.

Josh said, 'Could I get out of the car for a little while?'

'Oh, I think not, Josh,' Levrin said.

'Just to stretch my legs.'

'No, that's a comfortable car. No need.' Gazing over the car roof toward the entrance, he said, 'And the wait is over, in any case.'

Josh looked, and across the pale concrete parking area under the bright midday sun, here came Mrs Rheingold's big Marathon. When Josh next breathed, there was a little mewl sound in his throat that he couldn't suppress. He stopped breathing instead, and trembled, clutching the wheel with both clenched fists.

The Marathon approached, larger than most of the cars around it, then nearer, away from the other cars, and he could see two men in the front seat, strangers to him, men like Hugo. In the back were three people, in a row on the seat; Jeremy and Eve, huddled as far to the right as they could get, and on the left Mr Nimrin.

'Nimrin,' Josh said. His voice was dull, without resonance.

'Yes, of course,' Levrin said. 'This will be a reunion, will it not?' The idea seemed to please him.

The Marathon swung around to stop next to the Land Cruiser, facing the same way, its left side nearest. After an instant, the rear door on this side opened, and Mr Nimrin hurtled out, to grab the Land Cruiser's right-side door, yank it open, thrust his upper body inside, show his red-faced furious glare to Josh, and shout, '*Where are the uniforms?*'

43

'**O**UTSIDE THE BOX,' Josh said.

Mr Nimrin stared. Some of the flush left his cheeks. He said, 'What was that?'

Something had snapped inside Josh, maybe when he saw Eve and Jeremy, maybe when he saw Mr Nimrin's rage, some wire of tension had cracked apart, that had both held him together and held him down. Terror and despair still enclosed him like a shroud, but within that fog of hopelessness there suddenly hummed a brand new kind of energy. It had nothing to do with hope or anger or even hate. It was a kind of freedom, the freedom that floods in when everything has already been lost, when there's nothing left to struggle for, nothing left to protect.

He wouldn't play Mitch Robbie's scenario, the schoolboy deception of outraged innocence, the imp tweaking the grown-ups. Nor would he play Josh Redmont's scenario, the paralysis of fear. He had a new role now.

'Get in the car, Mr Nimrin,' he said, 'Let's talk.'

Mr Nimrin said something, angry, peremptory, some sort of demand, but Josh paid no attention, turning the other way instead to say to Levrin, 'You people move away, I have to talk in private with Mr Nimrin.'

'Well, Josh,' Levrin said, trying to retain control of the situation, 'I must say, I don't see a reason for that.'

'If you'll look at Mr Nimrin's face,' Josh told him, 'I think you'll see the reason.'

Frowning, Levrin stooped so that his face was disgustingly close to Josh's, so he could peer past him toward Mr Nimrin. Now Josh had them on both sides of him, Mr Nimrin leaning in the open door on his right, Levrin staring through the open window on his left. Not bothering to look toward Mr Nimrin, already knowing enough of what that face would show, Josh said to Levrin, 'See what I mean?'

Levrin straightened. He was doing his best to hide discomfort and confusion. 'You have one minute,' he said, to re-establish control.

'It may take longer,' Josh told him. He no longer would give any of them anything. Lifting his left hand from the steering wheel, not even caring that it didn't shake, he made a little shooing gesture in Levrin's direction.

For just one second, the jackal inside Levrin appeared, with a lift of the lip and a cold heat from the eyes, but then the louse turned away, abruptly, as though he'd done so before seeing that gesture, without in fact seeing it. He spoke gruffly to the other two, and all three went forward to stand just in front of the car, to throw sullen looks toward the windshield.

Josh said, 'Get in, Mr Nimrin. Shut the door.'

Mr Nimrin hesitated. He looked through the windshield toward Levrin, then gave Josh a questioning look. 'What has gone on here?'

Josh showed his right palm. 'I have fired a pistol.'

Mr Nimrin considered that, then nodded and slid into the Land Cruiser, shutting the door. 'You do not have the air conditioner on.'

'They don't let me have the key.'

'No, of course.'

Even-toned, moderate, Josh said, 'How long have you known?'

'*You* told me the target,' Mr Nimrin pointed out. 'When was that? Tuesday.'

'How long have you known what they meant to do to my family and me?'

Mr Nimrin pretended innocence, not very well. 'What do you mean?'

'Levrin showed me the suicide note.'

Astonished, Mr Nimrin said, 'What did he do *that* for?'

'I asked him.'

'Did I tell you he was an idiot?' Mr Nimrin shook his head, throwing a sour glance toward Levrin. 'Brutal, and an idiot.'

'How long have you known?'

Mr Nimrin looked back at him. 'An hour. No, less than that.'

'Hard to believe,' Josh said.

Mr Nimrin frowned. 'Do you believe, rather than that, do you believe, in all our conversations, I *knew* what was being planned?'

'Yes,' Josh said.

'I told you, from the beginning,' Mr Nimrin reminded him, 'that I was kept out of the loop, that they no longer trusted me and were holding my passport. When they activated you, I was outraged and baffled, you know I was. I couldn't think *why* they would bring you untrained amateurs into any operation at all.' The shrug and dip of the head he made might have

171

been a kind of apology. 'Well, now we know.'

'You told me at the beginning,' Josh said. 'Remember? "Lambs to the slaughter." '

Mr Nimrin had the grace to wince. 'Yes, of course. Unfortunately, we did not think it through as to who the butcher might be.'

'Yet,' Josh said, 'all of a sudden here you are. There's a little glitch in the program, and all of a sudden Mr Out-of-the-loop is the man in charge.'

'They came to me,' Mr Nimrin said, and shrugged. 'You know where.'

'Mrs Rheingold's place.'

'They said there was a problem with my moles. I had to solve the problem or face the consequences. Matériel that had been entrusted to you—'

'The uniforms.'

'—vital to the success of the operation, had been stolen.' Mr Nimrin was working himself up toward rage again. 'I have very little time, Josh,' he said. 'If I have to, I'll turn you over to Andrei to ask the questions. I must know, and I must know now, *where* are those uniforms?'

'You rode here with Eve and Jeremy,' Josh said, '*after* you were told what was happening.'

'Where are the uniforms?'

'Once you got into that car with them,' Josh said, 'you answered the question, is there any difference between you and Levrin. Other than that he's a bit more honest.'

'Where are the uniforms?'

'No,' Josh said. 'Not even if I knew.'

'You'll see if there's no difference between us, Andrei and I,' Mr Nimrin said, 'when I turn you over to him to force out the answers.'

'Make something of a mess of me, I suppose,' Josh said.

Exasperated, Mr Nimrin said, 'Do you think this a *joke*?'

Josh said, 'What I mean is, if he makes a mess of me, what happens to the suicide tableau?'

'You'll be just as dead,' Mr Nimrin snarled at him, 'no matter what the police think.'

'And so will you.'

'Where are they?'

'The uniforms may be gone,' Josh said, 'but the assault rifles are still there. Do you suppose you can slip them out unseen before the police start searching my apartment? After they've found us dead, I mean. And no longer a suicide.'

Mr Nimrin studied the dashboard, trying to formulate his thoughts. At last he said, 'If I can locate and return the uniforms, even if slightly late for the original plan, even if only for the alternative plan during the return trip from the stadium, *if* I can produce those goddamned uniforms, all other questions about me will be forgotten.' He glowered at Josh. 'Do you think I will pause in turning you over to Andrei, to save my *own* neck? And be damned to the suicide note!'

Josh said, 'I can see that. So it's a good thing I don't know where they are.'

Mr Nimrin reared back. 'Of course you do.'

'Actually, no. The nice thing is,' Josh told him, 'no matter how clever Levrin is at torture in a public parking lot in the sunshine, your deadline will be long gone before he can know for *certain* that I'm telling the truth.'

Mr Nimrin thought about that. 'You believe you are willing to go that route.'

'I believe that's my only route.' Josh offered Mr Nimrin a sympathetic smile. 'Also,' he said, 'I don't suppose I'll be able to keep *your* little secret to myself, not with Levrin being so insistent and all. How you got me into this in the first place. Me, and Mitch Robbie, and Robert Van Bark.'

Mr Nimrin waggled a finger at him. 'There's a new arrogance in you, Josh,' he said. 'It's an unpleasant quality.'

'Tough.'

'Do not think,' Mr Nimrin told him, 'you are in the driver's seat.'

Josh looked at the steering wheel in front of himself. 'Well, as a matter of fact, I am.'

'You know what I mean.'

'And soon,' Josh told him, 'you'll begin to know what I mean.' Glancing out at Levrin and the others, getting restive out there, moving from foot to foot, he said, 'Mr Nimrin, it's time for you to start earning that eighty thousand dollars.'

44

MR NIMRIN BROODED out the window, where Levrin now stood flatfooted, glowering at the windshield. 'He can't see us,' he said. 'You notice? Because of the sun.'

'He should have had me park to face the other way.'

Mr Nimrin sighed. 'So many details. I think I should go out there, talk to him, put him in the picture.'

'In parts of the picture.'

Mr Nimrin raised an eyebrow at him. 'I preferred your earlier manifestation,' he said, and got out of the Land Cruiser.

As Mr Nimrin walked toward Levrin, who waited for him, pretending insouciance by putting his hands in his pockets, Josh looked over at the Marathon. Eve and Jeremy took up a little more space in there, now that they were alone in the backseat. The windows were shut, so the engine and air conditioner must have been on. The two in front carried on an idle conversation.

Josh caught Eve's eye and tried a small smile and nod, hoping he looked encouraging. No response. Either she was too afraid to know what a right or wrong response might be, or she blamed him for where they were. Which she should.

Mr Nimrin and Levrin walked out over the sunlit concrete, away from the car and Hugo and the other thug. One spoke, then the other. Levrin's hands remained in his pockets, Nimrin's moved in front of himself, sculpting the story. Levrin's head was slightly bowed in the posture of one prepared to take whatever explanation, alibi, confession might be offered, while Mr Nimrin's head leaned sideways toward the other man in a posture of confidence-sharing.

What was going to happen now? Suddenly, there were no more certainties. *Everybody's* scenario had been scrapped.

It was only now, with a chance to think while watching Mr Nimrin and

174

Levrin stroll together like plotters in a spy novel, that Josh realized the true brilliance of Robbie's idea. The actor cannot perform without his costume. The costume is part of the role, because there can be no suspension of disbelief without it. You can have plans, you can have guns, you can have a script and an audience and a socko finish, but if you don't have your costume you can't go on.

So what would happen instead? Levrin would opt for torture, Josh was sure of that, and he supposed, Levrin being Levrin, he would immediately think he'd get farther if he tortured Eve, or possibly Jeremy, in front of Josh. 'Shall I do this again?' That was just another horror he could do nothing about, another repayment on the eighty-four thousand dollars.

What could he give Levrin? Mr Nimrin, of course, and immediately. It would offer them all, at the very least, a little distraction, a little delay while they sorted Mr Nimrin out. But then what?

He could tell them that Robbie had taken the uniforms, but that he had no idea where. All true. Possibly to that theater, but probably not. Robbie would know there was always the possibility he would be mistrusted and his home and theater searched. Probably Tom or Dick or Harry, whose names and addresses Josh did not know, had the uniforms now, to await a production of *The Prisoner of Zenda*.

Where was Robbie at this moment? Where was Tina? If she did go back with him to the theater last night – another reason for the uniforms not to be there – what happened next? Did she sleep with him, and then this morning kiss him a more serious goodbye than he could imagine? Or would his slightly mad sense of self-preservation come into play?

Levrin and Mr Nimrin continued their stroll in the sun. Whenever they were turned so that Josh could see their faces, Levrin looked discontented, irritated, frustrated, while Mr Nimrin looked like a con-artist selling underwater building lots, smooth and calm and endlessly patient.

A big sticking point for them would be the guns in Josh's apartment, or not so much the guns themselves as those large packing cases. With the original plan, the assassination team would have boldly walked out of the building wearing the uniforms and carrying the AK-47s, looking like people in costume, off to some sort of pageant or show, not dangerous or remarkable at all, not on a sunny Saturday in New York in July. With the original plan, after the Redmont family had been found dead, the police would have come across the empty gun boxes in their apartment, and that would have been merely one more proof of Josh Redmont's guilt.

But now? No matter what they did to Josh, the rifles in their cartons under his bed were going to be an awkwardness, an anomaly. Would the guns be traceable back to their organization, or their organization's employer? A dead family, for no discernible reason. Assault rifles in their home. No possible explanations, at least not on the surface.

Levrin will want to torture and murder me, Josh thought, for revenge and out of spite, even if there's nothing to be gained by it. It is Mr Nimrin's job to see and to explain that the plot has sickened, that they were not going to be able to perform their wickedness at Yankee Stadium after all, and that their only choice was to retire from the stage, await another opportunity, and not leave any mysteries for the American authorities to poke at. It is Mr Nimrin's job to convince Levrin that it is in Levrin's self-interest to leave the Redmonts alone, not exact revenge, and go away. It is Mr Nimrin's job to convince Levrin that a live Josh Redmont is no threat to him or his future plans.

No wonder it was taking such a long while.

45

AT LAST, THEY separated. Both faces, seen from the car, were inscrutable, grim, not showing satisfaction or pleasure. And they weren't staying together; while Levrin headed back to the Land Cruiser, Mr Nimrin strode directly to the Marathon. He passed close to Josh, but did not look in at him. There was perhaps an extra forcefulness in the way he opened the Marathon's rear door on this side – Eve and Jeremy slid away, into the same corner as before – but that forcefulness might mean no more than the tension everyone felt at the moment.

Meantime, Levrin had paused to discuss things with his two thugs. Josh watched, trying and failing to read the body language out there, then was startled when the Marathon abruptly drove away. He looked, to see it angle rapidly toward the exit.

They were taking Eve and Jeremy away? Where? Why?

When he turned back, the other three were approaching, all of them poker-faced. They came up next to the car and Levrin said, 'Get out of there now, Josh.'

What was going on? If there was a threat in this, what was it? The Marathon was already almost to the exit as Josh stepped out onto the concrete. He would have closed the door, but Levrin held it open and said, 'You will not mind if Hugo drives.'

Automatically, Josh said, 'Where?'

He never saw the punch, he only felt the pain, just above his belt buckle, shimmering out through his body in hard wavelets. His breath burst from his nose and mouth, black pinwheels crowded his vision, and the strength left his body. He dropped forward, arms folding over his stomach as Levrin held his shoulders to ease his fall. He landed on his knees, Levrin released him, and he kept going, toppling forward and then, when Levrin gave his right shoulder a little prod, toppling leftward, to land on the concrete on his side, head not quite hitting the pavement, body bent over like a shrimp.

Several legs stood in front of him, unmoving. At first, he couldn't breathe, and then he could, and that was worse, as though he inhaled nail files instead of air. Still, he had to do it again, a little less painfully, and again, a little less.

They waited for him, none of the legs moving, and finally he could straighten, could turn his head, look up at them, huge monstrous silhouettes against the sky. 'What—?'

It was Levrin's foot that came out to kick him, lightly, on the chest; not to hurt him but to attract his attention. He blinked upward, unable to make out their faces. Levrin's face. But he could make out Levrin's voice: 'You will never ask me another question.'

He nodded. There was nothing else he wanted to do.

'Stand up now, Josh.'

They didn't help. He clambered up the chainlink fence beside the car, wishing he could just keep climbing up and over the top and down the other side, to scamper away across that scrubby ground. But, no. He stood there, weaving slightly, holding the fence with one hand.

Levrin looked as amiable and unruffled as ever. He said, 'Do you know, Josh, the two results of what has just occurred?'

Josh shook his head.

Levrin smiled. 'One, it relieved my feelings. Well, to some extent, it relieved my feelings. And two, just as important, it left no marks.'

Interesting point. Believing Levrin wanted some feedback now, Josh said, 'I see.'

'Yes, of course you do. You will not mind if Hugo drives.'

'No.'

'Very good. Get into the backseat, Josh, you and I will travel there together. A new experience for you, I think, to ride in the backseat of your fine vehicle.'

46

WHEN, OUT OF JFK, Hugo drove first north on the Van Wyck Expressway, then turned east onto Northern State Parkway, Josh knew where they must be going, though he also knew better now than to ask. Mrs Rheingold's estate above Port Washington; where else?

They didn't know he already knew about that place, had seen it, at least from the outside. Was there any advantage in that? Was there any advantage anywhere?

Not that he could see. There was no conversation in the car this time, an angry and frustrated Levrin glowering out his side window at the towns and trees of Long Island, the two thugs up front sitting as still and as thick as a pair of frogs on a rock. So, with a quiet period at last, he tried to look back over his recent conversation with Mr Nimrin – funny how, even now, he couldn't think of the man without that polite honorific – and it seemed to him he had never actually admitted to being a part of the uniform-removal. He hadn't quite done Robbie's suggested portrayal of outraged innocence, but the confrontation had wound up in the same place.

So that would have to continue to be his story, no matter what. He'd been dragged into this, all unknowing, seven years ago, through no fault of his own (well, maybe a little fault), and no awareness of what was going on, because of Mr Nimrin's payroll-padding scam. (Explain in detail.) Once he'd discovered, through Levrin's appearance and annunciation, the fix Mr Nimrin had put him into, he'd done his best just to go along with the program, never dreaming *they* meant, as a grand finale, to doublecross *him*. Why, after two weeks of total obedience, would he suddenly do something so off-the-wall as to steal a bunch of uniforms? What were they to *him*?

What alternative explanation did he have for the disappearance of the uniforms? None. Alternatives were for other people. That was a part of the change he had felt inside himself when Mr Nimrin burst into his death scene. He would no longer go out of his way to please them, to be a good soldier, to go along and go along and hope for the best. There was no best, he knew that now, and no way out. He would not help them find their stupid uniforms, because he just didn't care.

And, in fact, he didn't even care if they believed him.

He knew the situation had changed now. He knew the ceremonies at Yankee Stadium were going forward even now without blood sports, that the whole scheme of these miserable evil people lay in shreds at their feet.

But that had nothing to do with his own situation. That didn't mean he felt an inch more hopeful about *himself*. Or Eve. Or, goddam them, little Jeremy. What would a gangster in an old-time movie have told him he knew? Too much. You know it.

Zipping along the Northern State, light traffic eastbound, heavier on the other side with people ending their weekends early, Josh tried to think what would happen next, what they might plan for the Redmont family now, and he thought he saw the way it would have to go.

The same triple murder as on the original menu, but no longer in public, and no longer part of a public massacre. No, they would simply be shot somewhere and be buried there, on Mrs Rheingold's estate, after Josh had dug their graves. And the rotten Mr Nimrin, once Josh had ratted him out, might well be buried next to them.

Then what? In a few days, when Josh and Eve's absence had been noted by enough people, the super would enter their apartment, find the AK-47s, and call the police.

And so what? Weren't there bizarre stories like this in the newspapers two or three times a year? Sudden violence, baffling disappearances, photos in the papers of an ordinary apartment house or nice-looking suburban home, and a thick mixture of mystery and shock. Almost never was there a follow-up, an explanation for *why* that person – so ordinary, so middle-class, so without any kind of criminal record – suddenly came up missing, or was found shot in that car or hanged in that kitchen or sliced up in that bathtub. Such things were impossible, and could not happen. Then they happened. Then they were forgotten, and became impossible again.

As for the villains, Levrin and Mr Nimrin and Tina and Hugo and the assassination team and all the rest would be long gone, completely off this continent, planning some different outrage, brightening some other corner of the world.

Any reason for them to delay? None that Josh could think of. Any way to get out of this, rescue Eve and Jeremy and himself? None that Josh could think of.

47

OFF THE NORTHERN State Parkway at Searington Road in Roslyn Heights, north to and through Port Washington, past Mailboxes-R-Us, past Revenge Estates and the world's biggest spite fence, to stop at that tall iron gate between tall brick gateposts topped by those gray stone balls. The nameless thug got out to walk heavily over to an intercom mounted on the left gatepost. He buzzed, waited, spoke, turned to come back to the car, and the big gates started to open, inward, the two halves receding like hands that beckoned into Hell. The nameless thug got back into the car and they drove through. Where Josh was seated, behind the driver, he could tilt his head a bit to the left and watch in the rearview mirror as those gates swung slowly shut, taking most of the daylight with them.

The road, old pockmarked blacktop, curved through scruffy woods under a thick canopy of midsummer green leaves. Almost immediately the high wall disappeared and there was nothing but the road and the woods. Then the house emerged, as large and as decayed as when Josh had seen it first, from the side fence, somewhere over to the left.

The house was stone, hadn't been cared for in years, was a mottled darkish gray, with black wood trim. Most of the windows were heavily draped in pale fabrics, so that they looked like rows of dead eyes, flanked by black wood shutters. The roof eaves were long, as though the roof were descending over the facade, to mask or blind it.

A detached three-car garage with rooms upstairs stood to the right of the main house, and here the road split. Half of it angled leftward past the house's elaborate dark front door to make a loop and return, while the other half went rightward toward the garage. That was the route Hugo took, to stop in front of the last garage door to the right, farthest from the main house. Again the nameless thug got out, this time to pull open a pair of wide gray wooden old-fashioned garage doors. He stood to the side, and Hugo drove in.

The interior was very dim, particularly after the nameless thug pulled the doors shut again. Immediately to the left, in the middle slot, a big boatlike Cadillac convertible, probably forty years old, bright red, top down, was parked like spoils from some happier world. Beyond it was the Marathon, empty.

'We get out now, Josh,' Levrin said.

Josh overflowed with questions, all of which he kept inside. He had no desire to help Levrin feel relieved again. So, silent, asking nothing about Eve and Jeremy, nothing about what was going to happen next, he got out of the Land Cruiser, next to the Caddie.

'Come around this way, Josh.'

Josh walked around the back of the Land Cruiser, and Hugo had opened a door in the side wall, to which Levrin gestured, as genial and as dangerous as ever. 'We will go upstairs,' he said.

Through there, a closed windowed door was to the right, stairs to the left. They went up, Hugo first, then Josh, then the nameless thug, and Levrin last; so that Josh could neither race ahead of them up the stairs nor attack Levrin below. The stairs were narrow, enclosed in wooden walls of a medium brown, all lit by a window high in the right wall. When they reached that window, a door stood opposite it on the left, which Hugo opened, and they all trooped through.

A living room, small, minimal, but in recent use. Coffee cups, newspapers, a gray cardigan sweater thrown over the back of the sagging sofa. Was this where the assassination team had been – what was Tina Pausto's term? – billeted?

'Straight through,' Levrin said.

It was a railroad flat, one room leading to the next, no hallways. Windows at left and right were near the floor, because the roof angled low. Beyond the living room was a small galley kitchen, also in recent use, with a bathroom off it to the right. Beyond that was a large bedroom, messy, with half a dozen cots, all recently occupied, and beyond that a much smaller room, with two narrow beds, a tall narrow armoire, an armless wooden chair, and a tall narrow window in the end wall, giving more light than the low windows at the sides.

This was where they wanted him, for now. 'We'll talk later, Josh,' Levrin told him from the doorway.

Josh said, 'I don't mean to ask a question, but I need to know where I can go to the bathroom.'

'Why, out the window, Josh,' Levrin told him, gesturing at the window in the end wall. 'Though you would not want to fall out. See you later.'

And he backed away to close the door.

Josh heard the key in the lock. He wouldn't want to fall out the window? Why not? Why not *jump* out the window, and run into the woods? Somewhere, somehow, he'd get over that goddam wall with all its broken glass on top, somehow he'd get to the police, make them believe him.

He heard their footsteps recede, and immediately went to that window, an old double-hung with smallish panes, four each in top and bottom. It had a simple latch that held the two parts together, which he twisted free with some difficulty, then punched the top crosspiece of the bottom window half with the heels of his hands until at last the old paint and the rust of years gave way and the window scraped loudly open.

Down below, Levrin and Hugo were just walking off, away from the garage, toward the main house. Hearing the window squawk, Levrin turned, looked up, smiled, offered an easy wave, and moved on toward the house. Hugo didn't bother to look up.

So they'd left the nameless thug here, to watch him. He moved away from the window, back to the door, where he put his ear to the old-fashioned keyhole and faintly heard the television set.

A railroad apartment, doors certainly open all the way through. No escape in that direction; but why not go out the window?

He hurried to the window, leaned out, looked down, and saw why not. There was a basement to this structure as well. Instead of ground, one story down, there was a flight of concrete steps descending to a basement door, with a metal pipe rail on the outer side. The window was directly above the basement entrance, the lowest point of that stairwell.

Not one flight down to ground, two flights down to concrete. And a window too narrow to give him a way to launch himself outward, over the concrete to the softer ground beyond.

He looked toward the house, but Levrin and Hugo had reached it, and disappeared. Were Eve and Jeremy over there? Where else could they be? What was planned for them all, now that the original scheme had fallen through?

Were Eve and Jeremy already dead?

Money for nothing.

48

THERE WAS NOTHING to do but watch the house, and wait. The two structures were angled so that he could just see that broad dark front door with the driveway curving before it. The side of the house facing him was four windows broad, all of them blank, shielded by faded curtains, with dispirited ivy, much of it dead, crawling on the stone.

It had been after one o'clock when they'd arrived here, and by three he was beginning to remember he'd had no lunch. He wasn't hungry, exactly, he was too tense and worried for that, but the growling in his stomach increased his nervousness, gave him more of a sense that his body was not completely under his control.

As he fretted, nerves more and more jangled, for two hours nothing happened over there, and then all at once something did. A vehicle he hadn't seen before, a black Lincoln towncar of the sort used in New York City by private car services, came crunching around the drive to stop at the front door. Josh had just noticed the distinctive design of the diplomat license plate on the rear of it when both rightside doors opened and three people climbed out. Two of them, from front and backseats, were more thugs, like Hugo, but the third, also from the backseat, being more tugged than helped by the thug who'd ridden in back with her, was Tina Pausto. She wore loose tan slacks, a lightweight cream sweater, and brown flat pumps; not at all her normal style. Traveling clothes?

First he saw that she was angry, and then, astonishingly, that she was handcuffed! The thug from the backseat grabbed her arm, to propel her toward the house, and as Josh leaned at the open window he could hear her enraged voice, very loud: 'Take me to Andrei! *He'll* know—' And that was all, as the front door was pushed open and she was pulled through into the darkness within.

Meanwhile, the other thug went around to the trunk, opened it, and took out two bags. One was a standard black wheeled flight bag with a handle that raised up, the other the small overnight bag he remembered from Jeremy's room, that had so upset Eve. The thug carried both into the house, leaving the door open. Faint exhaust from the tailpipe showed that the driver, still inside the car, had kept the engine on.

She'd been leaving. Her job finished here, she'd packed and started to leave, and they had intercepted her. At the apartment? At the airport? They'd intercepted her and brought her here. Intercepted her, *handcuffed* her, wrists behind her back, and brought her here. Why?

He thought again of that angry fragment he'd heard from her: 'Take me to Andrei! *He'll* know—' Angry, but was it also frightened?

What had she done to make them turn on her? From what Mr Nimrin had said, that time they'd sat on the bench pretending not to talk to each other, Tina Pausto was a longtime valued part of their group. What had gone wrong? Had she told Mitch Robbie the truth, so he wouldn't be killed? Had her heart swayed her head, and now she would suffer the consequences? Somehow, Josh doubted that could be true. But what else could have happened?

The two thugs came back out of the house, without Tina and without the luggage. They got back into the Lincoln, and it purred away around the driveway and out of sight.

Everything's getting unstrung, he thought, not just my nerves but everything. Out at Kennedy, at that parking lot, he'd decided he could no longer be passive, no longer just do what everybody else wanted, but here he was again. Stopped, static, waiting for *them* to act.

No more, he told himself, and at last turned away from the window. He looked at the door. It was time to get out of there.

49

THE ARMOIRE WAS essentially a free-standing closet, with two mirrored doors that opened to show a tall empty space within, a wooden rod for hangers across the top. Below the doors were two drawers, side by side, with ornate brass handles, in the same style as the knobs on the doors.

The drawers were empty. Half a dozen metal hangers hung on the rod, nothing more. On top of the armoire was a thin folded blanket. There was nothing under the bed, no other furniture except the chair he'd been seated in. The only electric light was a ceiling fixture, with a flat etched pink glass shade under it like a flying saucer.

What else did he have? They were so little concerned about him they hadn't even searched him, so what did he have? Wallet, keys, a little change, his watch. His clothes. Nothing else.

When he stooped to look through the keyhole, his view was blocked by the key, an old-fashioned skeleton key from the era when this garage was built, nothing ever renovated, updated. He could hear the television faintly, but couldn't see past that key.

He needed to see. Straightening, he examined his own ring of keys and chose the one for the mailbox, the thinnest of them, but also the shortest. Stooping again to the door, he slid his key in next to the other one and pushed it a little to the left, jiggling it, and the key in the lock turned. Just a fraction, but enough to clear the view.

Could he turn it the rest of the way, unlock the door? What if he broke off a piece of metal clotheshanger, bent it, used it to push the key up and around its orbit?

No. He might get it almost halfway up one side or the other, but then his lever would run into the body of the key and stop. He could only get at it from below, and that wouldn't be good enough.

But at least now he could see. He went to one knee this time to peer through the keyhole, and now he realized that, even more than a railroad apartment, this was what was called a shotgun apartment because the doors were lined up in a row and, with them all open, a person could fire a shotgun from the front and the charge would go through all the doorways and out the window in back. Which also meant he could see through the open doorways into the living room and look at the thug there, sprawled in an armchair he'd moved to the middle of the room, so he could keep an eye on this door. His right profile was to Josh as he sluggishly watched what sounded like some sort of sporting event. Saturday afternoon sports. Golf? No, it sounded a little louder than that. Tennis, maybe.

Josh straightened. If he were very silent and managed to get this door open, he might ease through and out of the line of sight without attracting that guy's attention. But the first question was, how to silently get this door open.

It opened outward, meaning the hinges were on the other side, so he couldn't get at them. The lock was old-fashioned, but it was still a lock, a metal bolt extended into a metal-enclosed hole in the doorjamb. How to get that out of the way, without making noise.

The keyhole and doorknob shared a decorative brass plate, held by two small brass screws at top and bottom. Josh put his keys away, took out his change, and found a dime. With that, which just fit snugly into the groove in the screws, and after trying for a discouragingly long time, he finally got both screws to turn. Once they started, they came right out, and then he could swivel the plate, still held by the doorknob, to expose the lock mechanism.

And there it was, a simple cylinder with the key in it, angled just slightly leftward from its bottom position. But still very tight in there, too tight for his fingers to reach in.

It was the mailbox key again that did it, pressing the skeleton key around to the left and up. At the apex, it met resistance from the bolt and he had to press steadily, teeth gritted, both hands on his key, afraid it might snap. But it didn't, and the skeleton key suddenly moved freely again, and he knew the door was unlocked.

This was the moment. He stooped again to look through the keyhole, now smelling the old dusty metal scent of the lock, and the guard was exactly as before. Commercials played on the television, but he didn't look away from the set.

Still peering through the keyhole, Josh slowly turned the knob. No sound. When it was turned all the way, he pushed slightly, and the door moved open an inch. Moving his head with it, keeping the guard in view, he pushed it a little farther, and just when the angle moved the guard out of his line of sight he had the door far enough open so he could release the knob. Then he stood, put both palms on the door, and took two deep breaths before pushing it open farther, just enough to slide through, not looking toward the guard now, not wanting to know, just sliding through, pushing the door gently closed behind him as he moved away to the left, not stopping until he was out of the guard's sight, standing next to one of the unmade beds in the larger room.

He looked back, and the door was almost completely closed, the faint angle of it probably not visible from the other end of the apartment. He hoped not, anyway. And in any case, the guard seemed very involved with his spectator sport.

Rather than risk showing himself too often, he climbed over three of the beds, then pressed himself to the far wall as he peeked cautiously around the doorframe there. No change. As he watched, the guard yawned and rubbed his face with both palms, then shifted his behind in the chair and blinked. Then went on watching.

This doorway was much closer, much more dangerous. Josh waited, and waited, and waited, and finally realized he was afraid to do it, so afraid that he might just stand here forever, or until they'd come for him. So don't think about it, he told himself, just *do* it. *Now*.

Into the kitchen, to the left, pressed against the refrigerator, then sidling to the right, hidden again. No reaction from the living room. He paused, facing the sink, both palms pressed down onto the front edge of the sink, looking into the sink. He could hear the television sound much louder now. Yes, tennis.

And now what? The stove was to his right. Above it was suspended from the ceiling an iron ornamental rectangle with hooks, bearing three pans and a spatula. One of them was a frying pan, six inches wide, cast iron, excellent for frying a couple of eggs. And for other things as well.

Josh carefully took down the frying pan, hefted its good weight in his hand, and it reminded him of the weight of the pistol Levrin had tricked him into firing out at JFK. Well, he'd learned something there, hadn't he? He wasn't violent by nature, had never thought of himself as someone who could do violent things, but he'd learned out there at Kennedy, hadn't he, at Levrin's hands? Learned, if he had to, he could shoot a gun he believed was loaded, shoot that gun and hope and believe it would kill someone. He'd learned that, hadn't he? So this was a piece of cake.

The handle of the frying pan grasped in both tense hands, he came lunging around the doorframe into the living room, not even hearing himself bellow, not even knowing the unearthly sounds he made. Two-handed, he swung the frying pan directly into that gaping, astonished, upleaping face, felt the impact, kept going, whirling like a dervish, all the way around, a complete circle, then tottering back, off balance, dizzy, thudding his shoulderblades against the wall behind him, the frying pan bouncing on the carpet as he looked down at the overturned chair, the man splayed out on his back, that ruined face gushing blood like a fountain.

That'll learn ya.

50

THIS GUY WOULD have a gun, of course he would. He'd feel naked without it. And now, Josh wanted it.

The man's face still bled, though less than before, oozing instead of spouting. Josh remembered something from his reading, that dead bodies didn't bleed, because there was nothing to pump the blood, so this one was probably still alive.

It was with a kind of dull surprise that Josh realized he didn't much care one way or the other. Dead or alive, it made no difference, just so the guy wouldn't go on being a problem.

And where would he keep his gun? Pants pocket, most likely. Josh patted, not liking to touch this body, but felt the metal outline, reached into the rightside pocket, and pulled out a pistol that looked too fancy to belong to somebody like that. It was small, an automatic rather than a revolver, pale brushed metal with paler marbleized sidepieces added to the butt. The barrel was encased in a rectangular metal sheath, with the word BERETTA stamped into it on the left side, near the front. A piece shaped like a metal lima bean that angled down beside the trigger would be the safety; push it up, and you're ready to shoot.

There was nothing else here he needed. His legs seemed to be trembling, but not badly enough to keep him from hurrying down the stairs and through the door at the bottom, which led him out to the end of the blacktop drive. The length of the garage was to his right, the main building beyond it.

Rather than go down that way, which seemed to Josh too exposed to the dead eyes of the house, he turned left, went around the corner, and hurried down the side of the garage to the rear, the gun in his right hand held at his stomach. Looking around this next corner, he saw the house again, beyond the garage, but back here the brush and spindly trees had not been cleared away. With luck, he could get to the house without being seen.

Before moving, he looked down at the Beretta. For a righthander like himself, that safety lima bean was perfectly placed, just above his thumb as he gripped the marbleized handle. Flick upward with the thumb, then pull the trigger. Simplicity itself.

Once he started along the rear of the garage, the trembling in his body grew worse, because he felt frighteningly exposed, but he bit his lower lip and stared hard at the house, and just kept moving. And, as he walked, staying close to the rear of the garage, eyes burning with the intensity of his stare at the house, a bit of doggerel circled through his head, written by some nineteenth-century British poet: 'Thou shalt not kill, but need'st not strive/Officiously to keep alive.'

So he must still be ambivalent about the guy he'd hit with the frying pan. But that was all right; he could be ambivalent all he wanted, just so he hit him.

He made it to the house without seeing any movement or causing any alarums. There were narrow basement windows at ankle-height, and the ground floor windowsills were on a level with his chest. The curtains inside there were old and frayed, gray with dirt, but lacy. He got an impression of what might have been some sort of living room, but there were no lights on in there and the interior was too dim to be certain.

He moved along the side of the house to the rear corner, looked around it, and saw no one and nothing. Just the blunt grim stone facade, holding its secrets. He set out along the rear, passed a window, a window, a window, and came to a door, up two shallow steps to a landing, flanked by wrought iron railing, to remind him all at once of the entrance to Harriet Linde's office. But he was a long way from that office and its implications now.

He went up the steps, peered through the windows in the door at a dim interior, not a kitchen, possibly a large pantry, but when he tried the knob the door was locked.

He needed to get in there, but how? To break a window in this door would make a sound that would be heard two or three rooms away. He had to get inside, but he had to be quiet about it.

Finally, he left that door and retraced his steps to the last window from the corner on the rear wall. Peering in, he saw some sort of library or study, unoccupied. Below that window was a narrow basement window, and when he knelt to peer in, he saw that a simple latch closed it, and that it was hinged at the top to swing in and up. Inside, the basement was very dim. No lights, no people.

The only way for him to keep going, he'd come to realize, was to act without thinking. Kneel by the basement window, see a dark empty interior, break the glass with the butt of the Beretta. A tinkling down below was quickly dissipated in the large empty space.

The latch opened easily. Pocketing the Beretta, Josh pushed the window in and up, and saw there was a metal ring on the inside of it, in the middle of the bottom strip of wood. Holding the window open with one hand, he reached the other hand up through the broken part of the glass, being very careful not to slit his wrist on the jagged pieces remaining, and found the hook suspended from a beam in there. It wasn't hard to push the window up far enough to slip the hook over the ring and hold the window open.

Rolling onto his stomach, Josh stuck his legs behind him through the open window and snake-crawled backward until he could drop into the basement. He paused to shut and latch the window, so it would look normal from outside, then turned to study where he was.

This was not the entire basement, but a very large room in it, extended from back to front at this end of the house, with a plaster interior wall to the right, creating a space forty feet wide and thirty feet deep. Much of the area was empty, but in the front corner were many wooden crates and cardboard boxes piled high.

Josh went over, to see if the boxes might contain anything of use, and they were all guns and hand grenades and ammunition and even small hand-launched rockets. Ordnance, this was called. Ordnance, two or three truck loads of it, all delivered through that basement window. What a lot of plans Levrin and his friends must have.

Josh turned away, wanting none of this stuff. The Beretta was more weapon than he'd ever had before, except for his rifle in the army, that he'd mostly ignored, occasionally cleaned, sometimes had to march with, and only twice (on the range) fired.

A closed door in the plaster wall led to another room, almost as large, this one containing a lot of stored stuff that probably should have been thrown away; old trunks, old armchairs and lamps, old television sets. In the middle of this room, an open wooden staircase led up. At the top, a closed wooden door was not locked. Josh listened, his ear at the door, then turned the knob and pushed it slowly open.

A hall. Extending left and right, it had a dark runner carpet, dark photos and prints on the walls, sconces with pink glass shades shaped like tulips. At the left end, it stopped at closed dark wood double doors. At the right end, a corner of kitchen could be seen. There were a few other doorways on both sides.

Josh moved leftward, wanting to know what was behind the closed double doors, but then he became aware of a voice, somewhere ahead of him.

Levrin? Low, conversational, coming from a room ahead on the right. Levrin and then, suddenly interrupting, Tina, much louder, angrier. Talking that other language of theirs. Tina's harangue abruptly ended, with the sound of a slap, and Levrin began again, just as calm and conversational as before.

Josh tiptoed forward, Beretta again in his hand. The first door on the right was closed, the voices coming from farther on. The second door was open. As Levrin talked, his voice seemed to move around the room. Clutching the Beretta to his chest, Josh inched forward until he could see around the doorframe and into the room.

Just the two of them in there. Her left profile to Josh and the door, Tina Pausto was seated on a wooden chair without arms, her own handcuffed arms behind the chair's back, so she was trapped there. Her traveling clothes had been removed from her, so that she was now barefoot. in bra and panties. Her expression was very angry, but even in that first second, Josh could see that the anger was a failed attempt to hide terror.

This was a small sitting room, with a few divans and overstuffed chairs and end tables. Levrin roamed among them, not bothering to look at Tina as he talked. His back was to Josh at this moment as he moved, waving languidly a box of wooden matches in his left hand. Josh could see on Tina's arm and leg where he'd been burning her.

Fortunately, this time he did think before he acted, because his initial impulse was to step into the doorway and shoot Levrin in the back. But that was the wrong thing to do. The house was full of dangerous enemies, who would be alerted by a pistol shot. In any event, he was not here to rescue Tina Pausto, he was here to find Eve and Jeremy.

In his strolling, Levrin turned, bringing himself closer to Tina and angling so he would in an instant see the doorway. His right hand was reaching for the box of matches in his left.

Josh ducked back out of the doorway. As he heard the scratch of match on striker, he turned to go the other way, past the basement door again. He needed to find Eve and Jeremy, and very soon.

If they were alive, where would they be?

51

BEFORE THIS HALL reached the kitchen, a second hall led to the left, broad at first, then narrower, and beyond the narrow section was visible the front door. The narrow section was a staircase, facing the front of the house. Josh was halfway up the stairs before he thought to wonder why he believed Eve and Jeremy would be on the second or even the third floor; he simply did. They wouldn't stash people downstairs, they'd stash them upstairs, he just knew that.

At the top of the stairs a hall went left and right, but straight ahead was a broad arched doorway to another sitting room, this one with a line of windows across the far wall and a distant view over the scrub to Long Island Sound. Closed doors were along both lengths of hall, and he'd decided to start with those on the left when a cracked old voice said, 'Oh, Charles, I'm glad you're here.'

He jumped, frightened out of his wits, and saw the withered old lady come out of the sitting room, smiling, gripping her ivory-handled black cane, holding a lorgnette to eyes like oysters. She was shriveled to shorter than five feet, surely less than a hundred pounds, in a long-sleeve black dress too large for her. Maroon slippers on her feet seemed as old as she was.

The Beretta! Quickly half-turning away from her, he pocketed the gun as he said, 'Oh, hello. Mrs Rheingold, yes, hello.'

'Oh, don't be formal with me, Charles,' she said, with a ghastly little playful smile. 'We've been first names with one another for ever so long.' That gesture must be what she remembered of how to curtsey, or as much of it as she could still do. 'Charles, Miriam,' she said, lilting, with what was probably not supposed to be a smirk, 'Miriam, Charles.'

'Miriam, of course,' Josh said. 'Lovely to see you again.'

'Come in, come in,' she said, waving the lorgnette at the sitting room behind her. 'I do hate to stand, you know. Come in.'

No choice. 'Well,' he said, 'just for a minute.'

The style of the sitting room was even older than Mrs Rheingold. Fabric balls dangled from amber lampshades, faces were carved into the leading edges of chair arms, a Persian carpet was casually tossed over a side table, and dark footstools were scattered everywhere, like markers in a boardgame.

Miriam Rheingold tottered toward a peacock-tail-backed throne near the windows, while jabbing with her cane toward a lesser armchair nearby and saying, 'Sit there, sit there, dear Charles.' She dropped like a bag of kindling into the throne, with a great whooshing sigh, then leaned forward to poke at something on the carpeted floor with her cane, saying, '*Do* sit down. Ah, there it is.' And she leaned back, smiling more or less in Josh's direction.

Seating himself, looking nervously toward the hall, Josh said, 'Well, just for a minute.'

'I do love this room in summer,' she said, and waved her lorgnette at the windows, or the view. 'North, you know. It never gets too hot in here.'

It was in fact very hot, though dry. Josh said, 'Beautiful view.'

'Fewer sails than in my day,' she said. 'Terrible little motors, so unattractive.'

'Yes. Well, I should—'

'We'll just have tea. So refreshing.'

'I really should—'

'You rang, muddum?'

The voice was familiar. *That's* what she'd been poking at on the floor with her cane! Wishing the Beretta were in his hand now, no matter what the old lady might think of it – worse than motorboats, probably, pistols would be – Josh half-turned, and approaching from the doorway was, of course, Mr Nimrin, obsequiously round-shouldered. His eyes never looked away from Mrs Rheingold, but Josh could feel them burning into his own eyes just the same.

'Yes, Roderick,' the old lady said. 'See who's come to visit. Young Charles. It's been ever so long.'

'Yuss, muddum,' Mr Nimrin said. The hands clasped before his crotch didn't tremble a bit.

'We'll just have tea, I think, Roderick,' Mrs Rheingold announced. 'And ask cook if she has any of those cucumber sandwiches.'

Josh said, 'I really can't—'

'Muddum,' Mr Nimrin said, 'I was in fact looking for young Charles when I received your summons.' Now gazing at Josh, those eyes as blank as fresh-laid tiles, he said, 'You're wanted on the telephone, sir. I'll be happy to show you where the instrument is.'

'Thank you, uh, Roderick,' Josh said, rising. He felt a formal bow was the proper leavetaking ritual with Mrs Rheingold; presenting it, he said, 'It was lovely to chat with you again, Miriam. But duty calls.'

'Don't be a stranger,' she said gaily, waving her lorgnette, as Josh followed Mr Nimrin into the hall and around the corner out of sight of the sitting room, where both spun and stuck their pistols into each other's bellies.

52

'TO BE SHOT in the stomach is a terrible thing,' Mr Nimrin whispered.

'But not immediately fatal,' Josh whispered. 'If one of us gets shot, so does the other.'

'You should not be here!' Mr Nimrin was so furious the gun in Josh's stomach trembled with his anger.

'Where are my wife and child?'

'Sssh! Come back away from the doorway, she has better hearing than you think.'

They sidled together down the corridor, each with a left-handed grip on the other's right elbow, both pressing the pistol tight against flesh. They moved fifteen feet along the hall that way, like students of a very peculiar form of ballroom dancing, and then Mr Nimrin stopped and released Josh's elbow long enough to push open the door beside him. 'In here, we can talk.'

They two-stepped their way in, both holding the position, and Josh pushed the door shut behind him with his heel. A guestroom, unmade bed, hunting prints on walls.

'You don't want to shoot, young Charles,' Mr Nimrin said, low and angry, with nothing of Roderick at all about him. 'The noise would bring them all.'

'I should think,' Josh said, jabbing the Beretta a little harder into the other man's midsection, 'you have enough stomach there to muffle the sound, if I have to do it.'

Mr Nimrin's brows beetled, they actually did; astonishing, seen from this close. 'This experience, Josh,' he snarled, 'has not improved you.'

'Toss your gun on the bed,' Josh told him, 'or I'll find out for myself how sound-deadening your stomach can be.'

Instead of obeying, Mr Nimrin tried to rear back so he could look down at the Beretta; but Josh stayed with him. Exasperated, Mr Nimrin said, 'Where did you *get* that ridiculous toy, to begin with?'

'From the guy I killed in the apartment over the garage.'

That stopped Mr Nimrin. All else forgotten, he stared into Josh's eyes, the two of them as close as the Smith Bros, Mr Nimrin trying to read if Josh were lying. His own eyes widened. 'And what have we awakened here?' he asked; of himself, presumably.

'Now,' Josh suggested.

Without further argument, Mr Nimrin swung his right arm wide and released his own small revolver, which bounced with a dull thud on the mattress on the bed.

Josh stepped quickly to the bed, grabbed the revolver with his left hand, put it in his left pocket, felt the weight of it tug downward on his pants, and turned back to the scowling Mr Nimrin. 'Why don't you sit in that chair,' he said, 'and maybe put your hands in your lap.'

' "Keep your hands where I can see them," is the cliché,' Mr Nimrin told him sourly; but he sat on the wooden chair next to the elegant ancient marble-topped dresser, and he did place his hands, palm up, in his lap.

Josh said, 'Where's my wife and child?'

'Upstairs.'

'I knew it!'

It irritated Mr Nimrin to be confused. 'What?'

'Nothing. How do I get there?'

'You don't,' Mr Nimrin told him. 'You told me to earn my money, and I am attempting to do so.'

Josh took a step backward, sat on the bed, and said, 'How?'

'You're all still alive,' Mr Nimrin pointed out. 'I am doing my best to arrange things, but this is a delicate moment. The operation, as you well know, is in a shambles.'

'I don't care about the operation,' Josh told him. 'How do I get to my family?'

'They are upstairs,' Mr Nimrin repeated, 'in a room, with the door locked, and with Hugo on guard outside.' He made a contemptuous flicking gesture at the Beretta. 'You wouldn't want to confront Hugo with that firecracker.'

'I'll use your gun,' Josh told him. 'Maybe I'll use both. They've got to be more effective than firing blanks.' Looking around, he said, 'Is there a key to this room? So I can lock you in instead of shooting you.'

'Don't get *too* impetuous,' Mr Nimrin advised. 'Hugo is seated in a chair at the top of the stairs. He is a marksman, and I suspect you are not.

If he sees you, he will shoot you dead long before you get close enough to harm him with *either* of those guns.'

Josh thought about that, and saw that, up to a point, Mr Nimrin was right. He said, 'This is a big house. There's got to be more than one staircase up.'

'Oh, come,' Mr Nimrin said, aggravated again. 'You're going to *sneak up* on Hugo? A man who has infiltrated armies, gone through the lines while a major battle raged all around him, killed a general in his villa while surrounded by four thousand enemy troops?'

Josh said, 'What's *your* idea?'

'Andrei Levrin,' Mr Nimrin said, 'as you and I both know all too well, is an idiot and a buffoon. Nevertheless, he is in charge in this house at this moment. None of us will accomplish a thing without his cooperation.'

'Cooperation!'

'Would you *listen* to me? Once Andrei gets those miserable uniforms back—'

'What? Get them *back?*'

'It turns out,' Mr Nimrin said, 'Tina Pausto took them.'

This so astonished Josh that he nearly blurted out the truth. Stopping himself, slamming the brakes on his tongue, he merely shook his head; then, when he felt it safe to open his mouth, he said, 'That's crazy. She's one of *you*.'

'A mercenary, no more.' Mr Nimrin shrugged. 'Well, most of us are, I suppose. Idealism doesn't last long in this business. But loyalty to your group, to your mission, to your comrades, that is supposed to last.'

Josh nodded. 'All right.'

'I'm afraid,' Mr Nimrin said, 'Tina went native.'

'She did what?'

'She became too much in love with *shopping*,' Mr Nimrin explained. 'She became corrupted by your western ideals. Self-indulgence. Fashion. Shopping sprees.'

Remembering the shopping bags the joyous Tina had brought back to the apartment, Josh could see what Mr Nimrin was talking about, and how it would look to people like him and Andrei Levrin. But still. 'But still,' he said. 'Why would she steal the uniforms?'

'To sell to someone else, naturally. She took you to the theater to make the coast clear so the uniforms could be taken.'

'Last night?'

'Of course. They were known to be there before that. And you were watched. It is known you did nothing after you returned home. Tina aban-

doned her post with you, and made a very severe security lapse in bringing you and Mitchell Robbie together.'

'But even if— Who would she *sell* them to?'

'Andrei will find out. My guess is, the Kamastanis. Sold them back
their own uniforms, as a way to thwart the operation. Andrei will find
out.'

'He's burning her with matches.'

'Yes, he likes to stretch these things out,' Mr Nimrin said. 'He has the
rest of the day and all night. Today's operation is destroyed, but we are
putting together an alternate for tomorrow, between the Mission and the
airport.'

Josh noted that 'we,' without comment. He said, 'I'm going to get my
family out of here today.'

'I'm sorry, Josh, that's not possible.'

'If I have to shoot you all,' Josh said, 'even that superman Hugo, then
that's what I'll do.'

'Be patient, Josh,' Mr Nimrin urged him. 'Andrei and the others will
not let you interfere with the operation. They've failed once, they can't
afford to fail again. Mrs Rheingold thinks you're Charles, go on being
Charles until tomorrow.'

Josh said, 'Who is this Charles?'

'Impossible to say.' Mr Nimrin waved a vague hand. 'Someone from her
past. Whenever she meets a new person, she turns him into someone she
knew long ago. The original Roderick was her butler who knows when.
Fifty years ago?'

'She makes a wonderful cover for you, doesn't she?'

'Dotty and harmless.' Mr Nimrin actually smiled, a rarity with him.
'And *we* would never harm *her*. Stay with her, be Charles, tomorrow we'll
lock you and your family away, the operation will be over before you get
out, and after that we don't care what you say or do.'

There was a time when Josh would have believed Mr Nimrin, but that
time was long past. He said, 'I tell you what. Get me that fake suicide note,
and I'll go along with you.'

The faint flicker in Mr Nimrin's eyes was all Josh needed. 'I don't know
if I can do that. How would I explain to Andrei?'

'Yes, you're right. Oh, good,' Josh said, 'you're wearing shoes with
laces.'

Surprised, Mr Nimrin looked down at his polished black oxfords. 'Of
course,' he said. 'The butler always dresses properly.'

'Take the laces out of the shoes.'

Indignant, Mr Nimrin said, 'Oh, *really*, Josh, are you going to—'

Josh was on his feet, the Beretta pointed at Mr Nimrin's face. The trembling in his arm now was anger, not fear. 'We are not debating,' he said. 'Laces.'

Mr Nimrin blinked at him. He *wanted* to debate, Josh could see that, but he could also see that Mr Nimrin at last did understand that the debate was over. Grunting a little, he bent forward and unlaced both shoes, then sat up and extended them toward Josh, draped on his palm.

'Stand up. Up. Put the laces on the chair. Lie down on the floor on your stomach.'

'I will *not* lie—'

'You will lie on the floor on your stomach, with a bullet in you or without.' Josh let Mr Nimrin see him push the little lima bean safety up. 'Now.'

'This is very undignified,' Mr Nimrin told him. Using the chair for a prop, he sank to his knees, then stretched out face down on the floor.

Josh walked around him and picked up the laces. 'Arms behind your back.'

'You're putting us both at risk with this,' Mr Nimrin told the floor, but he put his hands behind his back.

Josh went down on one knee, that knee in the small of Mr Nimrin's back. Ignoring Mr Nimrin's *ooof*, he said, 'Thumbs together.'

'This is outlandish.'

At some point, Josh would have to put the Beretta down to tie the knot, but not yet. Holding the gun against Mr Nimrin's back, he used his free hand to loop one of the shoelaces twice around those fat thumbs. Then, swiftly, he laid the Beretta on Mr Nimrin's back, tightened the lace, made a quick knot. Mr Nimrin twitched beneath him, wanting to take advantage, but the knee in his back held him in place. Josh made a sturdier knot, looped the lace twice more, made another knot, put the second lace in his shirt pocket for whomever he met next, then picked up the Beretta and got to his feet.

'Josh, it's too tight, there's no blood to my thumbs.'

'Tough. I'll help you up now.'

Josh put the Beretta in his pocket and rolled Mr Nimrin over like a Yule log onto his back, then sat him up by his shoulders, got his hands under those shoulders, and heaved him to his feet. Mr Nimrin would have immediately toppled forward, but Josh grabbed his linked hands and pulled him back.

Not looking toward Josh, a subdued Mr Nimrin said, 'This is extremely painful.'

'Good. It'll keep you focused. Let's go.'

Now Mr Nimrin twisted around to stare at Josh. 'Where?'

'To see Hugo.'

53

JOSH OPENED THE hall door. 'Which way?'

'If you insist on putting both our lives at risk,' Mr Nimrin said, 'we should go up the stairs Hugo is not observing. To the left.'

Away from the main staircase and the sitting room that contained Mrs Rheingold. 'You lead,' Josh said, and followed, his hands in his pockets, clasping the unfamiliar but really quite comforting handles of two pistols.

Partway down the hall, Mr Nimrin stopped at a door on the right. 'You'll have to open it.'

'Stand in front of it.'

Mr Nimrin gave him a look. 'You've become an excessively distrustful person.'

'I wonder why.'

Josh took the Beretta out of his right pocket, stood behind Mr Nimrin with the barrel pressed against the man's back, and reached around him to pull open the door, which revealed a utilitarian flight of wooden stairs leading straight up.

'As you see,' Mr Nimrin said.

'You go first,' Josh told him.

'I'm not sure of my balance.'

'I hope you don't hurt yourself,' Josh said, without sympathy. 'Go first.'

So Mr Nimrin went first, leaning far forward and frowning at the steps, so as not to topple backward. Josh followed, pulling the door shut behind him.

Midway up was a small landing, where the staircase turned right. Mr Nimrin was about to make the turn when Josh stopped him with a hand on his arm. Josh crowded onto the landing with him and whispered, 'What's up there?'

'A kind of dormitory,' Mr Nimrin said, low but not whispering.

'Who's there?'

'No one at the moment.'

Josh took the revolver out of his left pocket and trained both guns on Mr Nimrin's back. 'Go ahead.'

So, bent like an osteoporosis victim, Mr Nimrin went up the second half of the staircase, Josh close behind him, and at the top the staircase opened into the middle of a large low-ceilinged room. A railing ran around three sides of the stairwell. The room, as Mr Nimrin had said, was a kind of dormitory, with a dozen cots, a variety of mismatched armoires, an old wooden kitchen table, and a few chairs. Recent messy occupation was obvious.

Josh said, 'Who's been living here?'

'Part of the time, the assassination team.'

'Where are they now?'

'At your apartment,' Mr Nimrin said, sounding surprised that Josh wouldn't have realized that.

Josh was also surprised. 'What are they doing *there?*'

'The assignment is still to dispatch Freddy Mihommed-Sinn,' Mr Nimrin reminded him. 'They're already in position, so they might as well stay there until the new plan is finalized. With or without uniforms, they are determined to make that gypsy curse come true.'

'They? You were saying "we" a little while ago.'

'I am still a part of the organization,' Mr Nimrin said.

'Where's Hugo?'

Mr Nimrin nodded at a closed door in the left wall. 'That leads to a hall, paralleling the one just below. Storage rooms on both sides. At the end is the other staircase. Hugo will be there, where he can see the hall, the stairs and the room where your people are being kept.'

Josh nodded. 'Remember how we opened the last door?'

'Josh,' Mr Nimrin said, 'I know you don't trust me.'

'Of course I do.'

'Josh, please. If it is necessary for Hugo to shoot me in order to get at you, he won't hesitate an instant. Rethink this. You know where they are, you know they're safe. Why push the situation?'

'Because the situation,' Josh told him, 'as you know, hasn't changed. The deal is, my family and I are still supposed to be found dead with that suicide note, so your crowd can get off with no one the wiser. That's what *you're* planning, Mr Nimrin, just as much as Andrei Levrin or anybody else. If one of your co-conspirators wants to shoot you in order to get a clear shot at me, that just gives me a few extra seconds, and tells *you* you should have been more careful about hanging out with bad companions. Stand by the door.'

Mr Nimrin sighed. 'You're killing us both,' he said.

'Better than your idea.' Josh stood behind him, Beretta against his back, and reached around for the knob. 'I tell you what,' he said. 'When we go out there, you say, "We come in peace." '

'I think not,' Mr Nimrin said.

54

A SIMPLE, MORE rustic corridor, narrower than the hall downstairs
and uncarpeted. At some distance away, with more hall beyond him,
Hugo sat on an armless wooden chair, its back tilted against the left wall.
He was in right profile to Josh, not noticing them at first because he was
absorbed in an issue of German *Playboy*. His hand in Mr Nimrin's back,
Josh propelled him forward at a steady pace, not too fast, because he didn't
want his shield to stumble and fall and leave Hugo a clear view of fire.

At last Hugo did look up from his studies. He frowned, peering at the
odd couple approaching him. In no hurry, he got to his feet, dropped the
magazine onto the chair, and asked Mr Nimrin a question.

'In English,' Josh cried, compelling Mr Nimrin faster, needing to get
close, closer.

Hugo laughed. 'Oh ho,' he said, and spoke again, not in English.

Anticipating what was to come, Josh wrapped his left arm around Mr
Nimrin's torso, clutching him tight, at the same time keeping his legs
pumping, pushing them both forward.

Hugo was taking from his pocket a revolver Josh knew well; he'd
already fired that gun today, to no effect except to make a smudge on this
Hugo's white shirt. In fact, the slob still wore the same shirt. While Mr
Nimrin tried to twist left and right, tried to shake free of the arm holding
him, Josh reached over the other man's shoulder, aimed the Beretta the
best he could at that smudge on Hugo's shirt, and fired.

The sound was much louder in this enclosed space. Where did the
bullet go? Angry at himself, Josh saw the fresh scar of its progress. Wide
to the right, it had gouged along the right side wall far behind Hugo, then
angled out to the hall again and finally punched into the closed door down
at the very end which, not having been latched, now swung lazily open, to

reveal stacks of upright rolled carpets.

Hugo laughed again and fired at Josh's head, which Josh at the last instant had tucked into the back of Mr Nimrin's neck, like a chicken burrowing into a hen. The bullet too traversed the hall, ending its journey somewhere back in that dormitory.

Josh tried to brace himself against the side wall, but Mr Nimrin kept moving, vaguely but insistently, as though to dodge between all the bullets that would ever be fired anywhere, from here to eternity. Meanwhile, Hugo was moving forward, no longer laughing, saying one more terse sentence before firing deliberately into Mr Nimrin's torso, so that Mr Nimrin sagged backward against Josh.

Much better. With Mr Nimrin not squirming around like a baby during a diaper change, Josh could brace them both against the side wall, bring that left arm up across Mr Nimrin's now-bleeding chest, bring his right hand over Mr Nimrin's shoulder, clutch his right wrist with his left hand to brace himself, and this time aim *carefully* at that damn smudge. And shoot. Dust puffed from the smudge.

Surprised, Hugo looked down at his shirtfront, then glowered at Josh. Taking another flatfooted step forward, he fired his own gun again and Josh felt the heavy impact when it punched into Mr Nimrin's body. If the man got much closer, one of those bullets would go all the way through Mr Nimrin and into Josh.

'This is unfair,' Josh muttered, because he'd already *hit* the man. But, all right.

He fired again, and by God hit the same spot, and Hugo thudded to a halt. He looked confused, but he was closer. The gun in his hand weaved like a snake as he tried to find Josh behind Mr Nimrin.

Bullets stop people, dammit. Who did Hugo think he was, Rasputin? Josh fired a fourth time, and for the third time he saw the bullet hit home. That smudge was now red, and growing.

Hugo had stopped his advance. He took a two-handed stance, aimed very carefully, looking for some chink in the armor of Mr Nimrin, and Josh fired a fifth time, and then a sixth. Hugo weaved. His gun had apparently become very heavy; the angle of its aim drooped ever downward.

How many bullets were in this little Beretta? Josh stepped away from Mr Nimrin, who crumpled to the ground. Hugo, seeing his target in full at last, tried with both hands to lift his gun, but Josh stepped forward, stepping over Mr Nimrin, then one more step, and shot Hugo in the nose.

As Hugo toppled backward, his gun clattering to the floor, Josh leaned forward, aiming now at that exposed Adams apple, wanting the coup de grace, but this time the Beretta merely said *click*. A seven-shot magazine; who would have guessed?

But just enough.

55

NO TIME, NO time. All that shooting would have been heard all over the house. Dropping the empty Beretta, Josh ran forward to the closed door next to where Hugo had been seated, and of course it was locked, with no key in the keyhole.

Was this what life had become reduced to, searching unconscious and dead bodies? Josh pawed at Hugo's trouser pockets, felt a key – Yale, here in the main house, not the simple skeleton key of the garage – and as he reached into the pocket a hand snapped closed on his wrist.

He shrieked, biting it off after only a second, his feet scrabbling on the floor as he tried to get *away*. The hand gripped him, unchanging. He stared at it, and then at last stared along the arm and up to Hugo's face, which was sweating like a tankard of ale, the skin pale, metallic, the eyes unfocused around that punched-in nose, the lips parted, teeth clenched. No part of him moved, but the hand kept its grip.

Josh peeled the cold fingers back one at a time. They offered no more resistance than a flip-top ring, and stayed where he pushed them. Four fingers, then push down, the thumb bumped over the wristbone, and then he could reach into the trouser pocket to grasp the key.

At first he couldn't see them, in this storage room full of mattresses and Christmas tree lights. He stood in the doorway, peering in at semi-darkness, and was about to say Eve's name when a far voice called, '*What was that?*'

Mrs Rheingold. Josh turned away from the room, stood in the doorway, saw her there at the foot of the stairs, peering up, acting as though she might come up. From there, she wouldn't be able to see the two bodies on the floor.

'Just the plumbers, Mrs Rheingold,' he called. 'Blowing out the pipes.'

'The pipes?'

'Just getting them all unclogged, you won't have a problem anymore, be done here in just a few minutes, thank you, Mrs Rheingold.'

'A problem?'

She'd said that as though to say 'I didn't know I *had* a problem,' but Josh chose to hear it another way: 'Not much longer,' he called. 'Everything'll be fine in just a few minutes.'

'Josh?' Eve's voice whispered from somewhere inside the room.

'Everything's okay,' Josh called to Mrs Rheingold, and waved, and at last she nodded and departed, and he could turn to Eve, who thrust herself into his arms, folding in there, pulling him close as though to hide inside his ribcage. 'Oh, thank God, thank God, thank God.'

No time. 'Where's Jeremy?'

'He's—' Still clutching to him, she half-turned, peering back into the room. 'He's frightened.'

'No *time*.' Josh pushed her away, frantic, *feeling* Levrin pound his way up the stairs from two flights below.

She had Jeremy's hand now, out from behind a painted balsa manger. Josh pulled Mr Nimrin's revolver from his left pocket, switched it to his right hand, and stooped to gather Jeremy up, ignoring the child's cry of fear at the sight of the gun. He turned, Jeremy in his left arm, the revolver in his right hand, and raced back down the corridor to the dormitory, trusting Eve to follow.

In the dormitory, just in sight coming up the stairs, was a bulky man Josh had never seen before, who never saw Josh at all, because he ran to the railing, fired directly into the side of that head, and heard an echoing shot behind him. He looked back, saw Eve staring at *him* in horror, but it was Levrin and another stranger – how many of them were there? – who were running this way down the corridor.

'Fast!' he yelled, and raced down the stairs two at a time, jumping over the body crumpled at the bottom, turning left because that's where the stairs were to the ground level and the front door. 'Run, Eve, run, Eve, run, Eve!' afraid she was too far back, Levrin would reach her, a bullet from Levrin would reach her.

Down the main stairs, afraid to look back, and he hurtled out the front door and stopped dead, Eve running into his back. The two who'd driven the Marathon earlier were there, no more than ten feet away, standing beside the Marathon now parked in the drive, pointing guns directly at Josh.

And now Jeremy screamed and kicked out and punched his arms around and jerked his head from side to side so that Josh couldn't aim or hold his balance or think. He stood there, the screaming child in his arm,

Eve clinging to his back, until Levrin arrived to pluck the useless revolver out of his hand.

Josh looked at him, and Levrin was smiling. As ever, smiling. 'Well, Josh,' he said, 'you *have* been quite bad, have you not? But all is well that comes to an end well. Another idiom.'

Losing his smile, he barked something at the two in the driveway, who put their guns away. No longer needed.

Jeremy, feeling the strangeness in the air, became quiet, staring at Levrin, who looked again at Josh, his manner almost sympathetic. 'Come inside, Josh,' he said. 'Bring your family.'

'Say, chaps.'

They all turned, and around the corner of the house had come two of the Christian Capitalist golf carts, each carrying two suited and necktied and white-shirted and orange-capped Capitalists, one of whom had raised a hand for their attention. 'Say chaps,' he called again. 'Are we by any chance off the reservation?'

56

HOW HAD THESE retreaters stumbled onto this property? Josh watched them, the orange baseball caps, the simple smiles, and tried to find some advantage for himself in their intrusion. If he'd been on his own, he'd have used this distraction to run back into the house, hoping to find something in there to help him; but with a wriggling two-year-old hanging from his arm, and Eve clinging to his back, there was nothing to be done.

Meanwhile, Levrin, his genial pose under severe strain, was saying, 'What are you people doing here? You belong next door.'

'Oh, I am sorry,' said the spokesman, the heaviest of the four, while the other three climbed out of the carts to stretch their legs, bend the kinks out of their backs, gawk around at the house and grounds. There were four golf bags standing up in the racks provided at the back of the carts, each containing only one club, under a protective leather headcover numbered *1*. 'We were just tootling along,' the spokesman went on, waving vaguely toward Long Island Sound, 'saw the open door in the wall, tootled on in.'

'That door is kept closed,' Levrin told him, being more severe than usual.

'Not today,' the spokesman said, as the other three reached for their golf clubs.

'*And* locked,' Levrin insisted.

'Not today,' the spokesman said, and the other three lifted out the golf clubs, which weren't golf clubs at all. 'Take out the transportation,' the spokesman said over his shoulder, as Josh finally recognized him as Tom, the one who'd played Major Petkoff, Raina's father.

Levrin said, 'Take out the what?' but Josh had already understood that

213

last sentence, and had folded both arms around Jeremy, hands over the boy's ears as Harry (Bluntschli) turned with the golf club that was actually an AK-47 and laid a line of fire along the length of the Marathon. The rattle of the automatic rifle was amazingly loud, even out here in the open, but that was as nothing compared to the sound the Marathon made when its gas tank blew up. Everybody ducked and recoiled, Jeremy twisted around like a greased pig trying to see, and Marathon parts made a brief hot-metal sprinkle in the general area.

Into the stunned silence that came next, Mitch Robbie smiled over at Josh and said, 'Wasn't that nice? Harry was a Ranger before he found his true calling.' He smiled at the remains of the Marathon, the bottom of a twisted frame on four sagging tires. 'And here we have a barbecue pit with wheels.'

Levrin, flabbergasted, said, 'How can you have those weapons? The team is at that apartment!'

'Not anymore,' Robbie told him. 'I called them,' he said, and took a stance, as though about to say, 'I come to bury Caesar, not to praise him,' instead of which he said, 'This is Levrin,' sounding exactly like Levrin. 'Because of people here,' he went on, in the same style, 'I must speak in English. The Pausto woman has defected and informed on you. Leave at once, go to the bandshell in Central Park, I will meet you there.' He smiled, and spoke in his own voice: 'You should have seen them run.'

Levrin, spitting mad, said, 'That does not sound at all like me.'

Robbie smiled. '*They* thought it did.'

Tom had now taken out and unmasked his own AK-47, the last of the faux golf clubs, which meant there was an awful lot of weaponry out here in the driveway; everybody but Josh and his family. The cast of *Arms and the Man* were very well armed. The two men who'd been here when Josh and Eve and Jeremy had come out had pocketed their pistols, and so had the man who'd come out of the house with Levrin, but Levrin still had a pistol in his hand, and now he stepped closer to Josh, the trio of the family shielding him from the AK-47s as he grabbed Josh by the elbow and said to the others, 'Put down those arms, or I will shoot this entire family.'

Seeming to ignore him, Robbie looked around and said, 'We need more noise. We need to give somebody in the neighborhood a reason to call the cops.'

Pointing, Josh said, 'Behind that basement window, there's a whole lot of weapons and ammunition.'

'Oh, good,' Robbie said, and swung the AK-47 around. 'I've decided,' he said, 'to get over my fear of guns. To increase my range, you know. I never fired one of these things before.'

'*Stop!*' Levrin shrieked, and when Josh looked at him – he was way too close – Levrin was clearly a man in terror.

Robbie paused. 'Stop? Did somebody say stop?'

'That is a munitions dump!' Levrin yelled.

'Don't yell,' Josh told him.

'You'll blow up the house! You'll blow up the entire neighborhood!' He was still yelling. Jeremy kicked at him, but Levrin was just a bit too far away.

'Blow it up! Blow it up!'

They all looked up, and Mrs Rheingold was up there, half out a second story window, waving her arms, a huge manic smile all over her face. '*Shoot* it! Blow it up!'

'Never refuse a lady,' Robbie said, and squeezed the trigger.

As Levrin shrieked and cowered, and his three companions dropped to the ground with their arms over their heads, only the first bullet went through the basement window. Not prepared for the rifle's recoil, Robbie had been unable to stop firing until half a dozen shots went through the study window on the ground floor. 'Damn,' he said. 'Try again.'

'Hold it,' Josh said, and Robbie cocked an eyebrow in his direction, poised to go on. Josh said to Levrin, 'Give Eve your pistol.'

Levrin was still squinting against the expected explosion. Through the squint, he peered at Josh. 'To her? Why, to her?'

'She might not shoot you.'

Eve came around Josh to pluck the gun from Levrin's hand. 'On the other hand,' she told him, 'I might.'

'*Yaaaahh!*' The front door burst open and a six foot three inch naked woman with her hair half-burned away and a pair of handcuffs dangling from her right wrist next to the pistol she brandished came hurtling out, stopped, took a stance, and shot Levrin twice. He dropped like a piano out a window, and only then did she speak: 'Nobody move!'

Nobody moved.

Tina came warily down the steps, circling them all, and said to Robbie, 'You. Put down that weapon.'

'Yes, ma'am.'

'You will drive.'

'Yes, ma'am.'

Generally to the rest of them she said, 'You will not follow.'

Robbie got behind the wheel of one of the golf carts, Tina beside him. 'Go,' she said.

As the cart puttered away around the corner of the house, Dick (Nicola) said, '*There's* something the Christian Capitalists don't see every day.'

57

'S HE WON'T GET far,' Agent Schwamm said. 'Naked, and on a golf cart.'

'You just mean on a golf cart,' Agent Zimmer told him. 'Naked, she actually *might* get pretty far.'

'I know what I meant,' Agent Schwamm told him.

Josh knew what they both meant, that they were furious they couldn't arrest Josh Redmont, cuff him, and lock him up and put him on ice forever. Furious. Seething. Melting their shirt buttons. Causing the ends of their neckties to curl up.

They'd been on phones; Mrs Rheingold's and their own cellphones. They'd opened laptops and sent E-mails. There'd been dark discussions about calling something called *sog* to get a ruling at the very highest level, and they still entertained hope that one of their questions to higher authority would be answered their way. Because somewhere, somewhere in all this chazeray, these explosions, these illegally imported assault rifles, these payments to a mole – a *mole*, for God's sake! – these foreign agents with their plots and plans, their machinations and manipulations, some-where in this unholy un-American mess, there had to be some sort of Federal crime, please God, that they could pin on Josh Redmont, just so they could feel a little better, a little less like biting somebody's head off.

After all, look what he'd done, this Redmont. *Knew* about a planned criminal act – and a doozy of a criminal act, at that – and never reported it. (Of course, the criminal act had not actually occurred and now would not occur, in no small part because said Josh Redmont with others had foiled it, but still.)

All right, he had housed illegal aliens and illegal imported weapons. (Very well, his family had been kidnapped and he had feared for their safety, and at the first opportunity he *had* turned the illegal weapons, slightly used, over to the Nassau County police, who had turned them

217

over to FBI agents Zimmer and Schwamm, but still.)

Yes, but he had actually been a *part* of the planned criminal enterprise (yes, yes, noted above) for at least two weeks and should be considered one of the conspirators. (Yes, yes, the fake suicide note had been found in the dead Hugo's pocket, and its purpose, and its significance to the entire Redmont family, had been explained at length and at volume by Josh Redmont, but still.)

Speaking of the dead Hugo, the same Josh Redmont freely admitted to having shot the man six times, thus causing him to become dead. (Yes, at that moment the decedent Hugo had been firing his own gun at Josh Redmont and had been holding the Redmont family captive in a locked room, but still.)

He had taken *payment* to be an undercover agent of a foreign and presumably hostile power for seven years, at last culminating in the previously mentioned planned criminal enterprise. (That he was the inadvertent recipient of a monthly stipend because the scam artist Ellois Nimrin's payroll-hiking scheme had fallen through, which the wounded but not dying Nimrin had weakly admitted to on his stretcher while being carried out to the ambulance, and that accepting money even when you don't know what you are getting it for is not a crime – not even a Federal crime – were both apparently incontrovertible, but still.)

Redmont's Toyota Land Cruiser was at this moment parked in the spies' safe house's garage. (The dead Hugo had driven it there, as fingerprinting would soon show.)

Oh, *damn* it to hell! Agents Zimmer and Schwamm were not happy. They sat with Josh in the shot-up study in the long afternoon light, they never expressed anger or any other emotion, they never by word or deed put a single crease in the image of a professional FBI man on duty, but nevertheless they made it clear, in a thousand other ways, that they were not happy.

Others were happy. Josh, for instance, at last having no guns pointed at him or threats pointed at his family, and finally coming to believe he wasn't in terrible trouble with the law after all, was provisionally very happy, though it didn't seem like a good idea to express that thought too much in the presence of Agents Zimmer and Schwamm. Eve and Jeremy, both happy, or at least relieved, were elsewhere in the house, Eve chatting up Mrs Rheingold to help her get over the disappointment of not having her house blown up, Jeremy breaking some eighty-year-old toys. And Tom and Dick and Harry were presumably happy in a frantic sort of way, having been interrogated briefly by lesser FBI agents and then permitted to hurry back to the city, where they would do their best to find a new Sergius for tonight, since Mitchell Robbie and Tina Pausto had both disappeared completely, leaving nothing behind but a golf cart awash in the rocky water just outside Mrs Rheingold's back gate.

Which was something else getting up the noses of Agents Zimmer and Schwamm. 'Just what is the relationship between Pausto and Robbie?' Agent Schwamm asked, not for the first time.

'You'll have to ask them,' Josh said, not for the first time.

'I'm asking you,' Agent Schwamm said, not for the first time, but while Josh was trying to remember what his usual line was at this point the first notes of 'The Star Spangled Banner' emanated from Agent Zimmer's suit.

His cellphone, of course. He answered it, sitting at attention in the old tan leather armchair with the new bullet holes in it: 'Agent Zimmer.'

He listened, gazing intently at Josh, who looked away, to find Agent Schwamm also gazing intently at him. So he looked instead at the bullet holes in the oil painting – Hudson River school, Hudson River, mountains, sunrise, possibly sunset – over the walk-in fireplace.

'Sir.'

Josh looked at Agent Zimmer, who continued to listen to his little black phone while gazing intently at Josh. So Josh looked at the Hudson River some more. Sunrise, he thought.

'Is that the final word, sir?'

Yes, sunrise. Very nice, too.

'And the Pausto woman?'

Josh wondered what that part of the Hudson looked like today. Built up a lot, probably.

'Sir. We'll mop up here, return to sog in the morning. Sir.'

Josh looked at Agent Zimmer, who now sat with the little phone in his hand, dangling over the chair's tan arm. He had a bad-digestion look. 'You are free to go,' he said.

'I am?'

'He is?'

Ignoring Josh, as though he'd already left, Agent Zimmer said to Agent Schwamm, 'We'll mop up here, return to sog in the morning.'

'Fine,' Agent Schwamm said, as someone else might say damn-it-to-hell.

Rising, not wanting to move too fast or too abruptly, Josh said, 'I'll just get my, uh, my family.'

They didn't say goodbye.

*

In the Land Cruiser, Jeremy asleep in Eve's lap, Josh warily watching the light traffic of a late afternoon July Saturday on the Northern State Parkway, the sun sliding lower and lower over Manhattan far out ahead, he said, 'Never take a free gift, I've learned that much.'

'Always look a gift horse in the teeth,' Eve said.

'Boy, they do have teeth, don't they?'

There was a moment of silence while Josh thought about his close call – his series of close calls – and then Eve said, 'Poor Mrs Rheingold.'

'Poor *her?* She can afford to fix a few bullet holes.'

'But her staff,' Eve said. 'They were all spies, they're all either arrested or dead. She has to hire an entire new staff. *She* isn't up to that.'

Josh shrugged, and they drove in silence again. Then Josh began to notice that they were driving in silence again, with that last sympathetic remark about Mrs Rheingold just floating there in the car with them. He sneaked a quick glance away from the traffic at Eve's profile, which was beautiful and wonderfully familiar and just a little too innocent. Watching the road again, he said, 'Eve? What have you done?'

'I said I'd help out.'

'Help out.'

'She's going to need *somebody*, just for a little while. Interview staff, get the house tidied up.'

'Eve? What are you going to do?'

'Tomorrow,' she said, 'we'll all drive out there. Then—'

'We're going *back?*'

'It will be wonderful for Jeremy,' Eve said. 'Just like Fire Island in July, only now we'll have the north shore in August.'

'August?'

'We'll have our own wing of the house,' Eve told him, 'completely away from Mrs Rheingold. We can do the same as last month, only I'll need the car, we'll have to have a car out there, and you can take the train out on weekends.'

'Weekends.'

'There's swimming nearby,' Eve said. 'And it's a wonderful house, Josh, just full of antiques. You wouldn't want her hiring somebody who'd steal her blind, would you?'

'Another month alone in the city.'

'But *this* month,' Eve instructed him, 'you'll stay out of trouble.'

Late Sunday morning. While Jeremy watched something appalling on television – Tina was right, they had to get cable – and Eve in the bedroom unpacked from Fire Island and repacked for Port Washington, which they would drive out to later that day, Josh sat all unstrung in his chair in the living room, surrounded by all the many sections of the Sunday *New York Times*. He seemed to be gazing at the front page of Automobiles, without actually receiving any messages from it. If he had the energy to worry, he might worry about having no energy, but on the other hand this lassitude was certain to be gone by the next afternoon when, after a short train ride, he would return to his life at Sewell-McConnell, a life which at this point he could barely remember. But he was sure it would come back to him.

'Would you get that?' Eve called from the bedroom, which was when he realized that sound he was hearing was the telephone.

'Right,' he answered, but stared at the ringing machine for a long second of deep distrust. What fresh hell is this? he asked the universe. But it's all over, isn't it? Isn't it all over? So he picked up the receiver. 'Hello.'

'I will not be a coward and a trifler,' declaimed a sonorous voice. 'If I choose to love you, I dare marry you, in spite of all Bulgaria.'

'Oh, for God's sake,' Josh said, as *New York Times* sections cascaded to the floor all around him. 'Sergius.'

'At your service.'

'You got away?'

'Not away, exactly,' Robbie said, in his own voice; if that was his own voice.

Alarmed, Josh hunched over the phone. 'Is she still holding you?'

'Well, in a manner of speaking.'

'Mitch, you're not *with* her.'

'As a matter of fact,' Robbie said, sounding quite pleased with himself, 'I am.'

'The *police* are looking for— The *FBI* is— They'll think you're an *accomplice*, they'll throw you in jail!'

'No no no,' Robbie said, 'nothing that dramatic. We're in negotiations already with the Feds.'

'To give yourselves up?'

'For what? Tina will defect, they'll give her a transitional stipend—'

'*Money?*'

'More than we were getting, Josh. In return, she will spill the beans. Many many beans. You wouldn't believe the things that girl knows.'

'Yes, I would,' Josh said.

'She's a valuable asset,' Robbie told him.

'I'll take your word for it.'

'We'd have the deal set up already,' Robbie said, 'if they weren't being greedy about the movie rights.'

'*Movie* rights!'

'You can't get an agent on a weekend. Tomorrow afternoon, we'll call the Coast—'

'Agent? Agent?' Josh felt as though his head had become a jelly donut, with his brain for the jelly. 'An FBI agent? What do you—'

'Of course not,' Robbie said. 'A talent agent. Tina needs a major rep, and I'll see to it she gets one. There'll be something in it for you, too, you know.'

Money for nothing, Josh thought. 'Oh, yeah?'

'Well, you're a character in the story,' Robbie pointed out. 'Not a principal character, but one of them.'

'Oh.'

'I'll see to it they cast somebody good,' Robbie promised. 'Not a star, you know, but a rising young fella, maybe fresh off a series. Don't worry, I'll take care of you.'

'Thank you,' Josh said.

'Gotta run,' Robbie said. 'We're still in hiding, you know, until we cut the deal. Talk to you later.'

Click. Josh looked at the phone, then gently put it on its cradle. He sat there, thinking various thoughts, surrounded by a fall of *Times*es, and after a while Eve came in and said, 'Who was that?'

Josh shuddered all over. 'The future, I think,' he said.